HOUSE OF ASHES

By the same author:

Fiction
sun dog
The White Woman on the Green Bicycle
Archipelago

Non-fiction
With the Kisses of His Mouth

HOUSE OF ASHES

MONIQUE ROFFEY

**SIMON &
SCHUSTER**

London · New York · Sydney · Toronto · New Delhi

A CBS COMPANY

First published in Great Britain by Simon & Schuster UK Ltd, 2014
A CBS COMPANY

3 5 7 9 10 8 6 4 2

Simon & Schuster UK Ltd
1st Floor
222 Gray's Inn Road
London WC1X 8HB

www.simonandschuster.co.uk

Simon & Schuster Australia, Sydney
Simon & Schuster India, New Delhi

A CIP catalogue record for this book
is available from the British Library

HB ISBN: 978-1-47112-666-6
TPB ISBN: 978-1-47112-667-3
EBOOK ISBN: 978-1-47112-669-7

Efforts have been made to contact every copyright holder for material
contained in this book. If any owner has been inadvertently overlooked,
the publisher would be glad to hear from them and make good in
future editions any errors or omissions brought to their attention.

Typeset by Hewer Text UK Ltd, Edinburgh
Printed and bound in Great Britain by CPI Group (UK) Ltd, Croydon, CR0 4YY

AUTHOR'S NOTE

The City of Silk and the island of Sans Amen are ficti-
tious. The island is located in the northernmost part of
the Caribbean archipelago and was once a British
colony. However, the attempted coup d'état which
backfires so quickly and the ensuing events in this
novel bear some relation to an attempted coup which
took place in Trinidad and Tobago in 1990. Or the
events may have much in common with coups d'état
in other parts of the world, for example Latin America,
Europe or Africa. While on the decline, the coup
remains a common form of power change in the world.

For Ira Mathur and Raoul Pantin

The chant of the madman is the only salvation.

David Rudder

They are here with us now,
Those who saddle a new unbroken colt
Every morning and ride the seven levels of
sky,

Who lay down at night
With the sun and the moon for pillows.

Rumi

I. Jericho

WEDNESDAY, 3 P.M.,
A COMMUNE, THE CITY OF SILK,
THE ISLAND OF SANS AMEN

It was hot in the prayer room. Late July, and the air so thick with moisture every brother and sister gathered there glowed inside a halo of light. Some of the young boys occupied the front rows and Ashes was pleased to see most of them appeared clean. They looked reverent and alert, though he knew the truth was that most of them attended not just for prayers, but also for the football match afterwards. Ashes looked further forward and his gaze rested on the Leader's shoulders; as usual, he was dressed in robes of grey. The Leader was a huge man, six foot eight, with a broad and powerful back and a muscular neck. His skin was smooth, like a child's, the colour of caramel. His head was bent forward and he appeared to be fully absorbed, already prayerful. Ashes knew the Leader was asking for guidance for what was to come that afternoon, a plan which held elements of divine will and earthly chaos. His stomach constricted just at the thought of what lay ahead, and the lower parts of him, his loins, his thighs, felt weakened when he remembered what the Leader had said only the week before.

'Make sure you come in early next Wednesday, yuh hear? Nex week. It going and happen.'

With a hushed thrill, the ancient prayer ritual was upon him. Ashes bowed from the waist and uttered the holy vows of remembrance which lived in his chest and enriched his soul. These words were part of him, etched like a code, and they made him able to see straight and make contact with the supreme intelligence which lived in his heart. Something came down into him. Like a breath. Or a touch to the top of his head. It spread downwards, arriving like the quiet thrum of a hummingbird's wingbeat, like the whispers of a dense rainforest at night. The beautiful. The sensation was big and could often overpower him and it was difficult to contain for long. Now it descended, filling him with a lightness, a feeling of bliss – and he was grateful. He could never harness it. The beautiful touched on him as and when it pleased, always fleeting and temporary, like a kiss.

Two hundred souls stood in the hot, cramped room on the outskirts of the City of Silk, gathered in worship to the almighty. Around him others were whispering incantations; they held their hands out, palms up in worship. Others swayed and gazed upwards. This was his community; these were his spiritual friends on earth. Here they all met with prayerful intent and these prayers opened his heart and purified his being, *Praise be to God*.

The scent of the other brothers rose in his nostrils, their shirt sleeves pressed against his, their skin on his skin; some had oiled their hair, others had bathed with soap, others hadn't bathed at all, their clothes heat-stained and days old. Altogether their bodies gave off a smell like red clay earth after the rains fell hard from the skies above Sans Amen. The experience of being here, together, was always like this, intimate and intoxicating. Each of them was solitary and each was connected and surrendered to God. Ashes felt most alive here, called inwards, as though prayer cast a spell on him and the spell was to do with this invisible force. There was a longing inside him, since childhood, since his brother River had died, to be with the beautiful. The beautiful was always there, yet it could also be easily missed. Prayer reunited him with the beautiful. He felt aware and compassionate with everything around him, even the atoms in the air.

Ashes gave thanks and submitted his soul and said, *Praise be to God*, and felt kindred with the brothers and sisters around him, with the soul of every person who'd ever walked before him on earth. Again he bowed and uttered his prayers, an offering of devotion and surrender. He spoke to his God in the eternal verses and offered up his soul, and the dialogue between him and his God was awakened yet again through the power of ritual. The conversation was the same and the feeling was always wonderful and reassuring, and yet every time he worshipped it was like the first time.

When the prayers were over, some quiet moments of reflection followed. Then the Leader turned to them and spoke and his face glowed. The Leader often preached after prayers; he always had lots to say and everything he said felt important. He gazed at his followers and he smiled in his dazzling way.

'Brothers and sisters,' he addressed them. 'Amongst many things, our spirituality has been stolen from us.'

'Yesss,' a few voices responded.

'In times of slavery, it was taken away.'

'Yesss.'

'And so it isn't, for us, a matter of *con*version to this ancient path.'

He looked around. His voice was soft and clear. He

spoke like a man of great learning and wisdom, like a prophet.

'But rather, *re*version. We've had to set our path straight again.'

'Yesss.'

'This is a noble truth.'

'Praise be to God.'

'We had been lost, separated from our great teachings for many years. But now I have led you back, my brothers and sisters, and many of you have congregated together here, black people and brown-skinned people, Africans, Indians, a rainbow of colours have joined together here in this compound. This is unique, my brethren.'

Ashes nodded in agreement. The Leader was a remarkable man who'd brought together people from all walks of life. People of all persuasions, men and women who may never have come together, had all heard of his teachings and found their way to him of their own free will.

The Leader's face was gentle and his voice was measured, but his eyes were different today, hard as the hills.

'Now,' he said. And what came next was unexpected.

'Will the sisters kindly leave the room?' His voice

was polite and yet his intention was set firm. His gaze was fixed on some distant spot far beyond the walls. He nodded for his order to be carried out and the occupants of the room began to move.

'I ask the women to vacate the compound entirely. I have some matters to discuss with the men.' He spoke with his usual courteousness, the voice of a man who could charm the sun down from the highest level of sky.

Ashes watched as the sisters, who were in the back rows, their hair covered, most of them in long pleated skirts, began to depart one by one, silently, through the back entrance. Ashes' wife Jade wasn't among them. She was at home, cooking for that evening; she'd glanced up from her iron pot as he'd departed for the commune and blown him a kiss through the air and said goodbye.

The Leader had always applied the rule of *need to know*. The women of the community didn't need to know of this big plan yet. And so Ashes hadn't told his wife Jade of the evening's auspicious events, not yet; he trusted the Leader's motives. All was well in their household when he left his wife cooking by the stove, deep in the dreams she held for herself. His wife liked to dream a lot, of her future, of their happiness; she often conjured her ancestors, those alive and dead, and she liked to trace the patterns of their lives and connect them up. He was a lucky man. He had married a strong and gracious woman. Here, in Sans Amen, women were considered powerful; they were as strong-minded as men; they had as much courage, as much fire in the belly. Don't mess with the women of Sans Amen, everyone knew that. 'I'll be back for dinner,' he had said to his wife that afternoon, a small and necessary lie.

The Leader cleared his throat.

'Today,' he said, 'we will be making history. For ourselves, and our fellow countrymen of Sans Amen. We will be acting in accordance with the divine will of God. We will be doing what is right and necessary. We will be *removing* those in power.'

Ashes felt himself gently propelled backwards. Murmurs rose from the men, a mixture of agreement and barely concealed horror.

'The time has come, my brothers, to *rise up* and change our fate and the fate of this small country. We will be fighting for the oppressed and for a New Society, a fairer, more civil world. We will be liberating the poor man in the street, poor men like us. Common sufferers. And they will rise up and join our struggle. And this is the will of God.'

Praise be to God, murmured the men.

The beautiful had vanished. Ashes was feeling alone and a little awkward in himself. He tried to stand erect and ready for this mighty task but the air was heavier now the doors and windows had been closed. Then the brothers seemed to know it was time and they all moved as one in a slow swaying movement. They were all collecting themselves.

Ashes felt light in his head. His body seemed to vanish from under him. From the back of the room four brothers appeared wearing green army fatigues. The plan that had seemed so far off was now underway. Every man in the room stared in a kind of wondrous paralysis, not quite knowing their impending duty, not quite ready for all of this. Some of the brothers had been informed but most hadn't, and so a subdued chaos started to arrive in the prayer room; it was seeping into the bloodstream of every man and boy. One of the fighters wore a bandana around his nose and lower jaw. Another had put on a black woollen balaclava. Ashes could just about recognise them but didn't really know either of them in a personal way. Both these men were close to the Leader, they were part of the small group around him, the inner cabinet; these brothers had been chosen by the Leader and sent for training far away, to camps in the desert. That much he knew.

One of these fighters positioned himself to the right and another to the left of the Leader. Now the Leader looked even more distinguished than usual, like a movie star or some kind of cricket champion. Each of these new bodyguards held a rifle and wore a bandolier of ammunition across his chest. Each had cold eyes and looked proudly intent and serious as hell. They reminded Ashes of Sylvester Stallone. All of a sudden, he didn't feel good. He wanted to go straight back to his home, to his wife, their two sons Arich and Arkab, named after the stars they were born under; he wanted his life of books and medicinal plants which he cultivated in the yard. He had a sense that he was out of his depth, that he hadn't quite understood what this big plan was, not in detail. He had said 'yes' in principle.

'You will be useful,' the Leader had said. 'You have a part to play.' The Leader had name-checked his brother, River, and of course Ashes thought of the Phantom, and his Oath of the Skull, an oath sworn to destroy greed and avarice in the stacks of comics under his bed as a child. Yes, he was there for River and for the righteous notion of being of service and taking action. If words and prayers had no effect, then it was time to use the body. This was the time to secure a New Society for himself and his sons. He reminded himself of this, even though he felt uneasy. Ashes patted for his inhaler in his pocket. Quickly, he put it to his lips and pumped two jets of cold mist into his mouth. He held his breath and kept still, counted *one, two, three*.

Ashes watched as two of the brothers carried in a heavy metal locker and placed it at the feet of the Leader. The Leader bent, unlocked the clasps and opened the lid. Inside there were many long rifles and he picked up one and held it high above his head.

'Oh *Gooood*,' gasped one of the young boys.

Another let out a low whistle.

'Rambo time,' someone joked. But the Leader glared and the men and the young boys hushed.

'There are trucks waiting outside in the yard, just next to the exterior wall,' he instructed. 'You will each be given a gun and ammunition. Dress appropriately. We are an army. Once we arrive, you will be assigned a duty. Those of you with training have been prepared. You will take the lead and you will fight. You others, with no training, will follow orders. You will defend and guard. I will read out a list of names of those who will come with me to the television station, the rest will go with Hal to the House of Power.'

Ashes' vision blurred and sweat trickled from his hairline down the side of his face. He wasn't ready.

And yet he *knew*. He'd been told. He had come willingly, and he had lied to his wife in order to be here. The brothers now guarding the Leader seemed very organised; they began to take the rifles from the locker and hand them out. Some of the young boys who'd only really come for football seemed accepting of the situation. They had amazed smiles at the sight of the big guns. Others looked disappointed and a little lost. No football. Boys with no home, no mother or father; they were the foster sons of the Leader. Before they'd arrived at the commune they'd hawked sweets and plastic gadgets on street corners of the City of Silk or they'd run errands for the badjohns who occupied the pizzeria in the southeastern part of town.

Ashes glanced around him. Many of the older brothers seemed as anxious as he was. The room was full of nervousness. Only the four in the matching army fatigues were in tune with the Leader. Like him, they knew what was happening. Some of the men were older than Ashes and rougher than him; they had lived on the streets once too. But they were ready now, prepared for action of almost any magnitude. A few of the older men, Ashes knew, had been part of the earlier revolution in 1970; one, a feller called Greg Mason, had even shot a policeman dead and had done some time in gaol. This man had been part of the Brotherhood of Freedom Fighters and had known River.

But mostly, right then, seeing all those guns, everything was unreal. The world was hazy and far away and all the men were floating.

You coming, eh, the Leader had said. *I need good men like you.*

The Leader had rung him privately the week before. Ashes had been more flattered than alarmed by the phone call. It meant the Leader counted on his support, had his eye on him for backup in the ranks. Ashes hadn't even tried to be close to the Leader.

'Here,' said a gruff voice. It broke him from his thoughts. 'This is yours.'

A rifle appeared in front of him. Long black metal nose, a crutch-like piece of polished wood. The guns, he had known about them; they'd been shipped from Miami amongst piles of hollowed-out plywood. Hundreds had arrived some weeks ago and they'd been hidden in a warehouse near Cry-Town in central Sans Amen. Guns, ammunition, explosives, all in planks of hollowed wood. Ashes had never seen a gun before. He held it like he might hold a teapot. He had no idea how to use it; he hadn't been one of the brothers chosen for training. The gun was heavy and it frightened him. His wrists were thin and weak and he tried to hide this. His stomach was all curdled up. His armpits began to perspire. The gun grew so hot it seemed to scald his hands. His heart felt tight and closed up and he stood like a wooden man with a red-hot gun in his hands. One of the brothers gave him a bandolier of ammunition. With stiff hands, Ashes put the large bracelet over his head and one shoulder so it encircled his body. It was heavy and the bullets felt like sharp teeth. Now he looked like Rambo too. He wanted to call his wife immediately. He wouldn't tell Jade where he was or exactly what was happening. He would just let her know he wouldn't be home for dinner. That would be appropriate, that was all she needed to know.

Then everything began to move quickly. A hundred or so men were leaving the prayer room, wearing green army camouflage pants, big black boots, knitted hats, string vests; some, those who'd been trained, wore a version of combat fatigues they'd brought from home; all of them were armed with long metal rifles. The brothers began to file out the back door into the afternoon heat. They were fighters now, soldiers of God.

*

Two trucks were parked by the wall of the compound. More masked brothers stood by them. Ashes thought he recognised them. Most likely these men had also been trained. They looked fierce, almost like professional soldiers. Hal was with them and Ashes could see he meant business. He had on full combat fatigues and a black beret, neat and tilted sideways on his head. Hal was Number 2 to the Leader in the community. He was handsome, like the Leader, an educated man. Sometimes Hal gave talks after prayers, and sometimes he coached the boys because Hal was also good at football; he'd been away from the island to university to study 'computer science', something very new. In some ways he was even more qualified to lead than the Leader himself, but it was like Hal didn't want to. He liked to be Number 2. Seeing brother Hal gave Ashes a surge of confidence. He gave a brief nod and the two men exchanged looks.

'You, get in with me,' said Hal. Ashes was glad of this, that he would be with Hal.

One of the trucks had big white letters on the side: W. A. T. E. R. He knew that a brother in the community had a cousin or an uncle who worked for the water authorities; the truck must have been borrowed. The other truck looked like the kind of vehicle used to transport horses or farm animals. It had no windows. It was a metal box on wheels.

'I'm not going in the horse truck,' Ashes said to Hal. This assertion surprised him. Maybe it was because he had a gun in his hands. Already he had more strength. Hal nodded as if he had thought the same thing.

'The trucks are for camouflage,' said Hal.

Ashes nodded, but he still wasn't going in the horse truck.

Brothers began to line up, their guns shining in the sun. One of the men, a feller called Arnold, had put on a red Santa hat with a snowy white trim. Arnold was tall and his body was hard looking, hard as Pouis wood. He wore a green net vest and green army pants and black leather boots. He had bucked teeth. He was an ugly man, ugly like a vampire bat, but with the Santa hat on and his bandolier slung round his thin torso he looked dangerous.

Ashes stared at Arnold's hat. He wished Hal would say something. It was not befitting for a revolutionary soldier to dress like that.

'What you staring at?' said Arnold.

'You gonna make history in that hat, or what?'

'Yeah, man.'

'But we are not Christians,' said Ashes.

'Maybe I am.'

'*You?*'

'Yeah, maybe.'

'And you praying with us?'

'No. I never pray with you.'

'What you doing here, then?'

'I was invited, nuh.'

'As Santa Claus?'

'Captain Claus,' said Arnold, and he made a sharp mock-salute and laughed at Ashes like he was the arse.

Ashes steupsed. He didn't like this at all. More and more this was feeling difficult. He didn't want to go to a revolution in a horse truck with a brother dressed like Santa Claus. But Hal didn't seem to mind and no one else seemed to care or notice Arnold's hat.

Men were getting into the W. A. T. E. R. truck. Ashes realised he needed to move fast to find a space. He made his way towards the truck and put his gun inside and then heaved himself up and onto one of the bench seats lining the sides.

It was dark inside the truck and when he looked around he found he recognised all of the men and boys already sitting there. Most of them he'd seen around the compound for years; all he'd prayed with. They weren't friends; they weren't associates or colleagues either; they were brothers. One of the young boys, a street kid called Breeze, seemed to be delighted with his gun; he was alert, ready for action. Breeze was about fourteen, Ashes guessed. He got his nickname because he could run fast. He had dressed himself up in black: black pants, black sports shirt, big black army boots, a knitted hat over his razor sharp hair. The gun he held was thin and sleek and for a split second Ashes could see Breeze running fast with his gun.

Then Hal appeared, and Ashes felt relieved. Hal was like a big bull-terrier dog, strong, loyal, a fighter. He had two gold teeth in the side of his mouth and his eyes were a muddy green. Hal was a man a cut above the men he was leading. That was clear. Hal sat down on the other side of Ashes and switched on his walkie-talkie. He spoke to the Leader, down into the microphone. 'Yeah, yeah,' he was saying, listening to the final commands. 'Yeah, yeah, we going,' said Hal. Then he switched off the walkie-talkie and leant outside the back of the truck and shouted to the driver.

'Lehwego,' he commanded. The truck started to move, rolling out of the compound, straight past the army post stationed next door, the army that was supposed to watch the Leader closely and guard the country from the Leader's bad men.

*

The streets of St Jared's on the outskirts of the City of Silk were busy busy busy. It was late on a Wednesday afternoon, late in the month. Month end, payday soon, and people were out drinking beer. The W. A. T. E. R. truck rolled slowly past the people liming and the vendors out on the street. A parlour on the corner was blaring soca, and jerk chicken smoked on the grill at the takeaway next door. Ashes stared out into the world he knew well and it didn't feel real. Again he was far away. His head had gone soft. His heart had slowed down. He was barely breathing. The other brothers stared out the back too. They watched people walking across the street. They watched the maxi taxi behind them get a bad drive from another maxi, which turned in to the traffic. A vagrant with a big raffia bag on his head began to bawl in the street, for no reason but just to bawl. Cars beeped their horns at him, to get out of the way. Ashes felt like he'd gone deaf, like he'd come down with some kind of confusion of the head. He could feel Hal was nervous too. He was already showing patches of damp through his army suit. He wanted to reassure Hal: *I believe in you*, he wanted to say. *Everything will go okay.*

Then they were travelling around the big savannah parkland in the centre of town. The truck stopped halfway round, pulled over by the kerbside, and a few brothers, men he'd never seen before, wearing black robes and aviator sunglasses, were standing there. The men seemed to be expecting them; several boxes of rifles were piled up on the ground and they began to load these boxes inside the W. A. T. E. R. truck in broad daylight! Ashes rubbed his eyes as if he wasn't seeing right. Boxes of big guns were sailing into the back of the truck, right there, next to the savannah. It was like the guns were invisible, like this was some kind of sign or blessing from God. The rifles passed silently through the back of the truck. No one spoke. The boxes of guns piled up on the floor of the tray. Then they were driving again, and Ashes had a sense of leaving the world behind, of watching the world backwards from the truck which now smelled of gun metal and late-after-noon sweat.

The W. A. T. E. R. truck turned left down into the heart of town, travelling past the gaol, past shops, past people walking slowly in the afternoon sun, then right, then left again into Veronica Street. It wasn't a very long journey from the compound into town. Then Hal was giving them instructions as to what to do when they arrived at the House of Power.

'We going straight up,' he said. 'Up into the chamber. Up the steps to the public gallery. Security will be armed and they will try to stop you. Shoot them. Shoot them dead. They will shoot you if you don't shoot them. Do not shoot anyone else. We will be taking the Prime Minister and the other cabinet ministers hostage. We will round up as many ministers of the government as we can. Everything is in the first ten minutes. We will be taking them by surprise; people will try to run. The first thing we need to do is secure all the exits.'

And then the W. A. T. E. R. truck stopped. And Ashes could feel the air in his lungs had evaporated. Again he reached for his inhaler and pumped mist into his lungs and waited and counted and he said a brief prayer to his God. *Tomorrow, everything will be different*, he told himself. The skies were an empty chalk blue, the House of Power a stark and lurid magenta against it. The building was huge. There were striped-canopied windows, high arches and long balconies which made it seem like a palace of some sort. There was even a dragon on the roof, some kind of sea serpent, arched and hissing at them. It was a weather vane and it marked the direction of the wind but Ashes didn't like the look of it at all. It was like the serpent was vexed and cussing into the air. On the ground floor there was a wide wrought-iron gate which barricaded the street level, and next to it there were steps which led upwards into the balcony and chamber of the House. Five palms stood outside the gate like thin girls, showing their lewd red bunches of berries under their skirt-fronds. Ashes had never been so close to the House. He felt like he was near something very feminine and glamorous, like his wife's purse.

Hal jumped out and let down the back of the tray of the truck. And then it was like they were a thousand brothers and they were all running and shouting and Hal was yelling, *Go!*, and all the men and boys were running up the steps to the public gallery to the House of Power. Some of the brothers began firing their guns into the air. Arnold was ahead of him, with his Santa hat, strong and fierce now and he was shouting *God is great* and only God knew what else. Ashes didn't fire his gun; he could hardly hold it upright, could barely make his legs move. He could only just breathe and see what he was doing. All he knew was that he was in the pack, running, playing his part, and thinking of his dead brother, remembering those whispered conversations between himself and River, in bed at night, ideas of a New Society, the stacks of Phantom comic books under their beds. Those days came with him as he ran amongst the men who were shouting *Praise be to God*, storming the House of Power. The revolution was happening.

Then he heard loud screaming and more shots coming from another direction and he saw a security guard fly down the stairs and *bam*. He saw the guard fall back against the wall, a red spot on his chest. *Bam*, more shots, then he saw Arnold in his Santa hat. Arnold was still shooting the guard even though the man had slid to the ground and looked dead. Men were running past him, and there was black-red blood on the ground. And there was a sound like a loud woodpecker, *rat a tat tat*. Shots fired in the air, a woodpecker rapping on the glass as bullets ripped through the panes. Ashes saw a fat woman jump out the stately open window of the House of Power and fall crumpled to the ground, her feet bent beneath her. Her cries sounded like an animal in pain. And then he was up in the chamber and the screaming was so loud he panicked and started to yell out the name of his brother River.

*

Ashes hadn't expected to see women in the chamber. But they were there, three of them, youngish-looking, attractive women, dressed in jackets and skirts, actually in the chamber. He hadn't realised there would be women so close up in the politics of the day, so close that they could talk freely to the big men, the ministers and everyone in the House of Power. The women began to cry out in terror and they ducked under their desks. One of the male ministers froze and stood there like a ghost of himself. He was shot instantly and then he fell. Bullets ricocheted like grains of rice pouring into a deep metal pan. They flew everywhere in a hail and up into the air, shooting holes into the thick ornate white plaster which Ashes was also surprised to see, fancy, like a wedding cake. It was like heaven in there, another world to the one he knew. The House of Power looked just like a shrine or a holy place, all white and gold and tall columns, fancy *tra la la* and bows painted into the ceiling. There were high arched windows inside the chamber and a red velvet carpet. Ashes felt his insides melting. Then he flew upwards, out of his body.

He was on the ceiling then, watching everything: people were cowering under chairs, he could see their ankles, the heels of their shoes, their haunches not quite tucked under them enough. He saw two men dragged out from underneath a desk. One big man seemed to be protecting the other; he was covering this other man with his body; this was some kind of body-guard and the brothers told him to *Step aside or be shot*. Hal kicked the man he was protecting hard in the face.

Hal cussed at him, saying that *Everything is over, Prime Minister, we are removing you*. Then Hal struck this man, the Prime Minister, again hard in the face with the butt of his rifle and he groaned and fell unconscious. Hal and two other brothers hogtied the Prime Minister, yanking his arms behind his back, securing his wrists, and then they pulled down his suit pants so his white underwear was visible and his brown buttocks showed. Some of the brothers were shouting out names of ministers of the government: 'Where is Jayso? Where de IMF man? Where Cranleyson?' They kicked over chairs, pulling these men out, shouting *God is with us*, saying they'd caused pain and suffering to the poor man and now they were going to pay for it. Yelling came from down the corridors of power, the sound of gunshots, screams echoing and reverberating so Ashes had to put his hands to his ears. People who'd come to sit in the public gallery cowered. One man dressed up real smart in a suit and tie had urinated on himself. He blubbered and cried for mercy and one of the brothers swore at him and said, 'Fucking big man like you bawling like a cow,' and jabbed the man hard in the ribs with his rifle. Ashes didn't like the way the brothers were behaving at all; it was alarming to see such bad manners and foul language.

Government men and House employees were

escaping everywhere, running down the corridors and out onto the balcony; men were jumping down to the ground, out of the windows. Brothers with guns were chasing after them; two or three escaping people were shot in the back and fell down dead. In the tearoom next to the chamber, the tea ladies screamed as bullets zinged past them; there was a man amongst them undressing and pleading with them for help. They said, 'Yes, yes, quick,' and hid him in a cupboard. Policemen who'd been standing on guard were escaping from the chamber, running through the corridors away from what was happening; some were also shedding their clothes. The brothers didn't shoot them. They let them go free. There was a woman under a table in another room across the hall from the tearoom; she'd been shot and lay wounded and groaning and Ashes knew she was calling out the name of her son. Black-red blood was seeping from her stomach. No one but Ashes up on the ceiling had seen her. She'd crawled to a safer spot, but she wasn't going to live long.

Throughout, brother Arnold was jabbering and wild, shooting upwards and menacing anyone who looked like they might leave the chamber. His Santa hat had slipped sideways on his head. His skin shone and his hard muscles bulged and the whites of his eyes gleamed, and he looked like an escapee from the madhouse not too far way. Maybe, even, he was. That thought occurred to Ashes as he watched the chaos from the ceiling. The young brother called Breeze seemed well conditioned, very active and in step with what was happening. He was keeping close to Hal, going along with everything like he was a natural.

In the chamber Hal began to shout orders. The members of the public would be set free; they could go immediately.

'Go *oooonnn,*' he shouted. The brothers prodded them and these people began to leave very quickly, down the stairs and out into the draining evening light. They ran across the forecourt of the House of Power, out onto Veronica Street. The tea ladies were allowed to go and they fled, three of them in their aprons, muttering prayers. One of the parliamentarian women was allowed to go free too; she was a minister in the opposition party. Another man was told to go, a man Hal knew, a notable man in the labour movement. And then Hal weeded out all the men who were no longer high up in the government, those in a small group who'd split from the Prime Minister. He had them lie flat on the floor behind the speaker's chair; it was like they were a separate group of prisoners. The Prime Minister, already hogtied, he lashed to another minister, leg to leg, and he laid them flat on the floor in the centre of the chamber like the big prize. And then the other members of his cabinet, including the two women, were also tied with their hands behind their backs with tight plastic bands, face down, in the centre of the chamber; they were trussed up like blue crabs in the market. It was all happening so fast, like the plan was working. Ashes had a fluttering feeling inside, like the feeling of hummingbird wings, the feeling of God being present with them there, in their actions. Something important was happening and God was helping them. Ashes was impressed; Hal had been trained and it showed. Hal knew what he was doing, like he was a man of action.

Ashes felt sick and dizzy, but he was also proud of his friends. He was beginning to come down off the ceiling; maybe he could even walk around. Armed brothers were still running everywhere, but the shooting had quietened down. It had all been so quick. Everybody was either dead, dying or tied up and face down on the red velvet carpet. Ashes was surprised to find himself standing in a corner of the chamber, next to a wide open window which opened to a view of a samaan tree which spread itself like the green cloud of an atom bomb. He was holding his gun upright, his shirt was damp through and stinking of his own sweat.

His spectacles had fogged up. He had been weeping. His entire face was wet with tears. He was still shaking, but he was standing upright. No one noticed him there or seemed bothered with him at all. It was like he had become invisible.

*

One hour had passed. It was 7 p.m. Everything was different now in Sans Amen. One of the ministers tried to talk to Hal. 'Hey, Hal,' he said. 'I remember you from school. Maths class. Remember me?' Hal laughed and said, 'Yes. I remember you. But we weren't friends. Now shut up.' This was a small place, everyone knew each other. Ashes suddenly felt embarrassed that one of the ministers might know him, or worse, that they might know his wife.

In the corner of the chamber there was a television mounted on a bracket on the wall. Ashes made his way over to watch the seven o' clock news with the other men. They all gathered round. There was Justin Samaroo, the usual newsreader, looking very tense and serious. Next to him sat the Leader, dressed in his grey robes.

The brothers all stared at him, up there on national television. He had captured the country. No one said a word. It was like they were held captive too; so few of them had known of his master plot. Now they watched, some with loving pride, others with a new self-regard for what they had been part of. One feller raised his fist in a salute of solidarity like he'd all along been on the inside. All the brothers were glued to the screen, as if the Leader, there, dressed in grey, was indeed right-eous, an avenging angel. He'd seized power, just like he said he would only hours before. Some of the men clapped. Ashes stared upwards and he felt grateful he'd survived.

A dark woollen cap clung to the Leader's head. The Leader was always very well dressed and presentable, as was befitting of a man who was going to change everything around in the country. Now there, on tele-vision, was a man of the people, a man born to serve, a warrior and a man of God. The Leader, it was known, had many talents. It was said he could actually bake a cake and he did so now and then on important family occasions. The Leader had three wives, nine children and a hundred fostered sons in the commune. The Leader was loved. He was just and fair. *Do not under-estimate the complexity of this great man,* thought Ashes, as he watched the screen that evening. Ashes felt him-self regain his strength and sense of purpose just at the sight of him. Now he was relieved he'd been included in the plan, that he'd said 'yes', for River and for a New Society. The Leader was reading from a script of some sort:

'At 6 p.m. today, the government of Sans Amen was overthrown. The Prime Minister and members of the cabinet are under arrest. We are asking everybody to remain calm. The revolutionary forces are commanded to control the streets.'

Sitting there in the newsroom, the Leader looked calm and handsome. It was like a miracle. The revolution had happened. It had happened in an hour. Here they were, the brothers were now in charge, and there was the Leader, announcing the news. A few boys, a few guns – and a New Society could begin. It was so simple and so easy to overthrow a bad government in the middle of governing. Justin Samaroo didn't look so good, though. He looked frozen, like something had only just started. He looked like he might faint any minute.

Some of the brothers clapped and whooped. Hal, he could see, was visibly relieved. Ashes uttered words of thanks and said aloud, 'Praise be to God.' There had been some bloodshed, and yes, there had been some fatalities, but not too many. Ashes had understood this might be part of the proceedings. If words and prayers didn't work, it was appropriate to take action. The

Leader had marched for justice along with the labour leaders, petitioned for the poor; he had asked, pleaded, prayed for a new order – even made direct threats of seizing power. And now he'd taken the last option: force. Ashes wanted to ring his wife Jade to tell her the news; how proud she would be of him, that he had been part of such a thing. He wanted to apologise for his small lie, say that it had only been to conceal a larger surprise. He wanted to say, *Kiss Arich and Arkab goodnight, my love. I made history today.* One day I will tell them about their Uncle River and the great Fat Clay of Cuba, the other asthmatic revolutionary. Ashes felt for his inhaler and took it out and released two jets of mist into his lungs just for the hell of it, in celebration of this marvellous occasion.

Just then, bullets came in from the dark, like schools of barracuda, ripping up everything in their wake, shredding up wood, lodging deep into the walls. The air around him became smoky and peppery with gunfire and a brother next to Ashes, one of his fellow revolutionaries, was shot straight through the head. His skull split open and his face splattered into pieces and his tongue was shot out of his mouth. The tongue landed on the red velvet carpet. 'Everybody *down*,' screamed Hal.

Hal was on his walkie-talkie again, shouting to the

Leader who was no longer in the newsroom at the television station. 'What the *hell* is the army doing here so soon?' Hal shouted. 'It is Wednesday evening. We picked the day on purpose, they all supposed to be at *home*, month end, or at the football match in the stadium. Big football match and we already blow up the police headquarters. What the *hell* they doing here?'

The walkie-talkie buzzed. The army had stationed themselves right outside the House of Power and they must have been using bazookas because suddenly the whole chamber thudded and rocked. Chunks of plaster fell from the walls, fancy cornice work tumbled from the corners. A chandelier plummeted to the ground. Screaming now, a wild hysteria which belonged to every person in the room, the brothers and their hostages. Some of the younger boys wept openly. He saw Breeze throw his gun on the ground and cover his head with his hands and pray. Some of the brothers went to the windows and tried to return fire. Hal was on one knee shooting out into the dark. Arnold had gone mad and was belting out bullets from his rifle, and then it was clear no one had showed him how to reload; he was having trouble putting new bullets into his gun.

Ashes was up on the ceiling again. From there he could see outside. Hundreds of men in army fatigues had surrounded the House of Power. He was stunned. The Leader had said the army was *loyal* to him, that he had important contacts high up, that there would be no problems with the army. The police? They would all give up and run away. But the army would be supportive of the revolution: that was what the Leader had told him *directly*. The Leader had explained that on Tuesday night, the night before the coup, more guns would be handed out to well-known criminals the Leader had either paid off or who owed him favours, and these men would 'command the masses' in the streets in a popular revolt. He had said that the army too would join in this people's revolution, as it had done before in 1970.

But these plans had obviously gone wrong. When Ashes looked outside he saw an entire regiment of men, heavily armed, snipers in trees, men flat on their stomachs, army jeeps and trucks and men jumping out of them; the army had very quickly formed a cordon around the House of Power. Soldiers were everywhere, state-trained, expensive boots, soldiers obeying orders. A buzz in the air, a helicopter was circling overhead, and then he could hear a captain from the army on a megaphone shouting orders up at the chamber. But the brothers inside ignored this and kept firing out into the dark.

The Prime Minister was still face down on the floor
with his pants down by his ankles. All the other cabinet ministers were still on the floor too; they kept
quiet. Breeze looked startled and wild. He'd picked
up his gun and he was firing randomly; he had completely lost his cool. He was cussing loudly, saying,
'Oh, gorsh, damn frikkin muddecunts.' Arnold had
managed to reload his gun and was shooting his
ammo out into the night. The hard man, Greg Mason,
the man who'd known River from the Brotherhood of
Freedom Fighters, was with Hal, firing into the dark;
they were like real soldiers, together, steady and
focused. They'd been trained for this. Hal's walkie-talkie crackled and from it Ashes could hear the
Leader's panic and this panic electrified his nerves.

*

The shooting lasted for an hour at least. Men firing
and men returning fire and a clatter of bullet-hail and
it didn't seem to matter who was shooting at who,
just that a storm was going on and the revolution was
still taking place. Bullets were embedded in the walls
of the chamber and it was dangerous as hell to stand
upright. Most of the boys were flat on the floor with
the hostages. Ashes came down from the ceiling and

made his way on all fours to the tearoom at the side of the chamber. It was safer there, behind a partition wall. But the tearoom was ruined; every piece of crockery was smashed and shot up. There was a big urn on the counter and he reached upwards and touched it and realised it was boiling hot, full of water ready for tea. He could happily drink a cup of Lipton's right then, with sugar stirred in. His stomach was a tight ball; he hadn't eaten since lunchtime and he wondered if there were any plans for dinner in this revolution. On the side there was a small white cardboard box, like you might get from a bakery; he opened it and saw it was full of cheese puffs which were his favourite delicacy. He ate one quickly and shoved another puff into the side pocket of his camouflage pants, next to his inhaler. There was a fridge too; he opened it and saw half a carcass of roast chicken on a plate, a carton of UHT milk, three green portugals.

Then he remembered the man he'd seen from the ceiling, possibly a cabinet minister, who'd stripped and hidden in a cupboard in the tearoom. He turned and aimed his rifle at the row of cupboards which lined the other side of the room. A man, he was certain, had climbed into one. Ashes' hands were numb and yet he managed to aim his gun. He advanced cautiously. The man was in the middle cupboard, he knew that for sure. Outside, in the next room, he could hear shouting. Hal was giving new orders, more of the brothers were shouting too, 'Get down, get *down*.' Ashes went straight to the middle cupboard and knocked on the door.

'Hello,' he said. 'Come out.' He tried to sound officious. 'Come out now with your hands up,' he said again.

But nothing. The door didn't open. He realised it had been locked from the outside by one of the tea ladies now escaped.

He turned the tiny key in the lock. He stepped back and aimed his gun and again he commanded, 'Come out of there.'

The door didn't move.

Instead, the door next to the one he was aiming his gun at opened, slowly.

A man was stooping sideways inside the cupboard. He was wearing only his underpants and socks and he looked very scared. He held his hands up. 'Please, *please*, don't shoot me,' he said, his voice choked. Tears in his eyes. 'I have children.'

Ashes stared. He was almost on the ceiling again, out of himself. He nodded.

'I have little children,' the man begged. 'Two girls.

Please don't kill me.' Ashes could see the man was about forty-five, his stomach covered in black hair. He had a neatly trimmed black moustache and he looked familiar.

'You in the government?' Ashes asked.

The man nodded in a cringing way. 'Yes.'

Ashes lowered his gun. He reached for his inhaler and shot a quick puff of mist into his lungs. The minister began to sob. 'I want to see my wife again,' he stammered.

Ashes could barely stand up straight; his head swam and he wanted to see his wife too, but he was duty-bound to stay.

'Go,' he commanded.

The man looked shocked. 'Go?'

'Yes. Go.'

'Where?'

'Out there,' he pointed to the empty hallway with his gun. Beyond the hallway there was a labyrinth of corridors which led further into the House of Power, and out and away from all the revolution, out onto the streets of the City of Silk.

The man didn't wait for Ashes to change his mind. He stepped out of the cupboard with his hands raised high and then he fled, running down the wood-panelled corridor, and Ashes felt relief for the escaped man and a powerful surge of shame for his own cowardice. In truth he ached to flee. He wanted to leave. He had to pray, needed to pray, connect with the beautiful, the force that would take him away from all this, the heartsource he understood. He needed space and he whispered, *Oh, help me, oh Lord*. It had been hours now of this battering; he hadn't been fully prepared for all the noise and chaos. When the Leader had spoken to him, he hadn't painted this picture at all. He'd said it would all be well executed, straightforward. Everything had been planned for months, planned like professional soldiers, a militia of men. All Ashes had to do was show up. He had assumed it would be an easy takeover, and it had been, to begin with.

Ashes left the tearoom and walked into another large, high-ceilinged room which was also empty and ruined. Telephones lay strewn over the ground, their wires ripped from the wall; chairs were upturned all over the floor. The window was open to the night air. A chandelier gave off a pretty fairground-type light. Under a big wooden table lay the injured woman he'd seen from the ceiling. She was on her side and her stomach was now slick with blood; she'd been shot and was badly wounded. She was barely conscious; she was on the carpet under the table, bleeding to death. He bent down and looked at her and she made eye contact with him, but he could see that she was on the ceiling too, out of herself.

She whispered something and he couldn't hear what she said. He bent closer.

'My son,' she whispered. Blood came up in her teeth and spilled from her lips. 'The young man who shot me. The same age . . .'

Ashes saw River, then, bleeding, just like this woman, left to die with a hole in his stomach, left to die in the road.

Ashes recoiled and let out a gasp. 'I'm sorry,' he said, and left the room quickly and ran down the corridor and found himself deep inside the House of Power. All the rooms had been ransacked: papers everywhere, drawers pulled out onto the floor, overturned chairs and smashed-up glass, bullet holes where the army had shot in, and in the corners there was the acrid smell of urine. Some of the younger brothers had been in here and they had shot up the place just for the hell of it and relieved themselves in the corners. Someone had written *Praise be to God* in white Liquid Paper on the grey wall. Ashes stood in wonder and read these words over and over again. His heart felt sour and heavy: it was wrong to harm women.

The brother called Breeze appeared at the door with his rifle which was bigger than him.

'What you doing in here?' Breeze asked. The young boy seemed to have recovered himself from his fit of terror.

'I came in here to pray,' Ashes said. It slipped out. He didn't know that was what he'd come to do. Maybe he was even already deep in prayer, or had been praying all along, up on the ceiling and now in here.

Breeze gazed at him, unsure of what to make of this. He nodded and yet kept his expression neutral. Again, Ashes recognised that faraway look; he sensed the young boy was struggling, as he had been, that he was a little out of himself.

'What happen?' Ashes asked.

The boy steupsed. 'Nothing.'

But Ashes could see this was a lie.

'Nothing, nuh. Mind yuh Goddamn figging business.' The boy looked sullen and dangerous.

'Come and pray too, nuh.'

Breeze looked at him like he was crazy, as if this was no time to pray and the last thing he needed to do. 'You muddercunt,' he said and fled.

Ashes was left by himself again. He bowed his head and put the palms of his hands flat together and

opened his chest and his heart and waited and hoped.
He could feel water falling from his eyes and his nerves
were jangling and electrified. There was something
about the air, it was too troubled; something about his
head, which was too closed up; something about his
heart, which was all troubled up too and racing; something about the drawers strewn all over the floor. The
words on the wall swam, *Praise be to God*. Nothing
came; nothing he recognised, no connection with the
divine source, the beautiful. This had been his life's
inner work. This was what had made life bearable for
him since his brother had died. This quest for the beautiful. But there was no peace for him here, not now. He
shifted position and stood with his back to the wall.
He closed his eyes and counted his own breath. But
nothing came to him.

*

In the chamber the shooting had stopped. No one had
missed Ashes.

Hal said: 'Right, everybody reload.'

Hal found his walkie-talkie amongst the debris and
switched it on.

'Yeah, yeah, yeah,' he barked into it. The television
station had also been bombarded; the army had

arrived within an hour of the revolutionary forces. The Leader and his band of brothers were also under attack. They too were holed up and returning gunfire, but they were making announcements on television to the nation, telling people to remain calm, that they had taken power. The Leader informed Hal that there were a few cabinet ministers on the outside, those who hadn't been in the chamber that afternoon. They had immediately converged at the army barracks nearby; a small team had pulled together, and somehow a prized hostage, the Attorney General, had escaped from the House of Power. He had been spotted by troops running down the road in his socks and underpants amidst all the gunfire. They had saved him. Now there was a proxy government on the outside.

'How did the *focking* Attorney General get out?' fumed Hal down the line to the Leader. He glared around at the brothers and no one spoke. Ashes almost dropped his gun.

'The army is here when they were not supposed to be and the Attorney General has escaped. What de *ass* is all of this,' Hal steupsed. 'Big mistakes, man,' he said, and he walked off down the corridor speaking into the walkie-talkie.

Ashes didn't say anything; he went and stood next

to the less important hostages who were lined up, faces to the ground, behind the speaker's chair. He decided it was best to keep out of the way of everything and everyone.

Hal returned from the hall. He'd made contact with the army and had an officer on the line.

'Bring him,' he gestured to a brother guarding the Prime Minister. The Prime Minister was clearly in pain. His face was bruised and bloodied from the beating Hal had given him. He was still lashed to another minister, leg to leg. One of the gunmen pulled them both from the row of others.

Hal went over to the Prime Minister and knelt very close to his face. 'Now,' he ordered. 'Your troops are stationed outside. You are to command them to stop firing. Do you hear me?'

The Prime Minister looked like he might expire any minute.

'Yes,' he said, his voice muffled.

'Okay,' said Hal. 'I have an army officer on the line. He is one of the commanders of your army and he and his men are stationed outside. Okay? Now. Listen, here. I am going to count *one two three*, and at the count of three I am going to put the mouthpiece of the walkie-talkie to your lips. And you are going to tell this officer to call off his men and retreat. Okay?'

The Prime Minister nodded.

'Otherwise we will shoot every one of you and throw your bodies over the balcony. One by one. Do you hear that?'

'Yes,' said the Prime Minister.

'It will not be a pretty sight.'

The Prime Minister nodded again.

'Clear?' said Hal.

'Yes, clear.'

'Now,' Hal said, and he stooped close to the Prime Minister's head. 'Right, the officer is at the other end. Tell him what I told you.' Hal shoved the walkie-talkie receiver next to the mouth of the Prime Minister of Sans Amen, elected by the people for the people, a man who, it was commonly said, was a little stiff, perhaps, a bit like an old colonial. Ashes knew he was from a small village in the north of the island and had old-fashioned habits, old-fashioned ideas. He spoke very formally. He was a little bit out of touch, and he was obsessed with communists.

'Go,' said Hal. 'Say it.'

The Prime Minister of Sans Amen raised his head and bellowed down the phone. '*Attack*,' he roared like a lion. 'Attack with *full force*. These people are murderers!'

Hal's jaw fell slack. He dropped the walkie-talkie

and stood up. He kicked the Prime Minister hard in the ribs. The Prime Minister howled.

Ashes stared. Every one of the brothers stared too. What would Hal do now? Were they to kill everyone? Would the army attack with full force? Ashes decided then and there that he would take no part in throwing bodies over the balcony. He would say 'no' to that. That was a crazy idea. There were women hostages. He would not be part of shooting a woman and throwing her body anywhere.

'You have no concern, then,' Hal said, 'for your ministers, those inside here. You will get them all killed.' And with that he aimed his pistol and shot two bullets, *bam, bam*, into the Prime Minister's legs. The man screamed in pain. Ashes cringed. The bullets went through the Prime Minister's legs, also injuring the minister he was lashed to. Both men groaned in agony, both men shot lame. Blood sprang instantly from their wounds.

'Jesus *Christ*!' Hal threw his pistol to the ground and stormed off, out of the chamber and back down the corridor.

No one said anything. Every one of the brothers went quiet and stared. Some ventured towards the windows to see what the army would do. Ashes went close to one of the windows too. He could see the figure of a burly, very large brown-skinned man dressed in high leather boots and army fatigues, a green beret on his head. He guessed this was the infamous Colonel Benedict Howl, the head of the army. Howl was receiving the news of the Prime Minister's order to attack from one of his men. He was shaking his head, like this was not the right way to proceed. Howl then gazed upwards at the House and Ashes ducked from sight.

Ashes thought of his wife. Jade wouldn't like any of this. In fact she would cuss him if she knew he was here in such a mess. How would he ever speak to her about this? His brother had been shot dead in similar action and now this. He wondered too about Fat Clay of Cuba, who had written about revolution extensively, a whole handbook in fact. *The guerilla fighter is a social reformer*, that's what he'd said. Fat Clay had been asthmatic, true, so he wasn't the best soldier around, but he'd been a lot better prepared for a revolution than this.

Jesus Christ was a revolutionary, thought Ashes. He had revolutionary ideas. *The last will be first, the first will be last*. Jesus Christ was a born socialist. And they nailed his arse to a cross. The Buddha was also a great socialist; Siddhartha Gautama Buddha ran away from his noble palace life, donned saffron robes and wandered about learning how to live from poor men. And they poisoned his arse too, in the end. The world's great spiritual knights were often socialists on a quest for justice, Ashes had always understood that. And he had also understood that as a socialist too, he was above the average man in thinking, and to be above average was to think of others, not just oneself. That was the sign of a progressive mind. The self was selfish; a more developed man was one who could share his wealth and assets with others. And if he was to take his politics seriously enough, he could end up dead just like those great men. Not quietly dead either. All the world's great spiritual socialists had been murdered horribly; they'd been tortured and he had come to know that it could be the same for him. River had been gunned down in broad daylight. The coroner said the doctor had picked twenty-eight bullets out of him. Fat Clay of Cuba was shot dead by the CIA and then they cut off his hands so they could prove he was dead. He was that dangerous.

Ashes had made a conscious choice when the Leader had called him up. *You in or out?* the Leader had actually asked him flat in the end. The Leader was testing him because he knew about River and he assumed he could ask safely. And Ashes had said, 'Yes, I'm in.' And he knew in his heart that to be right-minded and to pursue a righteous quest for socialist convictions he would need to make right actions, and sometimes these actions were dramatic and sometimes they involved bravery and bloodshed. And so he agreed to take these risks for a greater society and for others to live well. The Phantom would have made the same decision. Phantom and the Buddha, and Christ and even Frantz Fanon, the great Caribbean philosopher and revolutionary, might have picked up a gun. They were knights, spiritual men.

*

The brothers had gathered around the television again and they were waiting to hear what the Leader would next announce. Ashes was sure he would persuade the army to back off, that they held hostages and that they meant business. This time the Leader didn't appear so calm on the television and Justin Samaroo next to him looked positively shaken. There was a fine white dust on his face. The Leader seemed tense and he began to read from a script in front of him, his face looking more and more agitated.

'We, the revolutionary forces, are still . . .'

And then the Leader's face and voice disappeared, *whap*, just like that. The screen turned to furious fuzz.

'Eh, eh,' said one brother.

'What de ass . . .' said another.

Hal made a low whistle.

The fuzz sounded loud, like a chaos from another galaxy.

'Like he get vapsed,' said another brother.

Ashes looked at Hal. He was shaking his head and his face was blank of expression, as if he couldn't believe what had happened and so soon.

'Jesus, Lord,' said Hal.

The Leader had just been wiped off air.

*

Hal was on the walkie-talkie again. Ashes could hear the Leader erupting like a volcano down the line. Hal was angry too, and for the first time he looked uncomfortable, even scared. Hal held the walkie-talkie close to the side of his head and put his other hand to his eyes and rubbed them hard. He took off his beret and stuffed it in his army pants pocket and Ashes thought Hal might cry. Things were that bad. The army had gone up to the big hill out of town, up to the old fort where there was a massive transmitter dish. They'd taken some television technicians with them. They had shut down the transmitter and so now the Leader could no longer broadcast the news to the nation that everything was okay and that the revolutionary forces were in control.

'Damn them to *hell*,' said Hal.

The gunmen looked at each other. Someone said, 'The Leader gone?'

Another said, 'Yeah, man. Like he get blocked.'

Ashes decided that it would be a good time to make a cup of tea. He left his post with the less important hostages and went to the tearoom and found some Lipton's tea bags in a glass jar. Much of the parliamentary crockery was smashed on the floor, which he now realised was a stupid idea. Why smash up all the teacups, what was the point of that? He opened two or three of the kitchen cupboards and searched for a cup which wasn't broken, finally finding a hand-painted mug. He put a bag in it and flushed boiling water into it from the urn. Cutlery had also been hurled from the drawers and he picked a teaspoon from the pile on the floor, rinsed it off and stirred a spoon of sugar into Hal's tea. He dared not make himself a cup of tea. That felt too unsoldierly.

He found Hal sitting in the room in the back with the words *Praise be to God* written in Liquid Paper on the wall. Hal looked upset and tired. Hours now of this. It was 10 p.m. The army had come when they were supposed to be asleep; the Prime Minister had turned out to be brave. Now the Leader had been knocked off air and they were caged up. Even the tea-cups were smashed.

'Here,' he said to Hal, offering the mug.

'What is that?'

'Tea.'

'I don't drink tea,' said Hal.

'You need something,' said Ashes. 'The sugar will help.'

Hal looked up at him pensively.

Ashes handed him the tea but felt awkward. Tea was women's business. He never made himself tea at home. His wife was good enough to make him tea.

'Your brother done dead,' Hal said as he took the mug.

'Yeah.'

'And so what . . . you come in here with us on some kind of family mission or something?'

Ashes felt embarrassed.

'Yeah,' he said. 'I figure so. You . . . knew River?'

'No,' said Hal. 'But I hear he was a good guy. Wild.'

'He was my older brother. I was fifteen when he died. I . . . never been the same person since then.'

'Howyuh mean?'

'I get sick since River dead.'

'How?'

'Wheezin and breathing get bad, and I get a pain right here,' Ashes pointed to his groin. 'It never go away. It get worse when it rain.'

Hal looked him up and down, thinking. 'You two nothing alike. That is what I hear.'

'Is true, I am quiet. I read a lot. They call me Books, sometimes,' Ashes said. He couldn't believe it, but his eyes were glistening.

'Your brother was a hillsman?'

'Yes.'

'Boy, them boys was the real thing,' said Hal with admiration.

'Yes.'

'Hillsmen. Flatsmen. Alluh them get shot in the end.'

'Yes.'

'The police shot up the women too.'

'Just one of them. Bathsheba. She was pregnant, though. So they shot two persons in one go you could say.'

'Lousy sons of bitches. Your brother was a hero.'

Ashes looked at Hal and he could see a kind of pity in his eyes.

'Hal,' he said, and he knew this was risky. 'We have shot a woman too, you know. That woman next door. She—'

'Look,' Hal snapped. 'Mistakes happen. This is warfare.'

Ashes shut up and tried to stay calm. Hal sipped his tea and looked far away and then his eyes went hard and he steupsed loudly. 'Fock this is shit,' he said aloud.

Ashes nodded but nothing felt clear at all. He had been disappointed in some of the brothers and their indecent and uncouth behaviour – and now it turned out that their well-laid plans had not been so well laid at all.

'Our plans fock up real quick,' Hal said.

Ashes nodded. Somewhere, he knew he was going to die. Maybe he even wanted to die the same way as River had, a horrible, noble, glorious death, the death of a fighter for freedom. He had achieved nothing much with his life so far. He had two wonderful sons, true, but sometimes he thought he would die from the pain in his groin. Only the beautiful saved him and even then, only sometimes.

Hal steupsed again.

'What we gonna do now?' asked Ashes.

'Ah thinking,' said Hal.

Ashes rested his rifle against the wall and perched on a desk next to Hal. 'The army weren't so loyal last time round. They mutinied and locked up their officers.

I guess the Leader figure the same thing go happen again. The army leave us to it. But no. Now they capture us.'

'We have the PM and we have important high-level hostages. We can negotiate,' said Hal.

'You really meant it about throwing the hostages over the balcony? If so, I ent doing that.'

Hal shot him a look of contempt. 'We going to do whatever we need to do to get out of here. I'll shoot you first and throw your damn arse over the balcony if you don't shut up.'

Ashes went quiet. He didn't feel brave. He was scared and unsure about being here; it wasn't what he had expected at all. He suddenly remembered a famous spiritual socialist in Sans Amen. He lived in the City of Coffee in the south, but he was a labour man, a trade union supporter and a man of the people. The Leader knew him and liked him too; they had been part of a big leftist umbrella movement. They had marched together only recently, a street march against the cutting of the Cost of Living Allowance. Maybe he might be able to help them.

'What about Father Jeremiah Sapno?' said Ashes.

'What about him?'

'He could help. You know, negotiate.'

Hal's face changed. 'Howyuh mean?'

'Everybody respect him. He could talk for us. Talk to them for us. You know . . .'

Hal nodded and looked far away again. 'Yes,' he said. 'Yes.' And then he reached for his walkie-talkie. 'Come in,' he said gruffly. 'Come in.'

THURSDAY MORNING, 2 A.M.,
THE HOUSE OF POWER,
THE CITY OF SILK

Father Sapno was due to reach the House of Power any minute to help negotiate how the hell they would all get out of there alive. Ashes stationed himself close to one of the large stately windows of the House, and yet partially hidden in the shadows of the long drapes. A ceasefire had been agreed. It was as if they had made the city quiet, all that shooting and noise and then quiet. His groin ached just to see the streets so silent. This was a different city, scared of itself and held hostage. It was clear to him now, and to the others, that the people hadn't risen up to join them.

Instead, people had already been looting. Out in the quiet dark streets he could see shops and banks and buildings and that everything had been smashed up;

he could see towers of smoke down by the docks hanging over the city, still visible in the street lamps. But now these looters had all gone to sleep. There was no one picking about. A curfew had been imposed. A State of Emergency had been declared. Now the city was very still. Usually at night, downtown was lively, especially at the Square of Independence where the vendors sold swamp oysters and barbeque ribs. Now all was quiet and the city smelled of sea breeze and petroleum and burning buildings.

Ashes knew the city well. He was born here, up in the hills to the east. Born and bred son of the City of Silk. He liked it here and had never left the island, no need to. He could see the big wide world on television and he saw nowhere else too different and certainly not any better than Sans Amen. Sans Amen was one of the northern islands of the archipelago; the other islands which ran in an arc southwards were similar, in a way, but also each one was particular. Some were more mountainous; one was entirely flat – that one was overrun by tourists. Different languages were spoken on the islands, Spanish, French and Dutch; each had its own creole language too. Trinidad, in the very south, had oil and carnival, it was the only island he was tempted to visit. Trinidad had also started the tradition of calypso, and those singers had always been – and some still were – revolutionaries too. They were the great bards of the Caribbean and they sang things like they were. They sang about life in the street and about corruption in their own House of Power. Generally politicians were afraid of them and what kind of songs they brought out around carnival time. Yes, he would like to go to Trinidad, if anywhere at all, and visit a calypso tent and listen to a great old calypsonian like Lord Wellington.

Otherwise, everything Ashes desired was right here. He hadn't even seen much of the rest of Sans Amen itself. There were remote parts of central and southern Sans Amen he would never know or see, quiet sleepy villages in the old sugar cane belt; places where men still gathered in gayelles on basketball courts to stick fight and bet on who was the best warrior amongst them. There were masjids and churches all over the island, temples to every version of God. There were mountains in the centre, full of deer and ocelots, and there were swamplands full of howler monkeys and anacondas to the southeast, and plains which still raged with fire every dry season, generations after the cane fields had disappeared. There were small fishing villages on the southern and eastern coast he would never know. Leatherback turtles came to nest on the beaches on the north coast, though he'd never seen one. He was a humble town man; so was his family. His wife's family came from nearby. It was like that – they were a clan, all neighbours. Everyone knew each other.

Then he saw the holy man. Father Jeremiah Sapno was walking towards the House of Power from the north side of town. The streetlights lit him up and it seemed like he was walking out from an orange haze. He had his hands in the air and he had a cross around his neck. He was walking down the street away from the soldiers.

A shot rang out.

Father Sapno ducked.

One of the young brothers had taken a shot at him.

'Hold your fire!' Hal shouted. 'Jesus *Christ*. Don't any of you know what is going on? There's a frikkin ceasefire. Don't shoot the man.'

Father Sapno had stopped walking.

'Come,' shouted Hal. He was up on the balcony above the wrought-iron gates which barricaded the main foyer on the ground level of the House, the side which looked down to the big square in the centre of town where old men gathered to play chess. But Father Sapno looked uncertain.

'Come, come,' gestured Hal upwards. Hal quickly moved back inside, out of sight of the army snipers.

When Father Sapno appeared in the chamber he looked very scared. His hands were still in the air and they were shaking. He gasped and crossed himself and said, 'Oh, Jesus Lord,' when he saw all the ministers trussed up face down on the floor and all the blood on the carpet. Everything was shot up. He gasped at Arnold in his Santa hat and at all the young boys with guns bigger than them, and at Greg Mason who looked like his very mother had taught him how to kill. Ashes felt ashamed. He didn't want a holy man to see him in this kind of situation. He couldn't look at the priest.

The House had already started to stink of death. Those who had been shot dead had been dragged to other rooms. The gunman who'd been killed had been taken away too, but his tongue was still on the carpet.

Father Sapno gagged and pointed at it. 'Have some common decency,' he said, and Ashes was glad because he had been thinking the same thing. It was an awful sight and yet he hadn't been strong enough in his stomach to pick it up. Hal ordered Breeze to take it away. Everyone looked at Father Sapno and Father Sapno looked at everyone else, all the brothers with their guns and the hostages. He was a man with a wide-open face, a shadow of a beard surrounding it; he was naturally jovial, it seemed, because gracious lines were etched on his face, even at a time like this. Hal looked disconcerted. The situation was a mess.

'Where do you want me to go now?' Father Sapno said. 'I only have an hour. The army wants to know your demands and I must then go back and report to them. An hour.'

Hal nodded and said, 'Come this way.' He had been on to the Leader and there was now a list of demands. They had untied the Minister for Health, Dr Mervyn Mahibir, and the Deputy Prime Minister, Mr Elias de Gannes, and there had been talks. Hal and Greg Mason led Father Sapno and these ministers and some of the ministers who'd split from the PM down the corridor; they went to the room with the Liquid Paper graffiti about God. Ashes felt glad. Also he felt disappointed. How had everything gone so badly wrong so quickly? Although he didn't know the exact plans, it was common knowledge in the commune that some of the Leader's men had been in training in camps in the countryside; some were even sent to the deserts far away. There had been ideas, plans, for a New Society. This had been no pot shot, no quick grab. He couldn't believe that the plans had misfired, that the revolution was already over. That couldn't be the case, so soon. They had boxes and boxes of explosives down the hall.

The Prime Minister groaned. Another minister,

Minister Sheldon, the one who'd frozen and remained standing rather than ducking when they stormed the chamber, was also bleeding a lot. There was a puddle of blood now by his ankle. Ashes worked as a porter at a health centre in his neighbourhood, but he wasn't trained to deal with medical matters; he was no nurse. Even so, he could see this minister was barely breathing and it worried him. It was possible he might die too if he wasn't seen to. The female ministers were very subdued. They were both hiding under chairs. One had urinated into a glass and it stood next to her. It looked very . . . intimate . . . and it made him feel unsure of going anywhere near them.

Many of the brothers were standing around. Some had forsaken their everyday names; they had spiritual names and they had shaved their heads and grown their beards and they were men with wives and families. The men who were trained for this looked more serious and mature. He could see a cold confidence in their eyes and in their posture, a seriousness of intent. None of these brothers had any questions or regrets so far, not like him. They were still following orders. If he didn't know who they were, he too would be scared of these men. They weren't fooling around. The Leader had attracted thousands of brothers and sisters over the years, but these men were a hand-picked bunch.

Ashes was now worried, scared for his life, and he promised himself that if he got out of there alive he would get off the island and take himself on a trip. He would take his wife and his sons, they would go to Trinidad. They would go for carnival, and he would go to Lord Wellington's tent and sit and listen to him and the other calypsonians sing. In particular he liked the song called 'Jericho', an old tune now, by Lord Wellington, but it was about a time just like when River was shot. It was a song about the guerrilla fighters of Trinidad, not so long ago fellers, all shot too. He liked the name of the hero in the song, Jericho, because it was the name also of a famous city in the Bible. Jericho was a town where palm trees spread their roots to an underground well in the desert and so the city was lush and green, an oasis in those arid holy lands. Jericho was known as the City of Palms. And yet the subterranean roots of the palms may have had something to do with why the walls of the city fell flat when the Israelites ransacked it, claiming it back and slaughtering everyone inside. Jericho, in his mind, was also a City of Blood.

THURSDAY MORNING,
THE HOUSE OF POWER,
THE CITY OF SILK

Dr Mahibir had arranged the cheese puffs on a chipped parliamentary plate. He had lined some of the less broken teacups up along the counter in the tearoom and he was making tea. Ashes noticed that the doctor limped around, but could see no wound. He hadn't been injured, yet something was wrong with one of his legs. It wasn't a new limp; his awkward manner of walking looked like an old habit. He seemed in quite good spirits considering everything. He had been the first hostage to be untied; he was useful. Hal had let him free in order to assess the wounded, hostages and gunmen alike. They had found a First Aid kit in another cupboard in the tearoom; it had bandages and ointments and so Dr

Mahibir had gone about attending to people as best he could. One of the young boys had accidentally shot himself through the foot and he had bandaged the wound. Several of the brothers had been nicked by bullets. But Minister Bartholomew Sheldon needed to be taken away to hospital immediately, he advised. He had been badly shot in the back of the thigh and he would bleed to death by lunchtime. The Prime Minister had stopped bleeding, but he was also diabetic and could lose his sight without his medication. They should take him to hospital too, but the PM insisted he would be the last parliamentarian to leave the House. Hal refused to let him leave anyway. The doctor had been up all night tending to the injured. Now he was making a tray of tea and cheese puffs.

Some of the brothers had eaten the chicken in the fridge. The woman under the table in the back room had died. Father Sapno had left hours ago along with the Deputy Prime Minister, Elias de Gannes, and they had a list of demands written down on a scrap of paper: 1) that the Prime Minister would immediately resign; 2) a free and fair election to be held in 90 days; 3) a reversal of plans for the IMF loan; 4) reinstigation of the Cost of Living Allowance; 5) a full amnesty for the gunmen. Under the list of demands were the signatures of every minister in the chamber, including the Prime Minister's, signed while Hal pointed a pistol to his head.

If these demands were not met, Hal and the Leader had decided they would blow up the television station and the House of Power with all the explosives they had with them. They would not be taken. They would kill everyone, including themselves, in the name of their righteous cause. They would go down fighting.

'Would you care for a puff?' Dr Mahibir asked Ashes.

Ashes stared at the tea tray. 'No thanks, I've already had one.' And then he remembered he hadn't yet eaten the puff in his army pants pocket and that now it must be very squashed. He couldn't eat anything. His feelings were very off centre and his heart was like a stone in his chest. Things were very badly wrong here in the House and he remembered the dragon he'd seen on top of it as they stormed in, hissing and looking threatening, and he'd thought this was a very bad sign. The House was protected. Ol time dragons – here, in the Caribbean. King beast. He'd seen plenty at carnival time, an ol mas figure. But this dragon was different; Queen Victoria had brought it with her. The Queen and the dragon were some kind of team.

And yet Dr Mahibir casually went about offering tea, like he wasn't worried at all. He had made a big metal teapot full of Lipton's and several chipped cups were stacked on his tray. He was offering tea and puffs to the hostages and brothers alike and this was very confusing, as though everyone in the chamber was the same when they clearly were not. Ashes wondered if any of this was correct hostage-taking behaviour; surely the tea and puffs were much too informal. And already Hal had agreed to cut free the plastic hand-cuffs of the hostages; he wondered if this was wise. Overnight many had tried to loosen the bands and they had only drawn tighter and begun to lacerate their wrists. The hostages were simply being guarded now, on rotation. The two female MPs should be let go, Ashes felt. They were having an effect on all the men.

Breeze was taking his role in the revolution very seriously; Ashes thought he looked like a miniature version of the Leader. His eyes were pensive and his lips were full; he was a serious-looking person already. His skin was very black and he was thin and stringy from a short lifetime of poor eating. Ashes knew he had come to the commune straight from court. Breeze had been bailed by the Leader rather than face six months in the overcrowded, rat-infested, lice-ridden gaol in town for petty theft and fraud – and for that he was loyal. Breeze was a street boy, wily as hell, an apprentice criminal already at fourteen years old; almost as hard as Greg Mason. If the Leader hadn't saved his arse from prison he would have become a common crook. Breeze had been given a dormitory to sleep in, albeit not much more than a scooped out abandoned bus, but he had been given shelter at least, three meals a day, free medical care, a peer group of other boys, also bailed from prison. And, most of all, Breeze had been shown the spiritual path, a way to purify his soul.

The City of Silk had many poor homeless boys like Breeze and no one but the Leader had shown any interest or care for them. They were nobody's concern. They had either run away or were put out of their homes early on, abandoned by their own families, and ignored by those in power. And so it was an act of divine will that Breeze now had power inside the House of Power. Ministers were afraid of him and his tall gun. He had recovered himself from the army's attack. He had removed a tongue off the carpet when no one else would touch it. He had refused puffs and tea. Hal and Greg had started using him as their chief assistant.

But now, despite Breeze's newfound respect amongst the ministers and top gunmen, Ashes noticed something else was happening to him, something Ashes found troubling: Breeze was drawn to the female ministers.

The female ministers were called Mrs Lucretia Salvatore, Minister for Cultural Affairs, and Mrs Aspasia Garland, Minister for the Environment, both African women in their early forties. Breeze had more or less appointed himself their personal bodyguard. Something else was strange too. The female ministers weren't scared of him; in fact they didn't show that they were afraid of any of the men. There was a softness in the way they spoke to Breeze and the other younger brothers; it was as if they were trying to befriend the young boys, as if they were trying to engage in a personal way. They were both sitting on the floor.

Breeze was standing tall above the female ministers, but if they stood up, the women would be taller than him. He was staring in a way which looked purposeful, as if he'd been given a rare and senior authority. He looked like he wanted to talk, and yet Ashes sensed that Breeze didn't know what to say.

The women regarded him in a half-bemused kind of way.

'So,' began the one called Mrs Garland, 'how on *earth* did you get into all this?' Her dark hair was straightened to curl in a swish. She had a thoughtful look in her eyes. She was conservative-looking in a way which said she meant business in the House, and yet her voice was husky-soft. She didn't look like a politician at all; she seemed too real and woman-like. Ashes moved a little closer so he could hear this conversation.

'We come for justice,' said Breeze. 'Alluyou is stealing money from the poor. I am a poor young man. You is stealing we money.'

'Who told you that?' said Mrs Garland.

Breeze steupsed. 'Is in the papers, nuh. And the Leader tell us is true.'

'What does the Leader tell you?'

'You is spending all the money in the treasury. Now you want to go to the IMF, because the money done. Is the people money and you spend it. Now Sans Amen go be colonised by the IMF. Is the same thing. Colonisation. First we get rid of the white man colonial in politics. Now you people go ask for the white man back in the country in the form of the big robber banks. We done with that. Economic colonisation. That cannot be. You spend all the people money; you cut the Cost of Living Allowance for poor people. You cut wages by ten percent; everyone know that. We must stop you. You ask why I get involved with all this. I is a fighter for freedom of the poor. You are the badjohns. You people in here with your fancy ideas. You is *thief*, you should be ashamed.'

By now a group of young brothers had gathered around the female ministers and they all murmured a *yesss* to what Breeze had said. Breeze looked pleased with his rhetoric; he had remembered it all and now glowed with pride. He looked defiant. Hal had heard this outburst too and looked on with approval. In fact everyone had heard what Breeze said; all the ministers were now interested. Along with three meals a day, Breeze had been fed doctrine.

'But listen here, young boy,' said Mrs Garland. 'You think is our government who spend all the treasury money? Eh? Think again, my young friend. The treasury was *empty* when we arrived two years ago. What we doing with cuts is for the general good of everyone. If we didn't cut back, then the country would bankrupt. That would be a big thing. Catastrophe. We had to make short-term cuts. Austerity measures.'

Breeze stared. He had nothing more than his speech. He looked like he needed more time to think.

'The Leader has come in and shot up the *wrong* government in my opinion,' said Mrs Garland.

One of the ministers laughed out loud.

Hal looked annoyed.

'Only yesterday afternoon we were debating this

very point,' said Mrs Garland. 'It was an important debate in the House, about corruption under the last government, just how much money was stolen by them, when you boys came in and shot up everything.'

Breeze looked lost.

Hal began to look uncomfortable.

'Young boy,' said another minister. 'My name is Mister Cordell Jayson. I am the Minister of Finance. I am the man who your Leader hates so much. I am the IMF man you were all calling for yesterday afternoon. Does your Leader have a substitute financial plan for how Sans Amen will recover its debt, how it will regenerate after the decades of corruption we have had?'

Breeze looked angry now. 'Your stupid government was going to spend fourteen million dollars on a statue of some dead woman. It was the last straw. We had to take action.'

'Actually,' said Mr Jayson, 'we had planned to spend one million on a statue of a woman who was a whistle-blower and had uncovered corruption in the past. She was a national hero. She fought for justice and was then ostracised by the men in power at the time. This new government stands for justice. We were elected to fight corruption. We have been in power only two years. Things take time.'

Breeze steupsed, not listening and not really understanding. 'So. Why you ent tell the people what you doing? All we get is bad news. Secrecy. Cut this and that. No explanation. The IMF is a bad thing. Meanwhile poor people cannot eat.'

'Well, maybe we could have explained things better ... yes ... and yes the IMF is a last resort. It is not something we take lightly ...'

Hal had had enough.

'Everybody SHUT UP,' he barked. 'Look, this is not Prime Minister's question time, okay. You boys, go stand guard by the windows. Breeze, get away from those women. We don't want the Special Forces coming up those steps while we discussing the price of bread. You,' he said to the female ministers, 'hush up. Stop speaking to my soldiers.'

Mrs Garland nodded.

Dr Mahibir had given out all the puffs by now; he was collecting the empty teacups. He was limping a little.

'What wrong with your foot?' said Hal. 'You got shot too?'

'No,' said Dr Mahibir. He lifted his pants up by the knees to expose his leather shoes which were attached to calipers and braces. 'I had polio as a child. I need help walking.'

Ashes felt like he needed to pray again. He needed a quiet private space. No noise, no others, no chaos. He started to collect up the teacups from those who were finished and he went back to the tearoom with Dr Mahibir and together they began to wash up the cups. He felt humbled being around Dr Mahibir; he sensed the goodness of this man who had been calm and helping everyone; he felt sick in his stomach at the injured and the dead. He felt hungry too and yet he could not eat. He was dizzy and hungry and now another feeling was creeping in, a type of feeling he associated with being in the wrong. He had that feeling with his wife sometimes, when she had to explain to him why he'd offended her or another person. The Buddha was big on teaching people how to refine their judgement; his wife and the Buddha had this fine judging quality. It was an important human quality to cultivate. Many a time he had praised God for the gift of his good wife. She was teaching him how to behave better than he generally could.

*

By midday the army were still encamped, and there was no news of the response to the demands they had put forward. Hal and the Leader had been communicating every hour. Colonel Benedict Howl was still outside in the streets around the House of Power, pointing a lot and issuing commands. He had a loud voice and didn't need a megaphone. Soldiers were scurrying around.

The attempted revolution had now become international news. Journalists were flying in from America and England, CNN, the BBC. A woman called Kate Adie had arrived; apparently she was already at the Holiday Inn. Hal was getting all this news from the Leader. The journalists wanted to speak to the Prime Minister on the phone, only all the phones had been ripped out of the walls. One of the brothers was now trying to reconnect a line. Mr Bartholomew Sheldon was very bad indeed, slipping in and out of consciousness. At 2 p.m. Hal allowed him to leave in a wheelchair in return for eight buckets of KFC chicken. Mr Sheldon went out, but no KFC arrived. Hal was furious. Furthermore, Colonel Howl refused to speak directly to either the Leader or Hal. Father Sapno was supposed to be the go between, only he had disappeared.

'You see that,' said Hal. 'They starving us out. They doing the textbook thing, nuh. Howl has been to hostage crisis school or something.'

Ashes cleaned his spectacles on his shirt and then put them back on his nose. It was like the freedom fighters were now hostages, Ashes realised. They held the ministers and the army was holding them. A double bind. The liberators were now being held captive and in turn were holding captive those who oppressed others. The army was loyal to the oppressors. The liberators were now being seen as oppressive. Some of the liberators were ex-army, Ashes knew that. The Leader himself was ex-police. The oppressed people outside, whose arses they had come to liberate, were all out looting; the brothers had seen them from the windows of the House.

Ashes tried to picture a bomb in the House of Power, with Hal pushing a red button to make the thing detonate, all of them blown sky high, the roof of the House of Power blown off, all of them dead, mutilated. Forty or so brothers and about twenty-five hostages. Sixty souls ripped to shreds in order to prove a point. Now it was hard to hold on to the point of it all. Perhaps Mrs Garland had been right. They had somehow arrived too late. They had captured the wrong government. When the colonisers left, a popular people's government were voted in and for almost thirty years they had simply replicated the mistakes and greed of the British. It was as if they had *caught* something, like a flu or a cold, except the thing they caught was corruption. Corruption had been caught and then continued to spread; the no-longer colonial government had carried on the same practices and the masses had remained more or less oppressed. Of course, as a result, there had been a popular uprising too, in 1970, but this was soon snuffed out. His brother River, twenty years old then, had marched and followed the young black leaders of the time.

At night, as they had laid in their separate beds, River had recounted his adventures of black power marches and the ideas behind them. *Sans Amen was part of a world struggle*, his brother had assured him. Revolution was everywhere in the world in 1970, especially in America; earlier they'd had something called a Civil Rights Movement and it had led to change for the oppressed. Even women had marched; they had called themselves Feminists. Musicians, artists, even white people had joined in. In other parts of the world, the big patches of pink or yellow on his small globe, revolution had made all the difference. River had called himself a fighter for freedom.

But 1970 all came to nothing in the end in Sans Amen. The then leaders of that black power movement were all tracked down, rounded up and locked away on a rock off the coast. Some wrote poetry; others broke down. Some never broke. But during their incarceration, the spirit of rebellion cooled in the City of Silk. Their ideas were ridiculed by the government and then forgotten by the people.

River had joined a small band of men who had fought on; they were called the Brotherhood of Freedom Fighters. It was as if the island of Sans Amen had been forever blighted with this flu called corruption; it had arrived with Christopher Columbus. Half the Amerindians were killed off instantly and then it had spread through the Caribbean; it had arrived in waves, with the Old World planters and the pirates.

Now it was 1990, fifteen years after River had been shot, and a new Leader had emerged on the streets of Sans Amen; a spiritual man who cared enough about boys like Breeze to rescue and educate them, give them a sense of self-worth. The Leader had also attended marches, he had self-organised and talked like River had talked, about a New Society. 'We *still* don't have enough men in society to respond to political oppression,' the Leader often said. 'We need to kill the very *idea* of oppression.' And Ashes had consulted his heart and knew that these words were true and just. Not enough common men stood up for what was right, or understood that they needed to fight for social reform. The people of Sans Amen were asleep; they had accepted too much corruption, they did not expect let alone demand fair governance.

*

Four o' clock on Thursday afternoon, and still no word of an amnesty or any of their demands. No one had eaten much, if anything at all. The hostages had been allowed water and if they needed to relieve themselves they did so in a teacup or a glass in the corner of the chamber behind the speaker's chair. Some of the brothers were openly relieving themselves against the wall. Some had defecated and Ashes was ashamed of this. Small heaps of human faeces had started to fester in the heat. That part of the chamber had become a latrine of smashed crockery and human excrement and piss. The two female ministers could not go there. Instead they used their own glass or cup. The chamber stank and what with the smell of the dead in the rooms behind and those lying dead on the steps leading to the gallery, there was a new concern: disease, an out-break of cholera or typhoid. Most of the hostages held a cloth or handkerchief to their noses. They didn't want to inhale the bacteria now airborne. The chamber was a hell. The fetid air was making Ashes' asthma worse. He had already used half the salbutamol spray in his inhaler; when the rest was gone he would be in trouble.

That was when he decided to go downstairs. He didn't need to ask anyone for permission or say anything about where he was going. He felt invisible again and quietly moved towards the back rooms of the House, the rooms with dead bodies, the rooms that were all shot up. Some of them contained gunmen sitting or lying on the floor; he walked past these and no one stopped him or called out. In the commune he was always the odd one out, quiet, aloof; he didn't live there, he came and went for prayers or to volunteer in the medical clinic occasionally. No one seemed to notice him as he passed. There was a staircase leading to the lower ground floor and he followed it, his feet slipping down the steps, his heart crying out for peace and solitude. But he knew downstairs there were barred gates, that he would still be surrounded and trapped. It was only just dawning on him what they'd done – what *he*'d done. He'd taken part in an armed insurrection. A coup d'état. Or at least a good attempt at one.

A fountain stood in the centre of the lower floor but there was no water flowing through it. He stood next to it and looked upwards to see a high vaulted ceiling, rows of opaque windowpanes and lots of green oxidised brass, all arranged in a square. He was under-neath the tower in the centre of the whole structure which was the House of Power. He realised the dragon was directly above him, pointing its scaly head towards the direction of the wind. He shuddered just to think of it; they should have taken more note of it and its spell. The tower and its structure reminded him of some kind of intricately woven ladder upwards to the sky, but it offered no way out.

Along from the fountain there was a cool corridor and many doors leading off the hall, most half open. The brothers must have come down here early on and rounded up anyone still in the House at 6 p.m. The lower floor had a deserted feel, like a museum. He walked past door after door, peeping into some of the rooms, feeling very small and like a burglar. And then he saw a door which looked older than the others, shut. He was still holding his rifle, which he had got used to, and yet still didn't know how to shoot, let alone reload. It stank in his hands of gunmetal and sweat. He opened the door, twisting the doorknob hard, and it opened with a push and he shrieked when a large ginger cat ran out, hissing. It fizzed its way down the corridor away from him, furious. Then it hopped up and sat on the ledge of the fountain and glared at him. It began to clean itself and glare and clean itself alternately and Ashes felt guilty to have annoyed it so much.

Ashes pushed open the door to find the room inside was very light, spots of colour all over the wooden floor. Ashes saw the coloured spots came from a stained glass window and in the window he saw Jesus Christ pinned to the cross gazing upwards. Ashes gasped and crossed himself as he'd seen Christians do. Jesus seemed to be blazing there against the afternoon sun, which was still strong. He was up on the cross on Calvary, the two thieves next to him, Jesus who was executed for treason, for preaching compassion and for challenging corruption. Ashes shivered and saw that to the right there was a wall of books, and the wall of books went around and encased the room and it was as if Ashes had been given a gift, a secret chamber in this vast monument built in the style of Victoria. The House of Power was a feminine place with its coolness and its fountains and fancy *tra la la* upstairs; all gold and white and embroidered with bows, the red carpet, the chandeliers. And at the heart of it, there was this library. A haven from the hell they had brought in. They had made a terrible mistake, he knew this now. They had injured and killed a woman, and others too. They had shot up the place and ruined the House. The City of

Silk was on fire. They had even locked up a cat. His wife Jade might never speak to him again.

Ashes leant his rifle against the bookcase and he allowed himself to scan the shelves. He saw history, law, encyclopedias, atlases, books of maps, books written by a famous ex-prime minister of Sans Amen, a book about the voyages of Columbus, and books full of old art plates, many files, papers and leather-bound books which looked meaningless, like a kind of wallpaper. Hundreds of books like these. But there were no novels or volumes of verse and the region had many fine novelists and poets. And nothing of Fanon or Fat Clay of Cuba, not even any words from Mahatma Gandhi or Martin Luther King. None of the great mystical poets, Kabir or Rumi or St Francis of Assisi, no books about living or dying well like those written by the holy sages in Tibet. There was no Bible, no Torah, nothing of the Quran or the Upanishads.

He turned around to face the window and Jesus there on the cross. He saw a man who said *The first will be last and the last will be first.* He crossed himself again and thought that somehow he did not feel righteous or noble or revolutionary. Somehow, his revolution had gone to pieces. He picked up his gun and he felt its weight and how useless it was in his hands; he didn't even know if it was loaded or not. He looked at the man on the cross and found himself saying 'sorry' aloud. It just fell out of his mouth because he felt so ashamed of himself. He left the room glad he'd found it, a place to be safe, away from it all; and yet in his heart, in the most intelligent part of him, he felt destitute.

*

Upstairs in the chamber the Prime Minister was still lashed to a man who Ashes now knew was Mr Bertrand Cranleyson, the Minister for National Security. Mr Cranleyson and the PM were the most high-level hostages they had captured. Both had been seriously wounded in the legs by Hal the night before. Though the blood had stopped seeping, both men were in poor physical shape. The Prime Minister's eyes were sealing up and his face was blue and purple from where he'd been kicked. And yet he had an air about him of being the victor. He had a rakish aspect about him too; his moustache was a thin line across his top lip, his sideburns were defined, like he had modelled his facial hair on a celluloid pimpernel. His skin was olive brown and his teeth were very white, and when he spoke it was as if he had been given elocution lessons. Also he had something that Hal hadn't counted on, a human quality no one else in the chamber possessed, and in some strange, unspoken way it was the very thing all the hostages and brothers were aligned with. The Prime Minister had stood up to the gunmen, to Hal's leadership, and he'd risked his life in doing so. He had been shot for his disobedience. But what he'd really been shot for was that he refused to acknowledge Hal's leadership. Under duress the Prime Minister had claimed his rightful authority. He would rather die than relinquish it.

The Prime Minister was suffering physically – and yet psychologically he was defiant. In some ways, he was still the most powerful man in the chamber. He had made sure everyone knew who was the official leader. His pants had been wrestled back up by one of the brothers and he was no longer so rudely exposed. But with his swelled up face and his legs caked with clots of blood, he didn't come across as vulnerable. He spoke like a dignified person, slow and articulate, and the brothers didn't know quite how to respond to him. The hostages were used to him and even seemed to like and respect him. Hal hadn't counted on all of this, and neither had Ashes or any of the other brothers. Half of those in the putrid, reeking, shambolic chamber still deferred to the Prime Minister. The PM had showed

Hal that his power was useless against him; Hal could go ahead and shoot him. Hal had threatened to do so and the Prime Minister had called his bluff because he had been willing to be shot. Now Hal knew he couldn't threaten to shoot him *again* without making himself look like an arse. The PM had shown he was prepared to die for his country and he had exposed Hal: Hal wanted to live and the Prime Minister was prepared to die.

So now the Prime Minister, all battered and bruised, an old colonial and yet dashing, had kept his power. And that power was greater than Hal's. The Prime Minister had demonstrated what power really was, that it was important enough to risk life itself for. And Ashes was stricken with a mixture of remorse and hopelessness for his own cowardice and weakness. He had fled upwards to the ceiling; he had vanished under duress.

The PM's bravery had had an effect on everyone. The hours dragged by. Parakeets squawked in the berries in the palms around the House. The ceasefire had lasted most of the day. No news from the outside. Hal kept in constant contact with the Leader but still neither of them had spoken to Colonel Howl, and Father Sapno was due to come back at 6 p.m. One of the brothers had brought a pack of cards and four of them played all fours. From the windows they had all witnessed the looting in the streets, the fires everywhere, men walking brazenly down the road carrying TV sets, beds, table tennis tables, boxes of expensive imported sneakers, standing fans, ladders, bolts of cloth, bags of rice, ironing boards, golf clubs, skate boards, tyres, boxes of rum. They spotted one man walking slowly down the street with a chandelier balancing on his head. The army couldn't stop the looting; the whole regiment was fully occupied with surrounding two locations in the centre of town. The police had all run away. The police weren't trained for this; they couldn't keep control of the looting even if they tried. Ashes saw that not one of the looters, his fellow countrymen, seemed interested in what was happening in the vivid magenta House of Power. They all walked past it. Some pointed and stared; one or two looked up. Fat Clay of Cuba had trained thousands to march on Havana in the end. The Leader had half-trained not even a hundred. There was a method to a successful revolution, Ashes was beginning to realise.

*

At five in the afternoon there was an important piece of news. Hal came into the chamber. 'Delta Force are here.' He announced this mainly to his men, but in some way he found the fact thrilling, that they had caused such a stir, like he was saying it to a larger audience. 'They Americans have landed.' Hal went over to the PM. 'You,' he said. 'You will make sure there is no foreign intervention, okay?' He kicked the PM in his injured legs and the PM howled.

Breeze looked worried. He walked over to the PM and prodded him with the nose of his rifle.

'What is Delta Force?' he said to the PM.

The Prime Minister regarded young Breeze with his august attention. He gave him a thorough looking up and down, enough to make Breeze squirm in his army boots.

'They are a specialist fighting force within the army of the United States of America. They have come to my rescue. They have come to rescue everyone here who you have barbarically captured and tortured, young man.'

Breeze swore, saying *muddercunt* under his breath. He steupsed and swaggered away, hiding that he was trying to think about this information. Everyone else also absorbed these facts. Hal disappeared with his walkie-talkie crammed to his ear.

Breeze came back.

'Why the blasted focking Americans interfere?' he

said. 'You tell them focking Yankee muddercunts to take their focking Delta focking muddercunt fancy specialist troops and stick them on the ground right here. We go blast their skinny white arses from here back to Washington DC.' Breeze aimed his gun out the window and made as if to pull the trigger. 'Pow,' he said.

Greg Mason whistled.

Arnold cackled and danced and said, 'Yeah, man.' Many of the younger boys laughed.

Ashes felt ashamed. This was no way to speak to the PM.

Mr Mahibir said, 'Young boy, have you not heard of the Monroe Doctrine?'

'The what?'

Now Greg Mason was paying attention.

'The Monroe Doctrine. It was penned many years ago. And it is a Doctrine which means that Latin America and the whole of the Caribbean region have a "special relationship" with the USA. They have sworn to protect us, you could say.'

Breeze looked suspicious. 'No. I never hear about that.'

'I'm sure neither has that arse your Leader,' said the PM.

Greg Mason said 'Ay,' as if to demand respect, but it

was clear Greg was interested and hadn't heard of the Doctrine either.

'The Americans saw off the Europeans in the end. They wanted the Europeans to stop all their warfare and land-grabbing in the New World and so they pledged to act as ... well you could say ... peace makers, in the Latin American and Caribbean region. They have done so ever since the treaty was signed in 1823.'

The PM looked at the small teenage boy with the big gun, the boy from the slums of Sans Amen who had no parents, who had little schooling, who was already hard as a bois man. He said: 'You cannot just take control of a country, my good friend. Even a small one like this. Sans Amen is part of the *world*. And the *world* cares. The world looks on and the world, most often, tends to get involved, tends to stop this kind of thing. Didn't you know?'

Breeze looked sullen.

Greg Mason said, 'Wait, nuh. That friggin Monroe friggin Doctrine is an ancient piece of paper. It mean the American imperialist superpower get themselves involved with everybody business. They are the *worst* colonisers. Breeze, you don't go listening to this crap. This black man is an old colonial. He 'fraid for his life. Delta Force can come right here and kiss my arse.'

Just then there was a heavy thud and the walls of the chamber shook.

'Get down!' shouted Greg Mason. 'We are under attack.'

II. Bathsheba

THURSDAY EVENING,
THE HOUSE OF POWER,
THE CITY OF SILK

I was thrown hard hard against the wall. I crammed my hands over my ears to muffle the sound of screaming and bullet-hail and the clamour of all the other terrorised people in the room. Plaster rained down on us from the ceiling. The room shook as if it had been punched from outside. The whole House swayed and heaved with the onslaught of that second attack. *Jesus Lord.* I crouched down low and tried to keep very small. I closed my eyes and counted, hoping the screaming would stop. It was a few seconds before I realised that the screaming wasn't just the others; I was screaming too, screaming for my children, 'I want to live, I want to live.' I needed to stay alive in all of this, somehow. That was all. I couldn't die. What would happen to my son and daughter? I urinated on myself, with shock. That second attack took everyone by surprise; no one thought Howl would come like that, so hard. A ferocious onslaught. It was late in the afternoon on the second day. Most of the women had been immediately let go; it was just myself and Lucretia they kept; we were also Ministers in the cabinet of government. It was just us in there with all those men and boys.

I glimpsed between my fingers and saw that the smoke was head high in the chamber, mauve and black, and it was like the air itself was alive and wailing a song, gasping for its own oxygen. The air was so thick with smoke and debris it was choking on itself. Chunks of plaster fell from the walls, big slabs of the cornice work had cracked and come plummeting down from the ceiling. One of the columns had keeled over, as if it had died on its feet. It had been shot to pieces. The air was all shredded up and bullets came again and again and again. They slammed into walls and sliced through window-panes, shattered glass rained all over the floor and then some kind of rocket was launched. A comet with a tail of fire hurtled through one of the windows and went down, down through the corridor. It exploded in the back parts of the labyrinth of the House. A savage fire must have started in there, which was a new terror, fire in the House! *Jesus Lord*. Fire. If they didn't kill us by bullets, they would smoke us all out. It seemed like a fire was raging in a far wing too, where the army was blasting rockets in through the windows. Everyone was on the floor, including all the gunmen; no one could move, let alone return any fire. All the young boys had thrown down their guns and I could see most of them were cowering in terror, just like us. Some of the gunmen were in the tearoom. I could hear one of the young boys crying for his mother. The army was attacking with full force. I was glad and at the same time it meant we were in big trouble. *What would happen to my children?*, was all I could think. They needed their mother. They say your life flashes in front of you when you think you're about to die and this is true. In those moments flashes came to me: a massive leatherback turtle I once saw with its fins hacked off at a beach on the north coast, flipped on its back, dying in the sun, its massive female head leaking tears; sleeping in our hammocks made from bamboo poles in the rainforest, hiking with my father, bathing in the waterfalls up in the mountains; the birth of my first child, our daughter Gloria; the first nervous and wondrous day I ever sat in this very chamber.

I want to live, was all I could think. Save us – and all of these young boys. Just where were their mothers?

The commander of the gunmen, the man they were calling Hal, was a man I'd heard of; everyone in politics had heard of him. He too was face down on the floor in the chamber, his hands over his head. The young boy called Breeze, who'd been watching me too keenly as far as I was concerned, was also flung against the wall. He crawled towards me for protection in all that confusion and I found myself holding him tightly as if he were my own son. He had wet himself too. He was crying and cussing and shouting for it all to stop. I was sure I was going to die, that we were all going to die at any moment.

The army had gone mad. Colonel Benedict Howl was a great man, but something of a colonial too, just like the PM. He'd been trained at Sandhurst in England I'd been told, and the PM trusted him. He was tough and dynamic. He and his men weren't taking any bartering or demands from this bunch of street crooks and criminals and half-baked radicals left over from 1970. *Thank the Lord* the army of Sans Amen was not only loyal but well trained. All the officers had been to England. That damn badjohn calling himself the Leader had been nothing but a pest for years, a vigilante and crook and a self–appointed spiritual leader of some hybrid religious order. God only knew who he thought he was and what they worshipped. But we had been watching him; we'd even positioned an army post next to his compound. But obviously the army on guard had been asleep the day before this outrage. Asleep! How had a band of heavily armed insurgents managed to leave the compound in broad daylight?

The army were attacking and yet they might kill everyone in doing so, including the PM and his cabinet ministers. The PM had already shown he was prepared to die – and that had been seen as a go ahead, *Blast them all*. But I wasn't prepared to die, not then, not for my country, not for anyone. I'd never seen courage before, but I saw it then, when the PM shouted *Attack* down the line. My blood ran cold.

And then I was holding a scared boy in my arms and for a few minutes it seemed like he'd fallen sleep or had fainted from shock. His body was limp. I was about to die with him, this hard little street boy, rather than my own son James. How had this happened? I prayed and closed my eyes and hoped it would all end quickly. But the gunfire continued and the walls thudded and shook. Fire and heat and thick gun smoke, and it was as if earthquakes were being hurled into the room. A tidal wave of bullets rolled in, the four horsemen had arrived, sailing through the windows of the House of Power on steeds made of ammunition. It was the end of the world as I knew it. A part of me was dying right then and there, with that little boy in my arms.

The bombardment lasted all of forty-five minutes. When it was over, I opened my eyes; I was still alive. The young boy Breeze revived and kicked himself free in a way which reminded me of seeing my son kick out in his sleep. He rolled away from me and began cussing his head off to the other men. I tried to focus in the smoke and saw that Mervyn Mahibir's calipers had been blown off in the attack. They were strewn a few inches from me and they resembled a heap of metal bones. The poor man was crawling on his stomach across the carpet towards them.

'Oh, God, Aspasia,' he gasped. 'You okay?'

'Mervyn,' I cried. 'Me? What about *you*?' And I realised my face was wet with tears, my nose was streaming. I coughed on the smoke and wiped the mucus from my face. Since it had started I had managed with the physical pain and various humiliations; I had coped. Now I was near the edge of my ability to stay centred. I was dizzy and faint and hungry and weak. In one day everything was different. I might die. This was a very real threat. I might never see my husband, my children again.

'Look, come,' and I held out my hand to help him across the floor.

'Jesus, Lord, what de *hell* are they using outside? I go speak to them when we get out. All that blasting was unnecessary. I took my braces off to give my legs a rest from standing. And then they shoot the place up.'

'Mervyn, they are simply following the Prime Minister's orders.'

'Well those orders not a great idea.'

'Well at least they are showing who's in charge.'

'And they going and kill us all in here if they keep this up.'

Mervyn crawled a bit closer, across shreds of plaster and glass, and then I helped him up on to the platform near the speaker's chair and together we buckled the braces back on to his legs and slipped his pant legs back down to cover them. I hardly knew Mervyn. He was one of those ministers who never made a big show of himself in the House. For a few seconds we just sat there and I squeezed his hand and he squeezed mine back and we didn't say anything, both of us silently recharging. Like the PM, I felt different about Mervyn now; I felt respect, and I was glad he was there. He always appeared to be jovial in the House, a reliable and steady type, clear-minded and well spoken. He was an experienced parliamentarian – but who would ever have guessed he was brave? You find out so much about people in these kinds of conditions. The PM and Mervyn were courageous. He gave me a look and I gave him back the same look. Would we ever meet and speak again on the outside? Would we ever work together again? This was the end of something, we both knew that. Right then, I had no real ideas about what was happening, only terror and despair.

'Thank you,' I whispered.

*

Day had turned to dusk. We were facing our second night under the gun. One of the gunmen had switched on the lights in the chamber and I wondered how long the army would keep the electricity supply connected. We were to spend another night on the floor, with the lights on, which meant no sleep would be possible. Chairs everywhere were overturned, everything was broken. People were still lying on the ground, afraid to move. The PM was covered in a fine silt which had fallen from the ceiling; *thank God* he was okay, thank God he was still alive. It was disgraceful what they had done to him, but he seemed resolute, as if he was still leading us. I knew his wife, we'd met many times at public functions, she was a good woman. She would be so worried but she would know him, that he would be strong like this. The gunmen hadn't got the better of him. He was almost as composed as usual, but I sensed his fury and indignation.

The young boys and men began to collect themselves again. Hal had roused himself and had disappeared to one of the back rooms to talk to the lunatic man they all called the Leader. The Leader was a famous man on the island; he'd made himself known with his marches and his posturing. It was said that he was squatting on government land, causing a great pain in the backside to our government and the one before. He had built a temple and a school and was preaching his mixture of ideas. Rumour had it he was a vigilante of sorts too, intercepting those who sold drugs on the street. Was that what all this was about? He wasn't really trying to capture power and reassemble a new order. He was just so damn vexed about the land. Or maybe he just wanted a job, high up; he wanted to be Minister of Defence, something so. Everyone knew who the Leader was.

I could see that Lucretia Salvatore, my colleague and Minister for Cultural Affairs, was handling things in her own way. She had been very subdued from the start, had tried as best she could not to get involved. I could see this was a good option. Everyone, hostages and gunmen alike, was coping in their own way. For my part, I had found it hard not to get caught up; my attitude towards the young boys and their guns had altered completely over just twenty-four hours. My fear and loathing of them had ceased, mysteriously. I found myself fascinated by them, and ashamed of myself as a minister. These were boys from the slums, from the east of the City of Silk, boys who still needed parenting. They needed help from society and the state. Their toughness was a kind of façade. They were loyal and obedient to Hal and the older men, and yet they were clearly out of their depth. Many of them had cried during the bombardment. The one that cussed a lot, Breeze, he was the one I'd actually grown fond of. It was strange to think this way. I had come to almost *like* one of the gunmen. He seemed so very, very serious, and yes, even dangerous in demeanour, and yet he didn't scare me. I saw flickers of concern in the young boy's eyes, like he was constantly trying to understand everything.

The older gunmen were different. They were hard-shelled men mostly from the streets and they were full of contempt and, yes, I was afraid of their show of discipline. One of them, the man wearing a Santa hat, was clearly deranged. He could do something very wrong at any moment – shoot us all, or even shoot himself. I noticed Hal was keeping an eye on him. The big guy they called Mason I also recognised. I was sure he'd been in gaol before, for shooting a police officer, or something that serious. He was very gruff and the one most obviously dressed like a mercenary or a bandit. And then there was the quiet, scholarly-looking gunman, Ashes; I'd heard them calling his name. He was tall and slim and wore spectacles, clearly the misfit of the bunch. He looked like a man who might work in a library, not the type I associated with this kind of thing. He'd been helping Mervyn with his doctoring and making tea. He was a mild-mannered man, the only one with a conspicuous air of spiritual intent. He kept slipping off and I wondered if he had been leaving the chamber to pray.

It was night again. The darkness activated my deepest fears. Would the looters be able to climb through the windows? Would jab jabs now show up in the dead of night? Would the gunmen shed their combat fatigues to reveal themselves as devils under-neath? All kinds of ideas came and played their own havoc. The mind gets messed up in conditions as bad as this. Who were these ruffians? How had they gathered and caused such chaos? They were men from a commune down the road, a spiritual community on the outskirts of town. Everyone was aware of them. The Leader often threw his weight around, making noise and threats, and it was true there had been times when government ministers had even hired his men as armed guards. Our government knew that some of the people the Leader had attracted were ex-criminals and ex-radicals. But none of us guessed they were *this* dangerous.

The room stank of sweat and blood and shit, and the shreds of glass everywhere meant it was best not to move. I could hear the groans and prayers of others and also long periods of a mournful, desolate silence. And when I closed my eyes the room swung about, and I spoke to myself saying, *Aspasia, the thing is to stay calm. Take every hour as it comes.* On the outside I knew there were ministers who were free; they and the army would be thrashing out what was best to do. Thank God the Attorney General had escaped; because of that stroke of luck a proxy government could be formed. The Americans had landed and now it was up to Colonel Howl to use them or send them back. The foreign press was on the island too, which meant the world was watching. Everything had backfired for the Leader and his band of men, and quickly.

I found it hard to concentrate for long; my mind

kept slipping and it was hard to stay focused. I felt like I wanted to go to sleep. Or as if the whole insurrection was all happening several feet away from me, or in another room. I wanted to disappear. It was all I could do to breath and stay aware. My children, *my darlings*, Gloria and James, I kept thinking of them. They were still young, fourteen and eleven. I ached to speak to them, to let them know I was okay. The army was in the process of rescuing us. But mostly, on and off, there was a nagging thought. *Was the young boy Breeze right? Was all this our fault?*

*

Hal had come back from his urgent meeting with the Leader on the walkie-talkie. He looked fierce.

'Right,' he addressed his men. 'The army have made their position clear. They want to intimidate us. They will be planning to storm the building at some point in the night. I want all the hostages on the floor, face down.'

At this command the men and boys began to move and shout orders to round us all up. By now almost all the ministers had been conversing with the younger boys; we had been having frank and open conversations about politics and there'd been debates about the nature of democracy and power. It felt like there was no reason to be so afraid of them, and yet now the boys were prodding us like cattle. They'd reverted to being killers.

The young boy Breeze had come to tie my hands back together and he was trying hard not to make eye contact. 'Keep still, Mrs Garland,' he commanded and I did as he said. He'd obviously denied or forgotten that I'd held him safe in my arms.

We were all lined up now, in the centre of the chamber, face down on the shrapnel-shredded carpet. The men and boys were standing above us and somehow this was even more frightening than the bombardment.

'Right,' said Hal. 'Each of you choose a hostage.'

This caused some prevarication, as though the men hadn't quite understood the command. It felt odd to hear the word 'hostage'. I wondered if the gunmen were as disorientated as I was. Had they begun to care? Had they seen we weren't so bad after all? Things were now much more personal. We were *all* hungry; all of us were frightened – and we'd talked, communicated, eaten puffs, shared the putrid latrine. Things were mixed up. Plus the army was now holding *them* hostage.

I could feel a gunman hovering above me.

'Now, I want you to mark your target,' said Hal.

I turned my head sideways, enough to see that young Breeze had chosen to mark me. I gave him a look I'd never given anyone, a stare of disbelief which was also a plea for mercy . . . for my children. *Don't kill me, little boy, I have to live for my children.* But this son of the city was about to shoot me through the back of the head. Prayers wouldn't come. The young man's face was locked down and his eyes were glazed over. He didn't see me. I was scared of him then. He could do it; he could shoot me dead.

Mervyn was face down next to me. The gunman, Ashes, the one who looked like he couldn't even hold let alone use a gun, had chosen Mervyn.

'We are going to wait,' said Hal. 'When the army storm the building, they will cut the power supply and the lights will go off. So. When the lights go off, I want you to fire and aim to kill. Each of you will mark your target and shoot to the head. Understand?'

I couldn't believe I'd heard correctly. We would be executed? If the lights dimmed? Mervyn's face was inches from mine. He didn't seem too perturbed. In fact, there was a smirk of mischief on his face.

'You,' he said, looking up at the guerilla soldier called Ashes. 'So is *you* who now coming to shoot me? You helping me to make tea an now you going and kill me? Eh, eh.'

111

Mervyn laughed, but I couldn't. His laughter was hollow and I knew he was scared too; he was attempting a kind of gallows humour.

'Mervyn, hush,' I said. I was scared he might be shot by accident; he was pushing his luck.

The man called Ashes was pointing his gun at Mervyn but his gun was shaking. I looked up at the boy Breeze and saw his gun was also shaking. He tried to hold on to his mean grown-up man's expression. But the boy had sweat on his face and he was squinting back tears.

My heart was racing, racing, racing and then slowing down, and then racing and then slowing. It was rock hard in my chest. The air in my lungs had evaporated and I could barely breathe. My head had filled with blood and the blood was pounding in my temples or it might even leak from my eyes. My body was rigid and yet the adrenalin made the terror inside me feel like liquid.

I felt the nose of Breeze's long, skinny gun in my back.

'Don't move, Mrs Garland,' he said, but his voice sounded weak.

The faces of my husband Marc and my children floated before me, my mother, my close friends. I was forty-two. Much too young. I imagined my soul floating upwards, to the ceiling. I could have gone to sleep right then, let go. I was flooded with the grief of my own death. I saw my own funeral, my family standing there, dumbstruck. I mourned myself, mourned with my loved ones the end of my existence. I wondered if or when I would find them all again, or who I would meet in my life after my death. This was my ending as a minister, as a public servant: being shot dead in the House by a street boy. A miserable event. I was only glad it wasn't that crazy man, the Leader. I wondered about the Leader, about his childhood. Had he been hurt too, neglected just like Breeze? It was commonly said about him that he'd had a knock to the head. Had he been hurt as a child in some way so damaging that he'd gone on to arm himself as a man, lead a small outlaw militia, lay such a grandiose claim on the politics of this small island? I was a woman in politics and I'd met all sorts of men in the House of Power, and many of these men I'd come to know, via cocktail parties, from their wives, had difficult personal stories. Somehow this all had something to do with a very personal abuse of power; it started at home, with bad fathering, bad mothering, with a lack of love.

*

We lay face down on the floor of the chamber for what felt like a very long time. Minutes elongated and strangled each other. Hal stood with his hand on his rifle, also ready to shoot. Then, from one corner of the chamber, mad-crazy laughter rang out; it sliced the air into pieces. Laughter and cussing, the laughter of jab jabs. Then there was gunfire. Plaster fell from the ceiling and sprayed us with powder. Laughter and gunfire, bullets hitting the ceiling, powder falling, and again my body was rigid and adrenalin coursed through me in waves. So it wasn't Breeze who would shoot me after all. The gunman wearing the Santa hat had started to shoot; he was cussing and screeching and had run to one of the windows, shouting, 'Allyuh, come, come, we ready,' and he began to fire out into the night.

'Get him *down*,' shouted Hal. I saw the man called Greg Mason leap across the room and round kick him hard, so hard there was a crunch. The shooting stopped and his body hit the ground. More gunmen went over to the man with the Santa hat.

'Tie him up,' instructed Hal. 'And take him behind.'

The Santa hat man had lost control of himself. The other gunmen struggled with him as he writhed and cussed and tried to fight them off. They beat him down and tied him up and I could see him still struggling as they took him away.

If I closed my eyes I could easily be drawn into sleep. I could fall into dreams and conjure up a different reality, *oh, if I could sleep*. But instead I was hyper-awake and over-anxious, my body's alarm systems on red alert. Mervyn lay next to me.

'Mervyn,' I whispered.

'Yeah?'

'You okay?'

He blinked and said, 'Aspasia, we need to keep our spirits up and our heads down. See that man who just went mad?'

'Yeah.'

'Well that madness is here in the room.'

I nodded.

'We will get out of here,' he said. 'The army would have stormed long time, if they wanted to. They playing games with these ruffians, cat and mouse. They could send Special Forces in. Or Delta Force. They in the stronger position. These fools grasping at straws. The game is over. Just keep your head down. We not near dying.'

'What about the lights?'

'They not storming down the place, Aspasia.'

I felt a wave of nausea rise. I hiccupped and coughed a little. 'You don't feel bad?' I whispered.

'About what?'

115

'About these boys.'

Mervyn thought for a few moments and then nodded slowly, like he knew.

'Yes.'

'The Leader captured them from the streets. Either they go dead inside here, or they going to gaol for ever.'

'Or worse.'

'What?'

'They will be hung.'

'What? All of them?'

'Yes. Treason is punishable by death. You know that.'

'How they go hang all this bunch?'

'By the balls, Aspasia.'

'Don't make joke . . . they can hang the leaders of this. But them boys is just boys.'

'And one of them had his gun in your back just now. He would have shot you on command.'

'It's not his fault.'

'So – you like them now?'

'No. But some are under sixteen. Surely different rules for them.'

'Maybe.'

'I pray for their souls.'

'Aspasia, right now, just think of your own soul.'

I was grateful for Mervyn's sense of reason and his wider view of things. Sans Amen still used the death penalty for murder and treason and I found this abhorrent in the extreme. It was ridiculous to demonstrate to the public that it was wrong to kill people by then killing people. But the citizens of Sans Amen had shown that they were thirsty for this kind of punishment; they were happy to see criminals hang. I tried to think of the logistics of hanging this crackpot bunch. How would they do it? First they would need to be tried before the courts, then sentenced. Would they do this in batches? If so, it could take years, maybe decades, and then carrying out the sentence . . . Just the very idea of seeing so many men and boys hung, what – in groups of ten or twelve over days, weeks? It would be a shameful thing for any government to do. Shameful. Hang all these boys?

I felt sick. I vowed then and there that I would do more if I got out of the House alive. Rather than slink away from politics, defeated, I would double my efforts. This tragedy wouldn't scare me off; instead it made me feel even more committed to my job. Our government had overlooked many things; we hadn't acted quickly enough to secure change, and it was true, we had made unpopular cuts. Austerity measures. There'd been marches, and this Leader of theirs had indeed made threats. We hadn't taken him seriously, hadn't taken the temperature enough. There were programs for the poor, yes, all in the pipeline, all to come. But these young boys – it was already too late for them.

Just then, Hal said, 'Okay. Looking like things are quiet outside.'

Mervyn mouthed, *Stay calm*.

'All of you can relax your position.'

There was movement above us as the men shifted about and started to move away from their targets.

'Can we move?' I said to Hal.

'Where yuh want to go?'

'These cuffs are digging in to me. Can you cut us free?'

'No, not yet, Mrs Garland. Not yet. You staying right there.'

With that Hal disappeared.

I tried to remain calm, hogtied with my hands behind my back. I craved sleep, but the chaos of alarm in my head made sleep impossible. I rested my cheek on the carpet. I imagined seeing my children; I hadn't said enough of a goodbye to them the last time I saw them. Brief kisses. If only I'd known. If only I'd had an inkling it might be the last time I'd see them. More plaster fell from the ceiling. It was about 8 p.m., I guessed. The chamber of the House was ruined now and I marvelled and thought, *How has this happened again?*

*

Later in the evening it felt clear the army weren't going to attack. Apparently Colonel Howl had disappeared from the street outside; it probably meant he'd gone back to discuss other plans at HQ nearby. Eventually, the gunmen untied us and I rubbed my wrists which had been so tightly tied together there were welts. There was a tight, screwed-up, empty feeling inside me which came from being so scared.

But I also felt release, a giving up, that feeling I sometimes get after tears, or after a sea bath. My bowels were also weak. I'd already relieved myself into a glass. Now I feared I might defecate all over myself. My legs were feeble; I hadn't walked around or used them since the night before. They were like phantom limbs, floating around beneath me. I'd been holding on, withstanding the situation. I had exactly twenty-four hours' worth of resilience stored inside me. Then I sensed all the different parts of me letting go. I needed to use the bathroom. I needed to defecate, cry, wash my face, wash my hands, blow my nose. I looked at my hands and realised they were shaking.

Breeze was still hanging round me, staring with open curiosity, and I found his gaze hard to tolerate. I glanced over at the latrine behind the speaker's chair and again I felt that caving-in feeling. A hot bile rose in my throat. I began to cough up whatever was inside me, a glue of bile and intestinal juices, strings of it came out onto the carpet and for the first time tears spilled down my cheeks. The air in my chest choked off. Tears rolled from my eyes and the young boy watched me and I wanted to shoo him away and say, *Get away from me*. I needed to relieve myself, but I couldn't face that foul heap of broken cups and piss-filled glasses in the corner. There were already piles of shit on the carpet; I couldn't see myself shitting in the same heap as the gunmen. I found a last shred of inner strength and I looked up at the boy-man with the gun as if he were my own son.

'You will take me to the washroom now.'

He gave me a look of puzzlement and then smirked.

'Don't just stand there. I want to use the washroom down the corridor.'

'No. You must go *there*,' and Breeze pointed with his gun to the heap in the corner.

'I will not relieve myself there.' I used my politician's voice. Stern, uncompromising. 'Help me up.' I began to struggle to my feet, but they were shaky. I had to steady myself with my arms. Slowly, I got to my feet and began to stumble towards the corridor and the tearoom where I knew there was a small toilet cubicle, and I felt the boy being left behind and then the nose of his gun in my back.

'Lady, you are not supposed to be walking around. Stop.'

I was dragging my legs and my ankles felt like rubber, like they could fold over themselves and I could fall. My ears had filled up with a ringing sound. I wasn't going to listen to this teenage boy's commands. I turned around. Hal looked across at me and so did some of the other gunmen. I put my hands in the air, just above my shoulders.

'You can shoot me dead right now. Okay?' I raised my hands higher. 'I'll give you that pleasure, if you like.' I was so damn tired, half-defeated already; I almost believed my own words. My hands were trembling, enough so the boy could see. 'Go on. Do it,' I cajoled. Right then I could have slapped his face.

Breeze frowned and seemed taken aback. Then he looked towards Hal, who was watching us.

'Shoot me dead, this minute, or let me be. I am a parliamentarian and you cannot take my status away.'

Breeze pointed his gun at my chest. 'I could do it, nuh,' he threatened.

I looked at him dead straight in the eye. Indeed he could. He was feral in some way; a child, but not like my son. He had a lack of being cared for about him and in that lack he didn't care for others.

'I'm going to use the washroom,' I said.

Hal gave Breeze a hard stare of disapproval and said, 'Ayyy. Not so fast. Let her go.'

I nodded at Hal in acknowledgement for his support. I limped forward, down the corridor. I hadn't left the chamber since the day before and now I could see the wreckage in the tearoom and beyond. It was the old anger, the barbarism and the torture once rained down on the black man that I saw there in this room. Bad energy: old, dark, rancorous; there was bad faith in there. Like a swarm of locusts had come and shredded the place up, leaving behind a pile of smashed crockery and the stench of urine. There were many words scrawled on the wall about God. And yet there was a desolate feeling of Godlessness.

I glanced left and seized up and let out a cry of terror. The body of a woman lay under a table in the room, sticky with blood. She'd been shot in the stomach and the wound was huge, like a giant mouth. I began to retch and panic and was near to lashing out. 'Jesus

Christ! What have you all *done*?' I realised I *knew* her; she was a clerk in the House. I saw that woman every day, though we rarely spoke as we went about our everyday business.

I glared at the boy with the gun. I pointed at the body of the dead woman.

'Go away! Get out of my *sight*,' I rasped. The young man-boy with the gun looked at the body of the woman on the ground and he winced as if she was a small mistake. He moved backwards a little but hovered, still, with his big gun . . . watching me.

I found the washroom and I turned the handle and let myself in. I gagged and vomited into the sink. I ran the taps and splashed water on to my face and tried to see, really see, who I was looking at in the mirror. Aspasia Garland, where was she? But I could barely see my face; it was as if I'd no head, as if it had been removed. I saw a blank space in the mirror. That woman's bloody and bloated body could have been mine. That body *was* mine. That woman *was* me. We were the same woman. Her body had been so casually discarded, a life thrown away; it could have been any woman, all women. The boys too, the gunmen. They were every boy. Tears ran and I saw that I looked very young, and also a hundred years old. I splashed water again so the water dissolved my tears. In the washroom there was a small window, but it was much too high up to escape from. I looked out into the night sky and prayed to God to be delivered from all of this. *Deliver us, Lord.* If I lived I would do better in this game of politics, which was mostly a game for men. I vowed to be there and stay there for the sake of the dead woman on the floor.

When I returned to the chamber I sat back down next to Mervyn.

'You didn't tell me how bad things were in there.'

'No. It's bad . . . isn't it?'

'Terrible. There's a woman lying dead. Under the table.'

He nodded, gravely.

'I think she was a clerk from downstairs. She must have come up here on Wednesday afternoon to deliver papers or something. A young woman, she has kids. I know her.'

I could see Mervyn was upset.

'They are crazy, these people, Mervyn. Their Leader, he gave a bunch of men some guns, he had some half-cooked plans, and now things . . . really, really bad. I wanted to be in politics since I was young, since I was about *twelve.*'

Mervyn looked impressed.

'I was one of the first people in Sans Amen to be a

member of Greenpeace in the early 1980s . . .' I laughed at this. It felt like a long time back; Greenpeace was then considered a kind of terrorist cell. 'I was an activist from an early age. Saving animals, you know . . . a conservationist. That was me. All I wanted to do was save the earth. It has been a passion of mine, since childhood . . . since I saw a turtle on its back on the beach, with its fins hacked off. It took hours to die in the sun. It devastated me to know humans could be so barbaric, to see the creature cry as it died. I went to school and university here on the island and studied politics. I was proud to be elected.'

Mervyn nodded. 'Not me,' he said. 'I fell into it.'

'Well I didn't.'

'I've never been an activist. I'm an observer. And a doctor.'

'That sounds pretty active to me.'

'No. I feel different, Aspasia. Quiet. I am a quiet man. I like to keep out of things. Really.'

The gunmen had been using Mervyn to help the injured and he'd been generous with his skills. Some more of the gunmen had been shot; one in the arm, another had had his ear badly grazed. Another had fallen on broken glass. None of the hostages, luckily, had been hurt by the incoming gunfire. Mervyn was asked to do what he could with the medicine kit and he freely obliged. One of the phone lines had been reconnected and I suspected this was how Hal and the Leader were communicating between the House and the television station. But Mervyn had also started to look a little shaky. He was less steady on his feet. Like me, he must be hungry and scared. The gunman Ashes was helping him tend the injured men. The pair of them made a rather well-matched team. In different circumstances, it was easy to see them as colleagues.

When he was done, Mervyn wrote a list of what was needed and gave it to Hal saying he should ring for supplies to be delivered as soon as possible. The gunman with the bullet in his arm faced gangrene within hours in the heat if he wasn't treated. Others needed stitches where he'd picked out large shreds of glass. But it was the Prime Minister he was most worried about.

'The Prime Minister is now losing his sight from his diabetes. If he isn't treated with his medication, he could slip into a coma. Then you will have lost your most valuable hostage. Then you will have a body to throw over the balcony. His. Then the army will come in here and kill everyone. Get him his pills or release him.'

'I am not leaving the House,' said the Prime Minister from the floor. He was curled up and looked like he was in pain. I could see he was still the great man I knew and respected, all curled up there, and yet I could also see, like everyone else, he'd made it for one whole day on his own reserves of spirit. His health was now declining rapidly and this could affect his valour, maybe even his ability to speak clearly for himself.

'No,' the Prime Minister repeated firmly, 'I'm not leaving.' He said this with eyes now almost sealed shut, his face swollen with the beating. The gunmen all stood round him in a circle. One kicked him in the ribs just for the hell of it.

The Prime Minister groaned.

'Leave him alone,' said Mervyn for the first time in a gruff voice. 'He is very sick.'

They moved away. It was as if the gunmen had lost their way a little, or they were no longer so sure of who they were. They hadn't just lost their purpose but their identity in this mad room; they'd gone a little astray. The atmosphere they had created affected *everyone*, including them. It was just as difficult for them being here where the air was mad, where the room was heavy with the smell of a bloated dead woman down the hall. Those ministers they were holding hostage had showed bravery and also kindness to them; the doctor had patched them up. The ministers, they now saw, were not such villains after all. It was easy to see that whatever was going on for me, the beginning of a failure to cope, was also happening to everyone, including the gunmen.

'The Prime Minister needs his medication,' Mervyn said to Hal. 'And he needs those pills by tomorrow morning latest, or he will comatose.'

*

The PM was very attached to the House and I thought about this. Of all the buildings on the island, the House had seen the most civil unrest over the years before and after Independence. There'd been ruination and violence in the House of Power before, every minister knew that; it was a historical fact. The House had been burnt to a shell of itself already. There'd been riots over the cost of water, decades ago. And for more or less the same reasons, the House had been violated. The government of the time had tried to tax the poor. Except the last time it was the colonials who were in power.

Back then, the British had passed an ordinance to increase the cost of water. They wanted to install water meters as they felt water was being wasted by the general public. Taps were allowed to run free. The British didn't like the sight of people bathing at standpipes by the road for too long. In response, there had been demonstrations and these had gone unheeded. Finally, the people had rioted and pelted stones and rocks through the windows of the House. They smashed up a stained glass window which celebrated Christopher Columbus arriving in the south of the island. They dragged the governor's carriage to the port and dumped it in the sea. Then they set fire to the ground floor of the House. The people were vexed, crazy like fire ants. When the police arrived they opened fire, openly shooting and bayoneting the crowd. Sixteen people were killed, including five women and a girl of twelve. Dozens of others were badly wounded. The House of Power was gutted.

Slowly, it was rebuilt. It was painted red at first, the colour of blood, in celebration of Queen Victoria's Jubilee. And then, in even gayer times, it had been through a range of colours: lime green, ochre, blue morpho turquoise, adapting to moods and eras. From working in the House I knew that parts of it were dilapidated and in need of repair. In the southeast chamber, there was a crater-sized hole in the ceiling where rain had soaked through and plaster had come down and pigeons had nested for decades. When the colonials departed in the early 1960s, they left behind this stately Victorian monument. And yet I had never understood why the new wave of independence leaders claimed it as their own; it didn't seem a good way to start a new era. The proud and hard-to-rule people of Sans Amen had already burnt the place down once. Now, they were attacking it again.

FRIDAY MORNING,
THE HOUSE OF POWER,
THE CITY OF SILK

In my dream there was a young woman lying dead on the ground. Her stomach was all shot up and slick with blood. The woman was called Bathsheba, and she was a fighter for freedom. She had a baby in her stomach. She lay face down, one arm clutching herself, the other flung forward as though she'd been swimming across the hot tarmac. Her body was riddled with bullets. There'd been a gunfight which had lasted for hours, men firing from houses, rooftops, the police were encamped. Now her body lay inert in the middle of the road; no one would touch it for fear of being shot too. Bathsheba was a woman who'd taken up arms to fight for a New Society. In my dream Bathsheba came awake. She stopped her slow crawl across

131

the road, struggled to her feet and dusted herself off. The bloody patch on her stomach began to shrink and she walked through the houses of that village in the hills and back to a more ordinary existence.

Then my dream started to blur and turn to chaos: people in the streets outside the House of Power were rioting. A young girl of about twelve years old, her eyes weeping tears of disbelief, a sharp bayonet rammed through her ribcage, in and up through her stomach. A long pointed blade glistened from her back. She lay dead from the wound in the street outside the House of Power. In my dream the City of Silk was now called the City of Riots.

My body was hot from the dream and I writhed with discomfort. It wasn't really sleep; for a couple of hours I'd drifted off. 5 a.m., or around there, I'd floated away from the chamber. My dreams were trampled up and full of dead women. The skin on my back, on my stomach was damp from the horror of these images. My eyes felt bruised and I touched around them, pressing gently to see if my skull was still there, under my face.

I opened my eyes. The young boy Breeze was standing above me and I had the feeling he'd been watching me for several minutes. His presence must have brought me round. His face was full of moodiness. It was a small, sullen African face; it carried questions and proud reserve. My city, the City of Riots, bred these difficult young men by the dozen; they were born of the mothers who were proud and dirt-poor and abandoned by their men, who, in turn, had been abandoned by other men. The City of Riots made boys who were resilient and who had patience and who could fight. This Breeze was a young poor man, full of insolence and posture, even grandeur.

'I see you before,' he said, looking down at me. He was only fourteen but possessed a manliness which came with everything else he was born to. It was every-where, this male charisma. It came from Africa; it was on the street and it was in the House. Sans Amenians were a charismatic people, men and women equally; it was our birthright and our strength and also our fool-ishness, for it was commonly said that God came from Sans Amen.

I tried to focus on the young man. My neck was stiff and I felt the skittishness of panic dart through me. He was standing above me in a way which threatened a sexual act. I had reason to be scared of this young man. He was a little too trigger-happy for my liking. He looked like his head was full of ideas, like he had more intelligence than the other boys, and yet he was also one of the most confused. I tugged downwards at my skirt. I didn't know what to say; my voice had turned to cotton in my throat. My dreams had left me weak and spacious.

'Where have you seen me before?' I said quietly. It was just before dawn; everyone was quiet on the floor of the wrecked House.

'On TV, the Parliament Channel. I does watch the *Saturday Night Review*,' he said.

I nodded. Recently parliament had agreed to being filmed in session and now debates and such like were shown on the news every Friday, and also once a week in a *Review* show.

'I see you making speeches and talking and having things to say.'

I nodded, hoping this wasn't going to go the wrong way.

'Allyuh chupid,' he said.

'Why do you say that?'

'I see you all eating nuts. Reading the newspaper. Sometimes I see half the men inside the House of Power asleep! Right here in the chamber.'

I felt ashamed. I'd often wondered if it had been a mistake to allow the chamber to be televised. This was Sans Amen. The ex-colonial citizens must have found the behaviour of some of the ministers in parliament a far cry from their fantasies. The House was Victorian;

they must have thought we behaved like Queen Victoria inside here, all formal and serious, wearing wigs and drinking tea. But that was not the case and I had also found it shocking to watch the footage of the debates. I'd seen the slumped ministers, the men I considered colleagues; some of them were quite good men, but they let themselves down by their casual habits.

'Yes,' I said to Breeze. 'Men in power are no different to any other men.' I wanted to say something general, placatory, but Breeze had a closed-up face and I felt his power and I felt judged and castigated.

'Huh,' he said. 'That is what *you* think. We is not like allyuh. We doh fall asleep when we meet to talk. We are men with discipline. Our Leader train us good. Not like this fool all roughed up so on the ground, none of you know how to behave.'

'You think your Leader is a good man?'

He nodded with a solemn certainty.

'You think your Leader could do any better than us?' The young boy continued to stare down at me as if I were less than him; he nodded again. I could see he belonged to a bunch of righteous men, vigilantes and crusaders. He'd been shown respect by the Leader and that acknowledgement gave him a sense of status, a place in the world. I could see they were a disciplined bunch, not like those men in the House. He had a point. Breeze was sure of his Leader. Not everyone in the House was sure of the PM.

'What do you do every day, then?' said Breeze. 'What is your job?'

'Me?'

'Yeah, when you not on TV, what do you do?'

'Well . . . I make decisions. I have a small team and we . . . make decisions for the country.'

'Tell me one decision you make.'

I tried to think straight. 'Well . . . I am Minister for the Environment. It is a new post, progressive thinking. We decide what is the best way to preserve our natural assets and that is both the hills and forests and the wildlife and also the sea life. We try to monitor the pollution in the sea, like mercury in the fish, like keeping the oilrigs from leaking. We work closely with the Ministry of Energy too.'

His eyes looked glazed and contemptuous. I hadn't answered his question. One decision.

'I made the decision to protect the leatherback turtles.'

The young boy's face creased.

'Turtles?'

'Yes. The northeast coast of Sans Amen is one of the largest migration grounds for leatherback turtles in the world. Our people haven't respected this. Often they kill them, or eat them, sell the meat. I have imposed a fine for selling turtle meat.'

The young boy laughed out loud.

'Didn't you know about the turtles?'

'I know nothing about no turtles. Turtles have nothing to do with politics.'

'Of course they do. Politicians are given the responsibility of caring for the whole country, that includes land and sea, not just people.'

The young boy looked incredulous.

I was vaguely embarrassed.

'Nah, boy. Allyuh *chupid*. You saving turtles? When people starving?'

I wondered about the size of this young boy's world. Had he ever swum in the sea along the north coast of his own island? Had an adult ever taken him over the mountains to get to the sea? If he was from the slums in the east of the City of Silk, there was no reason why he should know about, let alone care about sea creatures.

'Where did you live,' I pressed, 'before you went to live in the commune with the Leader?'

'I live in mih mother house.'

'And where is that?'

'Up so,' and he pointed eastwards to the hills, to the

slopes of shacks and old wooden houses; and then he looked at the slim metal barrel of his gun and he rubbed a spot clean.

'Do you have brothers and sisters?' I pushed.

Again, he gave me a look to say this was stupid. 'Mih mother have ten children.'

'Oh.'

'I number seven. She have three others younger than me.'

'Ten?'

He nodded. And then he looked distant . . . and then he looked alert, like a question had come to him. 'You ever speak to your children?'

I nodded. 'Of course.'

'Well . . . my mother. She busy, busy, busy. She have no time to talk to me. She busy, busy minding children. When she comes from work she only have time to clean the kitchen, go to sleep and then back to work. She ent tell me nothing about no turtles . . . I never have her to tell me about these things.'

I felt a shadow of guilt crawl across my back. I knew it would be very unwise to ask him about his real father. No wonder it was so easy for the Leader to make such an impression. People were like plants; they craved the sun and, just like plants, they grew anyhow they could. Unlike plants, people also craved love and knowledge; both gave them nourishment. Love, to humans, was like a food group. Babies denied love failed to thrive; children who'd grown up without love were forever damaged. The Leader had been giving Breeze knowledge and respect, he had been growing this young man. But I doubted the Leader had been giving him the love of a real parent. That true parental unconditional love, I could see, had been denied to Breeze.

The man they called Ashes appeared behind him.

'Come,' said Ashes, pulling the young boy away.

But the young Breeze didn't move and for a few moments both boy and man looked down on me and I felt their mistrust and condescension. They were from another life and set of ideas and they looked at me like I was a foreign type of human, and maybe I was very separate and hadn't been aware of just how apart it is to work in the House.

These two looked like brothers, Ashes and Breeze, two generations. I watched them back away and I saw that there was a familiarity between them, a gracious body language which I knew was unique for men in this town, a kind of modesty or self-respect.

Their Leader had given them this, too. They walked down the corridor together, past the tearoom, and I saw them kneel together and some of the other gunmen joined them. Six or eight of the men who were holding us hostage laid down their guns in the dawn light and prayed to their God.

One or two prostrated themselves fully, their stomachs flat to the floor; another knelt and bent his head to the ground. Ashes knelt and gazed upwards and held his hands to his heart. The young Breeze knelt and spread his hands flat on the carpet. It made me feel confused. It made this mad act of theirs look like it had meaning and substance behind it. And I could hear them chanting and it sounded beautiful, like a kind of music.

I curled up on my side and watched my captors pray and I felt desolate and lonely and this loneliness was nothing to do with missing my husband or children. I had a loneliness which was all of its own, a longing in my heart which I'd been born with; it accompanied my life. It was a thirst, and a sadness, to be loved . . . and when I watched these men I understood them and they made me feel less alone. I wondered if they were the only souls praying like this for miles around. Maybe the Leader had led them back to something good, to an ancient faith of some sort, to an original tradition of wisdom.

*

When Father Jeremiah Sapno returned to the chamber he caused a stir. He'd disappeared in the early hours of Thursday morning with a list of demands in his hand, scribbled on a piece of notebook paper. Now it was Friday, late morning, twenty-four hours later. There'd been big energy in those demands. But by the time the priest returned, the demands seemed lost, even forgotten. Howl was winning this siege already, hands down. The army had bombed the place, shown their massive potential, frightened everyone inside, including Hal. They had purposely kept Father Sapno back; they were forcing the gunmen to wait. The priest returned to the House on *their* terms. They were showing that they would decide when and if and how negotiations took place. They weren't hungry, weak, living cooped up in appalling conditions.

When Father Sapno appeared again in the chamber, it was clear he was very frightened by what he saw. I registered this with a mixture of understanding and alarm. I was no longer so frightened of the gunmen, or the situation. Me and my fellow captors had somehow, incredibly, acclimatised. We'd learned how to survive. The feeling of immediate danger had worn off, even though the actual danger hadn't. The guns, the bullets in them, no longer seemed so murderous. Again, my mind played tricks. They were like magic bullets that couldn't hurt or kill.

Bullets made of silk. That, or perhaps I'd been so scared for my life, for minutes, hours, early on, that there was no emotion left in me I could associate with terror. All my terror had been used up. The only loose cannon of a gunman, the one with the Santa hat, had been apprehended and tied up. There was a well-known madhouse in Sans Amen; I wondered if he'd once been an inmate. At that point the House was a madhouse too. I was an inmate.

*

My main concern was the split. In fact *the split* was at the heart of this whole outrage. A year earlier, our party had split into two. There was the PM, a good man, if a little stiff, and his faithful ministers, and then a small group who'd split away. It had caused the PM a lot of pain and made the party look chaotic. Those who'd divided from the PM were more extreme social-ists. They didn't like the way the PM ran things, his personal style. But the PM had seen them as dangerous and unstable with mad ideas; he'd viewed them as communists. These ministers had got involved with the labour movement and I was sure they'd even mixed with the Leader at times. Some of them had progres-sive ideas, like a new type of money, a bartering system, and buying land for social housing and setting up a type of co-operative system.

I suspected these ministers with progressive ideas knew the Leader and Father Sapno. I suspected they all had a lot in common. Those who'd split from our government were more like the gunmen in terms of their ideas. There were four or five ministers involved in this split and these were the ministers who were being detained separately during all this madness. They were kept apart and were being treated better in general, as if the gunmen hadn't meant to capture or hurt *them*. It was those ministers, who were out and out socialists, who Hal was prepared to negotiate with. The PM was entirely left out. He was still tied up on the ground, by then seriously ill; I was worried he might lose consciousness.

Father Sapno and Hal and three of the more socialist ministers disappeared down the corridor to talk. I turned to Mervyn Mahibir and said, 'Thank God the army are still loyal to the PM. Things could be very different now in Sans Amen.'

Mervyn nodded. 'Don't worry. This will all be over by the weekend, Aspasia.'

'How can you say *don't worry*?'

'Because I have faith.'

'You feeling faith right now?'

'Yes. Don't you? That's all there is. It has come on me the last day or so. Faith, the desire to live. I will be okay. You will be okay too.'

I felt very differently compared to two days ago. The world I knew was gone. I could remember being sworn into the new government, my sense of pride in the job, my feelings of being able to make a difference, to be of service to my country. Yet all along . . . this . . . this danger was the hard reality of affairs on the street. There was a chasm between my intentions and this small band of men with guns.

'I feel empty,' I said. 'Sinful and empty. And I feel like I've died somehow in here already. I can't think straight. I've been having dreams.'

'Yes. Me too.'

'I dreamt of that young woman Bathsheba who was shot years ago in the hills. A freedom fighter. Remember her? She was pregnant.'

'Yes, I do. I was a young doctor then. I was . . . well . . . involved in the case.'

'Really? Her child died in her stomach too. But now I see these young boys, I see that here is Bathsheba's dead baby son. So many riots in this city, Mervyn, so much violence already. Slaves have rioted, the canboulay riots, the water riots, trade union marches, black power in 1970. And now this crazy crazy . . .

what is this? An insurrection? Why does this keep happening, Mervyn?'

'It has something to do with renewal, Aspasia. Some kind of recreation of events so that people will learn. Eventually. They just don't learn fast.'

'Why did you ever want to be in politics?'

Mervyn laughed. 'I didn't. I told you. I'm no politician.'

'Then why? What are you doing here?'

'I'm a doctor, Aspasia. The Minister for Health. They need experts like me – and you. I am an expert on health. But that's not the same as being a politician. I'm a layman, a doctor. I have always worked in the civil service. I got offered a job in the cabinet. I go about making tea in the House. I'm not interested in politics most of the time. Haven't you noticed?'

'But you got elected, just like me.'

'Sure. But I see myself as a *public servant*. That's not the same thing as these men with guns down the hall; they from a different set of concerns. Those people with guns who care about "social justice" all end up causing trouble and violence. They want to rule. That is the politics of ego. Serving the public and ruling the public two different things.'

'Mervyn, I *wanted* to be in politics. I had ideas. I thought I was making changes. I even thought things

145

were going quite well for us until two days ago.'

'Look. Nothing stays the same, Aspasia,' said Mervyn. 'Everything is changing all the time.'

'That's not the impression I get.'

'That is a law of natural science. Once, there was no city here, for instance. Just swamp and silk cotton trees and red-skinned men and women from the mainland who arrived by canoe and they lived peacefully. Everything was different. I believe there is peace in the soil of this city, Aspasia. You are an environmentalist. Mother Earth. Gaia. The earth's soul is peaceful.'

I felt grateful to be reminded of this.

'Yes. True. But also I believe there is blood in the soil here too now, Mervyn.'

'Maybe there's both.'

'Maybe we laugh it all off once a year. At carnival time.'

'Or maybe we in Sans Amen have the enlightened gift of humour.'

'Or maybe we are a nation of gifted satirists who like peace and yet often cause bloodshed and once a year we wipe clean our memories.'

'Ha, ha. Maybe you and I haven't eaten for days, Aspasia. We are becoming philosophers.' Mervyn winked. I could see he wasn't scared. Mervyn was a gifted man. In this madhouse everyone was showing himself or herself. Everyone seemed bigger and more raw and more real.

I didn't know if I was hungry or not. I tried to look ahead, to allow myself to think that even this hellish situation could change. I would see my children; I clung to this belief. I would go home and start my life again. It was still happening, this attempted coup, or whatever it was; it was in progress. I must keep still and not act. I should only watch. I should keep out of things and be glad I wasn't involved in the negotiations. My children and husband needed me to be alive. I thought of bullets made of silk. Magic bullets that couldn't kill me. This was a very dangerous way to think. I would be okay if I stayed out of things and kept my eye on that young boy Breeze. I also wondered, secretly, if this was the most exciting thing that had ever happened to me and ever was going to happen in my political life. I wondered if this peace and blood was what politics actually involved. Turtles were indeed irrelevant.

*

The negotiations went on all morning. Twice Greg Mason came out cussing. Once Hal flew out from one of the backrooms on his walkie-talkie, swearing and speaking in terse tones down the line to the Leader. The white minister left the negotiations altogether, muttering.

I looked at Mervyn and he shrugged.

'These men seriously think they getting new elections?' I whispered. 'A chance to govern? Haven't any of them heard of democracy? A voting system?'

'They stuck now, Aspasia, they need to get out of here alive. Now they only bartering for their lives.'

'You think the Leader ever had any *real* plans to rule? He shoot up the place. But then what did he expect to do next? Did he have a further political agenda? Did he expect us all to become religious in the same way? They a bunch of mad hybrid mystics, or so they feel. A rainbow religion of some kind. What on God's earth did he want to do?'

'My gut feeling is that he wants Howl's job. To be top dog in the army or something like that. There were no other big plans.'

'Head of the army?' I laughed. 'Yes, I figure the same thing. He want a job. To be high up in politics. But that's like putting the Joker rather than Batman on guard.'

'Correct!' Mervyn laughed. 'But I figure he had a few plans to take control, but them plans not anywhere near good enough. After that he wanted the country to re-elect a government – and for him to be part of the new system.'

'Well, he get nowhere fast.'

Eventually Hal appeared looking distracted and jaded, a new piece of paper in his hands. He instructed Breeze to pass it round. 'Everyone here must sign it, words are no good alone,' he said, and he took a pen from his top pocket. 'Every minister must put his name to this document, in writing. We get told it have to be written down, that go make it legal.'

*

Around midday, Father Sapno left the House again. This time with only one demand written down on a piece of paper and signed by all the ministers, including myself; we were now three days with no food, still in shock, some of us injured. The PM had signed it too, half-blind and only half-conscious. This time when they put a gun to his head he easily capitulated. The army had made it clear via Father Sapno that the game was entirely over: there would be no political demands. There was no popular revolution, no bargaining with a bunch of armed boys and men.

I worried about the looting. This would put town planning and national spending back fifteen years. It would be a huge task for us, or any subsequent government, to rebuild. Not one man in the street had joined their cause. People in rural areas were probably living their lives as usual. They would have heard about this crisis, but no revolution had reached them. The army had acted impeccably; this was now a hostage crisis, a double hostage crisis. The Leader and his men had taken hostages and now the Leader and his men were surrounded and in turn hostages themselves. The army would not bend to threats. Colonel Howl still refused to negotiate directly with the Leader or Hal; negotiations were being conducted through the priest. Colonel Howl let it be known that if one dead body fell from the balcony of the House of Power, the whole game was over. The army would storm the building. The gunmen needed to relinquish their unworkable political ideals.

I'd read the piece of paper. It had only two lines:

We, the undersigned, do pardon and grant full amnesty to the Leader and his men in return for our lives.

We would surely be set free; the Leader and the gunmen would be rounded up and taken straight to prison and then to court. Of course this amnesty would be scrutinised by international experts and judges, and deemed invalid. It had been signed by the PM under extreme duress. It was a meaningless piece of paper.

But I thought it would help us to get out, and so I had signed it too; so had all the others. I shivered and felt sick in my heart. I knew that if these men walked out of the House alive, the courts would sentence them all to death for treason at the very least – also murder, arson and several other counts related to civil unrest. The courts of Sans Amen would be busy after this little catastrophe.

*

The conditions in the House were dire. Three days in, the latrine in the corner had become an open sewer and had attracted hoards of flies. No one had eaten, sleep was fitful. July, and it was humid in the chamber; the rainy season was upon us but it hadn't rained yet in those few days of terror. The lack of rain made everything seem more tense. The air was so thick in the chamber I could put my fist through it.

The young boy called Breeze was still eyeing me up and hanging around; it was like he wanted to guard me and also intimidate me at the same time. Sometimes he looked his age and rather unsure of himself; other times he was gruff, just like the men, a small boy soldier. He'd pointed a gun at me twice. He was one of ten children. I fought my instincts to mother him.

'What you looking at?' he said.

'Nothing.' I replied. 'I have nowhere to look.'

'Well, look somewhere else.'

I glanced towards the PM who was lying on the floor and very ill. He followed my line of vision and steupsed.

'You see that, that is your fault. You bring this thing on yourself, all of you.'

I felt so low and weak, I knew that somewhere this was true. We had somehow done wrong. I had little to come back at him with. He must feel very betrayed in his heart.

I looked up.

'Tell me about the kind of life you would like to live,' I said. 'Imagine you could have everything you want. What would it be?'

Breeze looked annoyed.

'Go on,' I urged. 'What do you want for yourself in life?'

His eyes narrowed. 'I have my freedom. I have my health and my God. I have so much. Is like you can't see it.'

I nodded.

He spat on the metal nose of his gun and rubbed it with his shirt.

'We going to get out of here, all of us. I will go back

to my life. I will be part of society. You will go back to what? To dominating it?'

'Right now you are dominating me.'

'I am a freedom fighter.'

'You have a gun. That is a means of terror not freedom.'

'State have guns too,' he steupsed. 'Is called an army. Your guns outside surrounding us. You too much of a coward to hold your own gun. You pay others to shoot. We do our own business.'

Again I felt penitent. It was all too hard. These men brought action and their half-baked theories crashing in through the windows. And the half-baked theories resembled the actual well-conceived theories. These men mixed it all up. Here he was, this young boy called Breeze, threatening to shoot me. Somehow he'd broken through all the red tape.

Breeze looked like he could read my thoughts. He looked satisfied with himself.

'Mih mother busy, busy,' he said, almost to himself. 'Busy life. Busy making business. I now here, making history.'

I wondered if his mother knew, let alone cared where he was. I was witnessing a young man currently being made, and currently ruining his already half-destroyed life. I had seen so much of this young boy. I'd witnessed him in the full surrender of prayer; I'd seen him pick up a human tongue off the carpet; I'd heard him spout forth his socialist politics, some of it text-book socialism he might have studied at the University of the West Indies. Then I saw the possibility that he would hang for his crime of being born poor and fatherless and easy prey for the likes of a politically half-baked egomaniac Father-Leader. I was sad about this. It *was* our fault.

The Leader. *Ha.* He had nothing new up his sleeve, nothing to say to a small New World nation which needed ideas as it emerged from under the claustro-phobia of colonialism. Sans Amen needed forward-thinking men and women, young men just like Breeze and these young boys, just like the son or daughter of Bathsheba the freedom fighter, the child who was shot dead in her stomach. 1990. The end of a century was looming, a century which had been bloody and devas-tating to the planet and its people everywhere. The age of 'computer science' was coming. Something called 'the internet' was happening, which meant that small islands in the New World would be joined up, con-nected to everything and everywhere. There were even women now in the House of Power in Sans Amen. There was no room any more for these antiquated Caribbean macho-men, these Father-Leaders. The Leader and this band of men would surely hang for their ludicrous act. Even the crazy one with the Santa hat; they would hang for being so out of touch with a world which was already changing around them.

*

At four in the afternoon on Friday we had a big surprise. Another hostage was found. She said her name was Mrs Cynthia Gonzales, that she was the mother of four children. The gunmen found her hiding in the cleaning cupboard. She had been there, undetected, for two days. She'd showed up at five o' clock on Wednesday evening, as usual, to start her evening job as a cleaner at the House of Power. She turned up every day at five – we all knew her by sight – and she left at ten and went home to her family in St Jared's. On the Wednesday of the attempted revolution she had been using the washroom when the gunmen stampeded the House of Power, shooting. She had run straight from the washroom to the broom cupboard and locked it tight from the inside, but the lock had seized shut. Two days later, one of the gunmen heard her hammering to get out. She'd had enough in there. Two nights and two days. They brought her a glass of water and then they carried her, weak and disorientated, from the cupboard into the chamber. When she saw the chaos and the mess and the vile stinking latrine and the PM of the country all tied up and with his eyes sealed shut, his blue-purple face, the plaster and the glass and the debris on the red velvet carpet, the carpet she vacuumed clean every day, when the House was closed, over for business, her face set hard. She seemed to grow, to experience a surge of strength. Mrs Cynthia Gonzales examined the filth on the carpet and then she glared at all the men standing around with guns.

'No,' she said, as if to herself. She stamped her foot and then turned around and glared at Hal. 'Allyuh damn chupid fools. Why you do this, eh, *why*?'

For a split-second, Hal looked cowed. Mrs Cynthia Gonzales had been hiding in the broom cupboard for days and yet she'd somehow emerged in pristine condition. She must have been in her late fifties; she had on a cleaner's gown over her everyday clothes. She was wearing comfortable flat-heeled ankle boots. I realised she was also wearing a copper-coloured wig, cut in a stylish short bob, and this was what gave her such a well-groomed appearance. Mrs Gonzales looked around the chamber and it was as if she'd stepped out from a parallel universe, one of order and normality; that or she refused point blank to accept the situation in the House. She spoke in a clear voice, not quite cussing, more like an impatient nurse.

'You are a damn chupid lazy man and you should feel shame for what you have done here. Big man, eh? Big so. Big boots. Army suit. Look at you. You feel you is playing soldier an thing. Shoot up de damn place. What de *ass* wrong with you, eh? You mash up mih carpet. Who you think clean this place every day, eh? You think is fine to come in here and mash it up? Eh? Well I clean this place every day, five days a week. For *fifteen* years. I consider it an honour to clean this chamber. This is *my* carpet. And you feel so free to come in here and ruin it. Eh, eh. Jesus Christ Lord in heaven. Where are your manners and where is your respect for civilisation?'

Hal put one hand up to ward off Greg Mason. The other gunmen looked to him to see what to do. Hal stood and took the dressing down like a man.

'Lady . . .' he began.

'You shut up,' said Mrs Gonzales.

Hal kept his calm.

The young boys stared. I almost laughed. One of them said, 'Oh, *gooood.*'

But Hal went closer to Mrs Gonzales with his pistol.

'Lady, you watch your language, okay?' He had raised his voice.

'Me?'

'Yes, you. We have no war with women. We come in here to save the country. Change things round. But our plans go wrong.'

'Plans? What plans? What you trying to change?'

'Lady, look, this is not your business . . . we come to liberate the people of the City of Silk who are oppressed.'

'Who is oppressed?'

'You are oppressed.'

'Me?'

'Yes.'

Mrs Gonzales looked Hal up and down. She steupsed at the ridiculousness of this idea. She looked around at the men and all of us ministers who were now watching her. Then, with a slow and mannered dignity, Mrs Gonzales took off her wig.

For a moment it looked like she'd taken off her own head. Her scalp was shaved down to a grey fuzz. Underneath the wig she was like another woman, sleek, older. Hal looked down at his feet, shamed by her nakedness. Breeze stared at this other skull. One or two of the gunmen backed away. Someone uttered the words 'obeah woman'.

My heart felt warm for the first time in days. Thank God for her, thank God for Mrs Gonzales. I was scared for her and also held mesmerised. They hadn't frightened her yet, or at all. She was a woman from Sans Amen. Taking no crap from no man.

'Listen, here. I am a grandmother,' said Mrs Gonzales. 'An old black woman.'

Hal looked like he was going to melt.

'You show me some respect. You see this?' she said, turning her head and pointing to a bump at the back. 'Mih skull split open once. Now mih head have a shape like an egg. A man cuff me down once and I end up in hospital. An you talk about me being oppressed today? I oppressed only once in my life, by a man I make the mistake to marry. That man now long dead. No man go oppress me again. None of you speak for me, yuh hear. I doh need no crazy bunch of boys with guns to come inside here on my behalf. I not oppressed. I have job, home, good health, family. You mad or what?'

I was worried. Despite their claims to have no war with women, these men could shoot women by accident. She was pushing her luck.

'Mrs Gonzales,' I chipped in. 'Mrs Gonzales, this situation is very serious. Please,' I turned to Hal. It was the first time I had said anything directly to Hal, the first time I'd had any cause to communicate verbally with him. 'Please, just let her go. She's been inside a cupboard for two days. No food, no water. Just let her go.'

Hal nodded.

'Eh, eh. I ent going *nowhere*,' said Mrs Gonzales. Her face was set in a cold and implacable fury; all the men and boys had seen this face before on a woman and it was trouble. No one said anything and everyone looked towards Hal.

Hal stared. '*Jesus*,' he said, shaking his head. But Mrs Gonzales was way ahead of him.

'You see that man over there on the ground? The Prime Minister?'

Hal looked over at the PM who had become more alert, who was watching everything now with more interest.

'He work here late too. Just like me. He often here all ten o' clock in the night. Often we does talk. I does bring him a cup of coffee. He does talk to me and sometimes we talk about politics in Sans Amen. So I staying *right here* with him till he leave this godforsaken place. Till allyuh go home. I not leaving you men in here to ruin mih frikkin carpet more than this. Me? I ent going nowhere.'

She gave Hal a look which told him not to trouble her any more than he already had. She tugged her wig back on her head. Somehow she looked less dangerous with it on. We were all struck dumb by her. She gazed around her at the debris and the tired, deranged hostages and she steupsed and shook her head. She knew many of the ministers by sight.

She said, 'Come, nuh, ah going over there,' and with that Mrs Gonzales picked her way over towards the Prime Minister and she sat down near him. She looked at his injured face and she said to Breeze, who'd been guarding him, 'Bring me a bowl of water and a sponge from the kitchen.'

Mrs Cynthia Gonzales seemed to have an effect on the young boys and even the men. Like the PM she was brave and it seemed that they didn't like how she appeared just like that from the cupboard and they didn't like her wig. They kept their distance and watched her with suspicion, and at the same time they didn't want to get involved with her. Again, Hal's authority had been usurped. He let this pass; he had no choice but to do so, and made a vague reference to 'upping the hostage count'. Her presence also had an inspiring effect on the hostages, including myself. Mrs Gonzales had decided to stay where everybody in the House was held hostage against their will. Breeze did as he was asked and watched over her as she sponged the caked blood from the PM's face. It was strange to witness her tenderness towards him. The PM looked at Mrs Gonzales with a kind of gladness and a small smile on his lips. It was clear they were friends.

*

Friday evening came about. A feeling of acute deadness had settled in the House. The situation was in the act of extinguishing itself. The revolution had no more incentive or motive. Hal had lost some of his power to the PM and then more to Mrs Gonzales. He looked different, thinner, tired. There was nothing for him to do but wait for the army to reply to their one last demand. Every now and then he retreated to the back room to speak on his walkie-talkie to the Leader. Sometimes they called each other on the one phone line available in the House. I guessed the situation at the television station was the same. Everyone cooped up, waiting.

At dusk half the gunmen disappeared to pray on a closed balcony wing of the House. They left the other half to stand guard. Their prayers were said on a rotation and their prayers were the only thing that made the situation feel endurable. The man called Ashes was leading the prayers, like the job had somehow landed with him.

That night, my third night under the gun, I felt like

I'd become another person. I ached for my children, my husband. Gloria, James and Marc. They were my heart; they were everything. I cried for Sans Amen, the other mothers like me. The City of Mothers: devastated, calling for change that had never arrived. I tried to review my life: my childhood had been happy enough, an older sister and a younger brother; I was the middle child, always different, always the one making a face in family photographs. Often, I felt on the outside of things. From an early age I was aware that I was wise. But I kept my wisdom to myself. Or maybe I was just shy and my feelings of being different came from just the opposite; I had the job of being ordinary, in the middle.

At school I'd done well academically; I excelled at geography and biology. My father was a hiker and often took us up into the hills of the northern range, up into the forest, and we often camped overnight, making hammocks with bamboo poles. In the dark we could hear agouti and manicou pass beneath us and this felt thrilling and also safe. We swam in the cold river streams which ran through untouched primary rainforest. Once we hiked up to where a famous pilot had crashed his plane, the rusted fuselage still there, bits of broken wing, the nose all crumpled up. He'd been trying to fly over the mountains and got snagged in cloud; the villagers nearby took ten days to find the plane, the bodies still inside, two young men, our first aviators. The empty mangled plane still ached with loss. I'd grown to love the land of this island from young. My father had taught me to respect it and to fear no animal or reptile, even the pit viper called a *fer de lance*.

I grew up and my chubbiness fell off. The younger, slimmer woman I became in my twenties met a man called Marc Garland, a handsome lawyer, and we married quietly. My husband knew of my dream of wanting to make a difference. He'd married a woman who needed to work, be of service. We honeymooned in a village called L'Anse Verte on the north coast of Sans Amen, in a house lent by a friend. It was then, aged twenty-six, I saw a leatherback turtle lay her eggs.

Female turtles have a tranquil grace born from their singular journeying across the vast oceans of the world. I saw her lumber from the sea, too big for land, too reptile for the daytime sun, and yet intent on settling to nest; she hauled her elephantine legs, her massive leather carapace. She came at dusk, the earth's wisdom in her eyes. They leaked a saline gel, and I wept and remembered the turtle I'd witnessed on the beach, as a child, its fins sawn off. Here was another, giving birth. As she dropped her blind, perfect eggs into the sand she slipped into a birth-trance and like that she was very vulnerable to attack. She let her treasure of future generations slide from her womb; a hundred eggs fell silently into the sandpit she'd dug with her hind fins. Only one or two of her offspring might survive. I remembered the turtle's determined crawl back to the ink black sea and tears streamed down my face. I was a young woman then, inexperienced.

In the House, all shot up and reeking of death, I felt old, old as the City of Silk. I prayed that my husband and children were safe and I remembered what Mervyn had said about change and thought about how much this situation gave me a new feeling about myself.

I sat on the floor of the House and listened to the sounds of tired, frightened men and boys as they prepared for another night. The chamber now looked and smelled like a battleground. The night-time brought all manner of intimate sounds. Many of the men snored in their sleep; there were loud farts, half-spoken threats; others whimpered into their dreams; some tossed and turned over in their nightmares. Everyone gave way as best they could for a few snatched hours of escape. I closed my eyes and I imagined myself slipping away from Sans Amen, heading north, into an ink black sea.

SATURDAY MORNING,
THE HOUSE OF POWER,
THE CITY OF SILK

The explosion sent me flying several feet into the air. I had been standing up when the army launched their rocket. I landed on top of Mrs Gonzales and the Prime Minister and we became a bundle of arms and legs. The air went white and the explosion was followed by another massive *boom*, and the building shook to its very bones. My bones shook too; the sound ripped through my body as it did through the walls. Plaster fell in a fine silt powder over us all. I looked at her watch. It was 9.15 a.m.

'Hold your fire, hold your fire,' shouted Hal to his men. Not one of them had run to the window to respond. All the young boys had hit the floor as had many of the men; many, like me, had been blown off their feet. The floor of the House of Power was now packed with men face down, covering their heads with their hands. Everyone inside was struggling to take cover. The army was attacking again.

'Do not return fire,' shouted Hal. This, I realised, was because it would be useless. Again, for the third time, they were up against the army's full vengeance. There was another *boom*. The House shook. I clasped my head and prayed and every cell screamed. They were using rocket launchers and firing into the walls of the House, blasting it away. Again, they were attacking with full force. They were carrying out the PM's orders. He was still the Head of State; he had ordered this from the outset. Now we were going to die once and for all. It was the end. Three days: enough was enough. The army were saying 'no deal' to their amnesty. No to letting these lunatics off. The modern world was watching what was happening on TV. Kate Adie of the BBC was here on the island. CNN was here too. The international media were watching. But many of the journalists of Sans Amen were at the TV station, held hostage too. The citizens of the island couldn't see the horror in the streets because of the curfew. Even so, there could be no pardon with so many people looking on; no one was getting away with anything, like in 1970. Now the army of Sans Amen were going to blow them all away. I looked across and saw that the PM was barely conscious. He might be dead soon; he was their prize hostage and he was already half dead.

Boom, another explosion followed by another massive jolt; it was as if the House was resting in the palm of a capricious giant and he was squeezing the walls and shaking it about. The ceiling groaned and dust fell. Outside I could hear a voice on megaphone shouting: 'Lay down your arms,' but the voice seemed tinny and distant.

Another *boom.* I wondered how the House could withstand any more pounding. This assault was even more fierce than the last. I imagined this was the final and total destruction of the House of Power. I hoped that those who governed Sans Amen in future would finally get the hint. They would build another place to govern from. There would be big changes after this.

Boom. The army guns outside were roaring, the sound resembling a massive sewing machine running on and on. I saw that the young boy Breeze was covering his head; he was screwed up in a ball. Next to him the man called Ashes was also face down. Greg Mason was down too. These men now felt known to me; not friends, but definitely people I knew and had some kind of understanding of. I found it hard to admit, but I had come to care for them.

Boom, boom, boom, then several rockets were released in one go. A part of the House fell off in a clump to the ground and then it was as if the chamber felt lighter. I looked up and gasped. There was a gaping hole in one side of the chamber. Sky. I could see sky, the outside world, and it occurred to me that freedom was beyond. I could leap out. They were blasting their way into the House; they didn't care. I looked at Hal and saw a wild and cold terror in his eyes. He was going to die after all. We were all about to die. *Boom,* a rocket flew like a comet in through a window close by and then there was the horrifying smell of burning wood.

'Do not return fire,' shouted Hal.

I was afraid for my life, but it was only then, at this ludicrous command, after three terrifying days, that I felt murderous. I could kill this bloody man Hal and his Leader with my own hands. I noticed that his soldiers were still with him, still loyal. Only one of them had cracked, even in all this, the one who was already cracked before he arrived. Not one other had mutinied or run away. Their prayers had held them together; their prayers would get them through all this. The pounding went on and on. From the way the House shook with every rocket, I was sure that parts of the building were falling off. The army were blowing off bits of the House. Soon they would be inside.

*

At 11.35 a.m., exactly, the army stopped. Everyone in the House was powdered white. Some of the walls were gone. Now there were only holes, which tempted the world beyond. There wasn't much left of the chamber. From the room at the back came the urgent sound of the telephone ringing. I realised it was the first time I'd heard the telephone in days. A normal everyday sound, while all around me an avalanche had struck. People were like ghosts, dusted white, coughing up the silt in their lungs. The phone rang on, an insistent solitary cry, impossible to ignore. The Leader calling Hal, I suspected. Hal got up and walked swiftly towards it down the hall. The dividing wall which separated the tearoom from the chamber had been obliterated. The latrine had been blown away with it. Faeces and silt ash were all mixed up.

'Lay down your weapons,' came the stern voice from the megaphone outside in the street. 'Come out with your hands in the air.'

Still the megaphone voice sounded far away.

No one moved in the House. Only Greg Mason got

up and dared a peek outside. A shot rang out from a sniper in the street and he ducked back down.

'Them boys serious now,' he muttered.

I glanced across at Breeze. He was looking at the PM with a perplexed expression in his eyes; something was dawning on him. The Prime Minster was dawning on him, what and who he was, that all this firepower was about coming to save him, about obeying his orders. I registered this newness of awareness in the young boy and I thought, finally, the Leader's spell has been broken. Finally, he can see the bigger picture.

Mrs Gonzales' wig had been blown off in the attack. She was on her hands and knees searching for it, cussing now, cussing the men who'd come to liberate her from her oppression. 'Mash up mih damn carpet,' she kept muttering.

Hal came back from his phone call and there was a mild triumph in his manner, in his step.

'We have an agreement,' he announced. 'The army will be sending a convoy of trucks to take you away this afternoon.'

III. Mercy

SATURDAY AFTERNOON,
THE HOUSE OF POWER,
THE CITY OF SILK

Ashes woke with a start. In his dream the Phantom had been digging under the House of Power. He'd tethered his horse Hero to a silk cotton tree and he held a spade in one hand like a staff. With the other hand he was pointing, saying, 'Look, there is the beautiful.' And there, in the red soil under the House, he had uncovered the bones of many bodies, the remains of Amerindians from centuries back. The bodies were all laid out in trenches, dozens of them. There was a small burial ground underneath the House. Men, women and children had been laid there to rest. Ashes woke up sweating, a heavy feeling of dread in his chest. Somehow he'd forgotten about them, the first people of Sans Amen, and how he was related to them.

The Phantom then did something unthinkable. He removed his mask. Behind the mask Ashes recognised a familiar face: that of his dead brother, River. River was smiling and there was a circle of light blazing around his head. His spade then turned to a long rifle, silver-grey and threatening. 'I'm always here,' he said. 'We all are.'

Ashes rose from the small nest he'd made on the floor of the library and prepared himself for prayer. His watch said 6.00 a.m. and a dawn light was filtering in through the stained glass. He could feel the City of Silk all around him, jarred, frightened by what had happened. It was a city on edge. Their doing. He had followed in the footsteps of his brother and the Phantom, but they were somehow good and he was somehow wrong and stupid. He knelt on his haunches in front of the coloured glass and he looked up at the martyr nailed to a wooden cross. He closed his eyes and opened his chest and very soon he became aware of the feeling of lightness and peace. The beautiful; it came down into him, spreading a tender and glorious love and he bent forward, open and receptive, and he pressed his arms and face flat to the floor, beneath the holy prophet, the revolutionary on the cross. Somehow it was all connected. Somehow he hadn't understood this. He uttered the words of holy remembrance, and when he said the words his spirits lifted and he felt drunk with love and connected to his heart.

*

Upstairs, the chamber was an open cavity. Brothers were tired and starving; the hostages were starving too and beyond their wits. Ashes remembered the first hours after they had rushed up from the street, how he'd been shocked at the smashed crockery, the cussing and the dead bodies. That felt like weeks ago. Now everything was pulverised, walls blown away. The younger brothers shifted from room to room. They were looking for things to do and he had a feeling that their sense of reality had been altered for good.

The last three days of revolution had shaken him. Ashes felt he'd become a crude, simple man again; he had succumbed to all the lowest emotions. He'd been scared almost every minute of the last few days. He'd been anxious, riddled with doubt. He had been angry with the others, with most of the brothers, in fact, including Hal and Breeze Arnold and Greg Mason. Anger was never a wise reaction to events; anger shut out the light. He'd felt ashamed, too. At first he was disappointed and then disillusioned with what had happened in the chamber of the

House. The dead woman on the floor, the dead men lying all over the place, in other rooms, on the balconies, on the ground outside, on the steps, their bodies now defiled. Arnold all tied up in one of the back rooms; Arnold who'd gone mad, overwhelmed by the *nafs*. The lady appearing from the broom cupboard; she had made him feel guilty and bad. And then there were the terrifying guns and rockets, the army outside. Ashes had suffered actual pains in his chest. Panic attacks. Even though he had been praying several times a day, but it was hard to open his heart in these conditions.

Greg Mason was one of the few that remained intact. His eyes were still mean and full of intent; his righteous fervour hadn't died. He had survived 1970; he had shot at least one man dead; he had served years in gaol for his crimes. He was the Real Deal: a guerilla fighter. Ashes looked out the window and saw the army and the ruined streets and he felt un-free. He doubted he would ever be free again. He knew his personal freedom had ended. But Greg still seemed crazy with zeal, committed and self-assured. They had kept each other at a measured and respectful distance throughout the last few days. Now it felt impossible to avoid meeting him.

'Ayyy,' Mason said, by way of stopping him in his tracks.

Ashes froze. He was holding his gun. For some reason he'd kept it with him all along. It had given him something to hold on to. He hadn't fired a shot. He carried it with a kind of tired resignation and yet he didn't want to put it down in case it was loaded and went off. He didn't know if it was loaded or not. He'd held onto it just in case.

Mason gave him a look which meant that he wanted to talk. He was one of those men in the compound Ashes had kept clear of. He'd kept clear of men like Mason in life, too. They were men of action who other men respected and women found attractive. Mason had that energy. Men like Mason made him feel weak. They didn't read books; they read magazines, if that.

'You use that thing yet?' Mason said, and his eyes were like they didn't see him.

Ashes shook his head.

'Give it to me.'

Ashes complied.

Mason weighed it in his hands and steupsed. He opened the chamber of the gun and peered inside.

He looked back at Ashes with a knowing and disappointed expression. 'It empty. W'appen, you doh figure to load the damn thing?'

Ashes cringed.

'You were given ammunition. Why didn't you load your gun like you were ordered to?'

Ashes had forgotten this command in the heat of it all. He had been wearing his bandolier of bullets, but had taken it off to sleep. The bandolier was now downstairs in the library. Besides, no one had shown him how to load his gun.

Mason steupsed. 'Come.'

In a back room there were boxes of ammunition, more guns, bullets, hand grenades. All unused; it was like they had brought too much; like they had decided they were going to save the rest for another try. Mason reached into a box and said, 'See?' And he opened the chamber of the gun again and loaded six bullets into the holes inside. He gave Ashes a look which said something to him about his brother River. Ashes' spectacles began to fog.

Mason glared at him. 'Your brother, he showed *me* how to load a gun,' he steupsed. 'You two like chalk and cheese. How your mother born two sons who get in to so much trouble, eh?'

It was a good question.

'River was a soul man, a man who saw the light.' And with this his eyes fired up and Ashes could see that Mason had loved River too. 'You two are so different. Is like you are him in reverse.'

At this Ashes bowed his head, feeling ashamed. He was no fighter. He had a few reasons for being here, but they had evaporated almost immediately. He wanted to be at home with his wife. He wondered if Mason was married or had children he loved. He wanted to say to him that heroism could also be quiet. He had made a family and that was enough good work for a man.

Mason passed him back the rifle and he weighed it like he was trying to measure the difference but it felt the same, with or without bullets. Now his gun was loaded. Now he was dangerous, just like Fat Clay of Cuba. It felt very late in the day to be so dangerous. He nodded at Mason and said, 'Our mother is very proud of us.'

*

Apparently, it was all over now. The army was sending a convoy of trucks to take all the hostages away. But by now he had overheard the ministers whisper amongst each other, using words like 'treason' and 'murder' and 'hanging' and 'prison'. And these words had been the reason for his attacks of panic. What would his wife think? He'd sunk to the lowest, crudest possible human form. He had deceived his wife – and his country. He was a common betrayer. *Treason*. It was a word he must look up in the dictionary. He hadn't even considered this. It was a crime he didn't know much about. He hadn't left the compound three days ago in a W.A.T.E.R. truck to commit an act of treason; that wasn't his motive at all. He wasn't a 'treasonous' man. One act, depending on how you looked at it, could be both positive and negative. Now he didn't know which way to look at what they had done. It was clear he had let himself down. And his spiritual aspirations were failed too; they hadn't just ended, they had reversed.

Jade must now know where he was. All the wives must have known since the first night. After the two-hour bombardment that morning, and the news of the hostages being taken away in army trucks, Ashes decided he would use the telephone. Everything had been smashed up and blown to pieces; everything was over. He would call his wife. He would apologise and beg her for forgiveness. And so, when Hal was issuing orders to the men in the chamber, Ashes went into the ruined back room where everything was smashed up and there was more graffiti about God on the wall. The phone was on the floor and he sat down next to it and he picked up the receiver and felt relief at the sound of the dial tone and dialled the telephone number to his home.

The phone rang and he felt a slow rolling oceanic wave threaten to engulf him, a wave of dread and fear and sorrow.

'Hello?'

She sounded unhappy. Even with this one word he could tell. He had expected it to be a relief to hear her voice. But he didn't feel anything like relief. He felt dead.

'Jade.'

'Hello . . . Ashes?'

'Jade, yes. This is me.'

He could hear her heart beating, and he could imagine her love for him now ruined. He had ruined it. He had ruined his life, their life together. His sons' lives. He had made an irretrievable error.

'Ashes, where are you?'

'I'm inside the House of Power.'

She didn't respond and for a few seconds he thought of telling her again, to make it clear.

'What you expect me to say, eh?' There was a thick sob in her voice.

'I'm sorry.'

'*Sorry*?'

'Yes. Please forgive me.'

'Ashes . . . at this stage forgiveness is high talk. They going and kill allayou. They going and kill you all.

Blow you away. That . . . or send you to prison for the rest of your life or hang your arses.'

A hard lump formed in Ashes' throat and tears fell. He could feel his breathing begin to change, his heart speed up; he patted for his inhaler and pumped spray into his mouth. But the spray had run out. He had none left, his secret air.

'Ashes, why you never tell me about this?'

'Jade. This wasn't supposed to end this way. This was all supposed to go well. It was a good plan which the Leader thought would work. He is not a bad man. He is not a treasoner. The Leader had been planning this event for months, even years. He send people to train in camps in the desert.'

'Plan? Desert? Are you all mad in the head? None of the wives knew about this. The Leader, he a madman. Allyuh crazy or what? I should never let you get involved with him. He mad. You mad too. Ashes, *oh God* . . . why didn't you tell me . . . the whole country in state of emergency.'

'You seeing it on TV?'

'No. They block it all out. Nothing on the TV but one show. *The Little Mermaid.* Running over and over again. Nothing else. We get the radio, though. One man still in the radio station across the road from the television station. He lock himself in and he broadcasting the news every day. We get the picture. This is a terrible thing. All of town in chaos I hear. Looting everywhere. Looters carrying TV and furniture all up the street by us. One man walk past just now with a bath tub on his head. The City of Silk is on fire, people dead. Utter lawlessness. I keep the children in and all they do is ask for their father and all I tell them is that I don't know where he is. They ask if you is with the Leader. I tell them no. I say you gone down south for a trip to visit your uncle. I tell Arich and Arkab you gone to stay with him. What else I go tell them, eh?'

Ashes groaned.

'You think I proud to tell them where they father is?'

Ashes took off his spectacles and rested them on his lap. His breathing was becoming uneven; he mustn't panic or get any more upset. He must say goodbye to his wife.

'You did this for your brother, River. You did this for some crazy idea. Family redemption. Sompthing so. I know is for River you do this. Well River dead. An you go dead too just now. The Leader use you. You think he care about you or about us?'

'The whole thing is over now,' Ashes said. 'The army coming for the ministers. Soon it all over.'

'Oh,' Jade said and her voice plummeted.

Ashes realised that this ending had no meaning for

her. She wouldn't be seeing him soon. He wouldn't be coming home. He missed his life. He hadn't reckoned on losing it. He looked up out of the window and he could see a magnificent sky, and he wondered about the impossibility of reaching the seventh level, or ever ascending to any higher level of selfhood than level one. He was a man. He had tried to grow but he had missed something.

'Goodbye,' Ashes whispered, his breath now very thin.

'Ashes, what? Goodbye? Are you mad? Come *home*. I want you to get out of there in *one piece*, yuh hear? We need you. I ent going an be a single woman, no husband. We need you and you must come back. Immediately. Get out of there, okay?'

'Okay.'

'Get out of there and come home.'

'I'm sorry,' Ashes whispered.

'I'm sorry too.'

'Can I come home?'

'Yes. Come *now*.'

Ashes put down the receiver and he sat very still with his back against the wall and tried very hard to breathe, but his lungs had constricted tight and it was very possible he might die right there sitting on the floor after three days of revolution. Fat Clay of Cuba, he had similar health problems; he had coughed and wheezed his way through weeks of active revolution. But unlike him, Fat Clay was a hero. He wasn't a treasoner. He had been a liberator, stamping out oppression; he had got things right. They had cut off his hands in the end. Ashes closed his eyes and tried to breathe through the rising panic in his soul, but he couldn't and then he saw Breeze staring in at him from the door and he gasped, 'Get the doctor.'

Dr Mahibir came quickly and when he saw Ashes breathing like a crapaud fish on the sand, he sat down opposite him and said, 'Look into my eyes.' He picked up Ashes' hands in his and said, 'Do not panic. You are having an asthma attack.'

Ashes nodded, knowing this. It rarely got this bad, but now it was happening and he had no secret air to save him. If he died here like this he wouldn't face what the others had to face, courts and treason. He wouldn't have to face his wife, his sons. It would be a natural way to disappear.

'Keep looking at me,' said Dr Mahibir. 'Look at me and breathe, keep breathing.'

Ashes looked into the doctor's eyes. It helped a bit.

'I know you,' Dr Mahibir said. 'They call you Books, don't they?'

Ashes tried to keep his breathing even. He nodded.

'You keep medicinal plants in your backyard. You read a lot.'

Ashes nodded and kept holding the doctor's hands; the doctor was kneeling in front of him.

'You work as a porter in the health clinic in the east side of town. I hear about you and about your plants from a neighbour of yours, a trainee doctor who works in my department.'

Ashes kept his slow, shallow breaths going. In, out, in, out.

'I heard you had a famous brother. River, right?'

Ashes wanted the doctor to stop talking. He wanted everyone to stop talking about his famous brother, the one who got shot up.

'I was the one who wrote his medical report for the coroner. I was a very young doctor then. I had my first job with the government. They needed all those men looked at, proper certificates. Everything above board even though they had shot them all dead. I was the one they called in. I removed twenty-eight bullets from his body.'

Ashes could feel the air in his lungs begin to surge. Air, the source of all life, was returning in small measured doses.

'You?'

'Yes, me. This is a small place, you know that. We

are all related in some way. I am sorry about your brother. I was shocked at the time, deeply shocked. Now I meet you here. Your poor mother. Two sons active in revolution. I guess having a strong political conscience must run in the family. I guess all this, guns and . . . everything must be exciting. Breathe,' he said.

Ashes breathed in slowly; he was feeling a little better, more air now.

'You know . . . I think we don't need guns to change anything. Change is upon us all the time. Change is natural and ever present. Nothing stays the same. Everything is always moving. We are always growing. Our hair grows, our skin flakes, we grow each day. Every situation moves forward in its own way. Look, you see, even this situation has changed. When I arrived you were breathing your last breath. You were dying. Now your breath is returning.'

Ashes nodded.

'All it took was a bit of . . . regulation. You are breathing again. See?'

'Yes.'

'The biggest part of the self wants to live,' said Dr Mahibir. 'Not one part of the self wants to die. We desire to live. That's a very basic rule of life. Being too reactive is not the way of the natural world. The natural world is slow and often abundant, it can heal itself.'

Ashes nodded. He was breathing again. And yet he felt profoundly confused. Love. Just like air, it was an invisible force. A cohesive agent in the world. In the last three days this love force, one he usually had access to, could find within himself, had vanished. Love had vanished into thin air. And then he had no access to air. Both air and love had cut him off. He put his hand to his heart and breathed in deeply and it felt like a miracle to be breathing and to be alive. He breathed in and out, in and out; his lungs were working again, just. If he'd found his way back to air, maybe, just maybe, he could find his way back to his own heart. *Go through the phases of life without losing yourself,* said the Sufi mystic Hazrat Inayat Khan. Yes, he had lost himself; he had lost the heart of self. He breathed, in and out. In and out.

*

There was no place to go; everything was wrecked. The tearoom had been blown to smithereens. There was debris everywhere. The dead lay under the debris. Three days. Ashes felt there was a sense that they, the men with guns inside, were hiding now; they had no power whatsoever. The army had not yet sent their convoy of trucks. Soon after Ashes had used the telephone, the army had cut off this line so that Hal and the Leader couldn't communicate. Hal's walkie-talkie had more or less died. Hal was on his own now. But the agreement, generally, was to get out of there alive.

Ashes tried to think it out: the elected Prime Minister of the country had shown from the outset that he was prepared to die. The head of the army, Colonel Benedict Howl, had shown that he was loyal to the PM and the country; he had followed orders and attacked. The army had shown discipline and loyalty. They had backed up the PM and Howl. These two men, the PM and the head of the army, had worked together in some mysterious way. They hadn't been speaking to each other like the Leader and Hal had been talking every hour; none of that was going on. And yet they were somehow working together, decisively, without needing to talk. It was becoming clear that this collusion was something Ashes didn't know about, had overlooked; and so had the Leader and Hal.

Power. In some way these two men, the PM and Howl, knew what it was and what it meant. It had been allocated to them. And they had both been trained about power. They seemed to have some kind of secret knowledge about events like this which both had put into action separately and together. It was as if this covert complicity was only needed once in a lifetime, perhaps – but it was vital. They both knew how to act when power was under threat. The thought of all this made Ashes' head spin.

Breeze had been behaving differently since the attack that morning. He looked like he had been doing some thinking too, and he'd been hanging around Ashes as if wanting to share his thoughts. Now Breeze came up to him with his hands empty. Breeze had stopped carrying his gun, maybe because it was bigger than him.

Breeze cornered him.

'What? What going on, my friend?' Ashes tried to sound encouraging.

Breeze crossed his arms over his chest. He was trying to maintain the posture of an urban guerilla fighter still.

'What is a Prime Minister?' he said. The question was more like a command.

Ashes laughed. Where had he seen Breeze before?

'The Prime Minister is the head of government, the head of the country.'

'Oho.' Breeze looked suspicious, as though this was a trick statement. He re-crossed his arms and struck the same pose from another angle. 'I thought *the Leader* was the head of the country.'

Ashes stared.

Breeze glared back, a small shyness now breaking out on his cheeks.

'Howyuh come to think *that*?'

Breeze shrugged. 'I ent know. Everyone think so. I does talk to alluh de men, everyone in the compound, they say he the real Leader of the country.'

Ashes steupsed. This was bad talk. 'No,' he said. 'The Leader is *not* head of the country. You making no sense at all.'

'Then *who* he is?'

'The Leader is himself.'

The young boy's eyes went hard and dark; suddenly he looked all boiled up and vexed. Like this was all the wrong information.

'He lead his followers, like us.'

'So how the Prime Minister get to be so important? I figure he an old man. I never figure he so important they go blow down this whole friggin place.'

'Well, yes . . . he is important. He is the most important and powerful man alive in Sans Amen.'

'Only now you telling me this.'

'You didn't know what a Prime Minister is?'

'No. Is only now I figuring it out.'

'Only now?'

'Yes.'

'Who you figure the Leader is?'

'I figure the Leader is the Prime Minister.'

'*No*,' Ashes sighed and wanted to weep. 'You have to be *elected* to be Prime Minister. Votes and elections. Official things must take place. The Leader, you know he doing his own thing. Freestyle. He is . . . well . . . he is spiritually inclined.'

'Why you follow him?'

'Same reason as you. He a good man. Spiritual.'

Breeze steupsed.

'He just make a mistake is all.'

Ashes looked at the young boy and it was then he saw himself, his fifteen-year-old self, the young boy who followed his brother around, who followed River everywhere. River his hero-brother. River who was cunning and smart, who ran off to the hills to take up arms. Breeze looked like River but he was as foolish as Ashes was at his age and even now. Breeze was like the two brothers melted into one, a young innocent boy with a gun.

But Breeze wasn't finished yet. Something else was stored inside. Now Breeze looked different, softer. Like a tear might fall and he was keeping it back.

'I want to tell you something.'

'Oh?'

Breeze looked down and said, 'I shoot someone.'

Ashes felt bad. Hot and dead in his arms and legs.

He had wondered if this might be the case. He nodded but he didn't know what to say or do. Unlike the PM and the Colonel, he didn't know how to act in these circumstances. River had also shot people. He knew that, but River never talked about it.

'I shot the woman in there,' Breeze pointed to the room behind, now blasted to pieces, the room where Ashes had bent down and seen the woman's body slick with blood; she had still been alive then. Then he remembered what she'd said to him.

'I sorry, yes,' said Breeze. 'I sorry.'

'You shot the woman?'

'It was an accident. It happen in the first ten minutes we get inside here. I was running and she appeared and I was shooting up the place. I shot her. She fell down. She was in the room trying to get out of the window and I doh know how it happen. Everyone was shooting everything. I doh know what I was doing. I shot her. She was trying to escape. I sorry.'

Tears fell down his face.

'I like the women inside here. Mrs Garland, she a good lady. She kind. I almost shoot she as well.'

Ashes felt his heart thunder around inside him.

'I have a bad feeling,' said Breeze. 'Right here,' and he relaxed one arm and let it hang free and with the other hand he patted the area around his groin.

'Come,' Ashes said.

'What?'

'I taking you to pray.'

'Where?'

'Somewhere quiet. Away from here.'

He put one hand on the young boy's shoulder and squeezed. 'Come with me.'

Ashes took Breeze down along the blasted, blown-up corridor, past all the smashed-up rooms where clerical support staff had been going about their business only Wednesday last, past the cases of unused guns and ammo the brothers had brought with them, past the room with the last telephone line, now dead, past the broom cupboard where Mrs Gonzales had been hiding, past the room with Liquid Paper graffiti about God, and then down some mahogany stairs in the middle of the building, down two flights to the cool terrazzo ground floor of the House of Power where there was a fountain in the centre but the water had stopped its flourishing dance. Although down there was quieter, the signs of the mayhem above were evident: broken glass and planks of wood were strewn across the floor. They had to go carefully so as not to be seen through the wrought iron gates by the army encamped on the streets. They were unarmed and couldn't return fire. They both looked upwards and gazed at the vaulted ceiling.

'This place huge, man,' Breeze gasped.

'Yeah.'

'It haunted, no arse.'

Ashes looked at him. 'Maybe,' he said. He thought of the burial ground under the House which had appeared to him in his dream. Could there be Amerindians buried beneath?

'Why they build this place so big?'

'So everyone can see it, nuh.'

'Who build it?'

'The Queen.'

'What Queen?'

'The Queen of England. Victoria. She dead long time. Is in her style.'

'Well she had good style. Fancy.'

'Yeah, but she have plenty power. And they stick one big dragon up there on top this place. To defend it. That dragon *serious*, no arse. Is why this all go wrong. Like this place cursed.'

'A dragon?'

Ashes said, 'Yes. Come.'

They walked along one of the corridors and Ashes pushed open the wooden door to the library and behind him Breeze let out a low whistle. There was his nest on the floor made of some curtains taken from the window and the cushions from the old leather arm-chairs. Ashes felt awkward; now the library had an intimate feel, like he'd made it his own bedroom.

They shut the door behind them and stood there on the deep blue velvet carpet and for a few moments it was like the world was normal again. None of the other brothers had been down here. No one else had thought to snoop around this far away from the action.

'What is this place?' Breeze asked.

'Is a library, nuh. For books.'

Breeze looked around, his jaw set in a held-in wonder. In the window Jesus Christ was nailed to the cross and was gazing up at the skies. Ashes had found himself talking a lot to Jesus on the cross. Mostly he had gone over the rights and wrongs of fighting for freedom and its cost. Now he stood there with Breeze and he felt self-conscious. Breeze was inspecting Jesus.

'That is Jesus Christ?' Breeze asked.

'Yes.'

'The prophet?'

'Yes.'

'He not looking healthy.'

'No.'

'He get his arse killed in a bad way.'

'He get executed.'

'Howyuh mean?'

'The Romans, they punish him by death.'

'For what?'

'For what he preach. It was treasonous.'

'Shit, man. Why you bring me here?'

'To be quiet.'

'You 'fraid to die?'

'Yes. Course I 'fraid. The doctor tell me is natural to want to live. Is like a rule. We all want to live.'

'I only ever want to die. Since young.'

'Since young?'

'Since I was very small. Mih mother, she had too many of us. She always telling us so. She tell us if only God would take some of us away. If some of us dead, then she could be happy. So I run away.'

Ashes didn't reply.

'Mih mother's name is Mercy. Mercy Loretta Green. Ten children. Ten different men. Ten fathers. I never go know who mih real father is. But mih mother is called Mercy Green.'

'And you? What your real name?'

'Joseph. Joseph Green. I get mih nickname on the street.'

Ashes said nothing. The City of Silk was the City of Nicknames. Everybody had one, including him.

'You want to know the truth?'

Ashes turned to look at him. His face was serious and full and sad.

'When I shoot that woman upstairs, it was like I shoot mih mother dead. I shoot she for . . . not wanting me. I shoot she in a fury. Something come over me.'

Ashes said, 'Come, nuh.'

He knelt down in front of the stained glass window and waited. Breeze followed his example.

'Jesus won't mind if we pray here?'

'No. None of them God fellers care who praying to who, really. They all friends up there and none of them are like . . . casting for votes. Is just good we pray anyhow.'

'You sure?'

'Yes.'

Ashes relaxed his chest cavity and he closed his eyes. Tears fell. 'I sorry too,' he said.

Then that feeling came, the wingbeat thrum of a hummingbird, or a quiet, gentle feeling from outside passing in. The world seemed to change colour; it became brighter and he felt light and clean, and then came the opening, the porous feeling of another part of him, the part which was soul. He connected with that part of himself, the part which was like God, all Gods, any God, with the divine soul of the world. He sensed that part of him swell and he put his hand on his heart. He looked across at Breeze and saw a sullen face, silver with tears. In Breeze he saw another soul, another boy who had replaced him and his brother River. Breeze, who had shot his mother dead, would somehow live. He felt sure of it. And with this Ashes felt an old anguish lift upwards and he said *Praise be to God*.

SATURDAY EVENING,
THE HOUSE OF POWER,
THE CITY OF SILK

In what used to be the tearoom, Hal and Greg Mason
and two of the other men had set themselves up as a
band. Hal was using his gun like a base cello, balancing
the butt on the floor and playing an imaginary bow
across the slim neck of the gun. Greg had the butt of
his gun cocked against his chin, the nose pointed out-
wards. He was playing his bow like the gun was a
violin. The two other men, two fellers from the compound Ashes barely knew, had balanced their guns
across their knees like guitars. They were laughing
and singing and Ashes thought that seeing Hal behave
all jokey like this was so very disappointing. For the
first time since it all began, Ashes felt let down by him.
Maybe Hal wasn't a cut above. Maybe he was just a

common man. The four fellers sang an old American song . . . *baby, baby, baby* . . . rock and roll or something, and they laughed and Ashes could see that Breeze also looked disappointed.

Hal and some of the brothers closest to him knew the game was now completely over. It had been over within twelve hours of the revolution. Things had dragged out. Now they'd really given up. No army convoy had come that day to pick up hostages. The army were now demanding 'unconditional surrender' through the megaphone. *Lay down your arms and come out one by one*, that was the only deal now available to the brothers. They weren't going to start shooting anyone in there, no bodies thrown over the balcony on Day Four. The place was a wreck and the gunmen and the hostages were all exhausted. The brothers were too demoralised for anything so dramatic. Besides, if Hal now issued such a command, he faced resistance. Ashes had had enough. He wanted to go home now, back to his old life. The stench in the place was the worst part. Everyone now wore a handkerchief over their mouth and nose. It wasn't possible to be inside of there without this protection.

The sun began to go down and as it did the wind picked up. The City of Silk was a city which had grown itself on the swamp flats of a curved lip of a wide bay.

Now and then it was possible to smell the sea in the gulf, even from the hot, busy streets. On Saturdays he would go down to the vegetable market on Chanders Street to buy yams and patchoi and pumpkin and he would stand for a few moments with his head raised so he could catch the scent of the sea not so far away. Now Ashes could tell it was going to rain by the sound of the ruffled up wind and the slight saltiness in the air. The sea in the gulf would be getting a little churned up. Finally, some rain. The pain in his thigh would start up again.

He thought of his wife Jade and their sons and he imagined the possibility of slipping out of the House of Power and past the army outside to pay them all a visit. Or maybe he should just give himself up and walk out. He had split himself from his family. His soul had followed the Leader and the part of him that was man had put his family second. Now he'd lost his family and his Leader was trapped in the television station and Hal was playing his gun like a cello.

Maybe a strong political conscience runs in the family, the doctor had said. He wondered about this. He remembered how River had infected him with his stories about black power in Sans Amen and ideas of a New Society; how, in America, black people had marched, had been changing everything. He and River had stacks of Phantom comic books under their beds. Mostly they admired his Oath of the Skull, an oath which Phantom had inherited from his father, to do battle with the forces of evil forever. That was the Phantom's job. Every son of Phantom inherited this position, to be a fighter for freedom and justice. It was like a line of spiritual freedom fighters, the mission of fighting for social justice handed down generations from father to son. Ashes and River had talked a lot about where and how to get a Phantom costume, if they could ask their mother to sew one for them in purple silk. But then there was the problem that they both wanted to be the Phantom. There couldn't be two of them. So they agreed that as River was older, River would get the costume first, if they ever made one; they agreed that Ashes could borrow the costume now and then.

That idea of a costume died because River soon took to the hills; he got swept up with the likes of Greg Mason and his band of men. Greg Mason was the only member of that gang still alive. During the last few days Ashes had come to understand that he himself was a revolutionary in spirit only. He had been afraid of his own gun. Unlike Breeze, he hadn't shot anyone, not by accident or on purpose because his gun hadn't even been loaded. Only now Ashes knew that he would never make a good Phantom or wear a purple suit. That was all childhood rubbish. His brother was dead and many years later he had got himself into a hell of a messy situation.

It began to rain. A faint velvety roar from the dark skies over Sans Amen. Rain always made him feel guilty and aware of his sins, the *nafs*, the way he could be overrun. Rain made his groin sear with pain. The wound he had received as a teenage boy ached, the pain of the death of his innocence. His desire to be alone with his thoughts was overwhelming. He could no longer tolerate the claustrophobic conditions and the stench of the chamber. When no one was looking, Ashes quietly slipped away and headed to the ground floor of the House to sleep. It wasn't safe descending to street level but the solitude was worth the risk.

In the library with the blue velvet carpet he lay himself down to sleep. His thoughts drifted to his own mother and father; they had been wise parents, happy with each other, fair. He had been lucky; they had been good to him and his brother and kind to each other. There was a contentment in their lives together, as though they had chosen right and had been pleased with their lot in life; that ended when River was shot.

Ashes drifted off. In his dreams he saw a car, a big, stately, official-looking limo with the Prime Minister inside. It was travelling down a dirt track past a green field. A flock of big black birds were attacking it for some reason. The driver got out and tried to shoo them away, but the birds kept pecking at the windscreen and the driver said aloud, 'Something terrible is going to happen today, Mr Prime Minister.' Then he saw his wife, Jade. She was climbing up a ladder and waving goodbye to him. She had his sons with her and they were waving goodbye too. They climbed all the levels of the ladder up to the sky and disappeared, waving. And then the dream was filled with trees, silk cotton trees, and he saw thousands of them, and from each one dangled a purple suit. The silk cotton trees had spun these purple suits of their own accord. They had sprouted the suits, and then Queen Victoria came into the dream and she cut all the suits down off the trees, harvesting them, and saying, 'This won't do.' She threw the purple suits into the gulf and said, 'Now let's drink some tea.' She began to drink tea with Hal and the Leader and then the three of them were painting the House of Power red and then Queen Victoria said, 'This colour won't do either' and the Leader shot her crown clean off her head. The Leader said, 'Ha, you see I know how to use a gun.' Queen Victoria looked stupefied and then the Leader said, 'Tea? I can bake a cake too. Let's have tea and cake.' Then the silk cotton trees appeared again, thousands of them along the banks of the City of Silk, and from each one hung the body of a man. The men's bodies were dangling in the breeze coming in off the gulf. In the hands of each of these men was a long, slim violin.

SUNDAY MORNING,
THE HOUSE OF POWER,
THE CITY OF SILK

Rain. A moody, grisly rain had moved in over the City of Silk. Rain like millions of needles in the air, steaming up the place. It was everywhere, rain swarming across the city like bees scouting for a new home to settle on. The clouds were smoky and dark. The City was empty now except for the army; streets upon streets of blackened, shelled-out buildings, sheets of galvanised tin pelted on the ground. It was as if barbarians had sacked the city, but instead the city's own residents had risen up and gorged themselves on the everyday items they couldn't afford: beds and tableware and microwave ovens and toasters and groceries. They had debased their own city. No one had joined in the efforts of the gunmen. Not one citizen had so much as paused to throw a stone or sing out a cry in solidarity for their bravery and their courage or their ideas. It was apparent to Ashes that people weren't as oppressed as he'd imagined. They were just poor. Maybe that was different to being oppressed. Maybe he would have to read more books about the subject of poverty. The poor had risen up, indeed. But only to grab what they thought they needed.

Inside the House they had switched the lights on. It felt chilly too. All of a sudden the city was in no mood to play host to a revolution. And the Prime Minister, it was also apparent, was dying. He was shivering uncontrollably and was more or less blind. He still didn't want to abandon his duties, he still planned to stay, but now everyone, even many of the brothers, felt he should be released. For humanitarian reasons. Mrs Gonzales had been nursing him as best she could. But now she broke.

'Ayyyyy,' she said to Hal. 'You. Mr Big Shot. Mr Army Suit.'

Hal came over to where she was sitting with the PM.

'You see this?' she said. She meant the PM; he looked three quarters dead. He would be dead soon if not medically treated. His face was a blur of purple and mauve.

'If you doh let him go *now*, ah go jump out de damn window of this damn place.'

Hal looked as though he was listening closely to this new threat.

'Ah go strip naked an ah go jump. Plain so. In protest of your barbaric ways and your lawlessness. You all can go to the devil. I happy to take mih own life to make this protest.'

With this she began to rise up to her feet and pluck at her clothes.

'Ayyyyy, lady. Stop.'

'Stop?'

'We going to send him out, doh worry.'

'You do it now or I go jump and put one hex on allayuh. I'll cuss you to high hell an back. Ah go jump if you doh release the PM. Ah go die with putting one hex on your arses.'

The men didn't like the sound of this threat and neither did Hal. The men were convinced Mrs Gonzales possessed obeah powers by then. Some of them said they'd checked the broom cupboard before she appeared and no woman had been inside. Others said she had the foot of a goat in one of her boots, that she was concealing it, that she was a Diablesse. Many of them had started to call the PM 'Mr Prime Minister' since the bombing the day before. The army had come to rescue him and this, at last, had provoked some respect. Some saw that if they got rid of the PM then the army wouldn't bomb them so badly again. Giving him up meant the army might leave them alone for the time being. It would buy a little more time. Others felt to hold on to him meant they would be safer.

Hal seemed to know it was time to let him go. He called Breeze to him and said, 'I need to ask you to do something.'

Breeze had a new demeanour. He was plainly not so enamored with Hal anymore.

He came and said, 'What?'

Hal said, 'Ay.'

But Breeze didn't correct his attitude.

'You need to take this flag here, see, and wave it from one of the big windows over the balcony in the front. We go call a truce. We handing over the Prime Minister. He need to go to hospital. We need to send him out.'

'You want me to wave a peace flag?'

'Yeah.'

'When?'

'Now.'

Ashes felt relieved. At last a giving up, this was progress. This is what the army were hoping they would do; it was a wise decision. It meant the PM would live.

Breeze took the stick and two of the armed brothers went with him through the maze of corridors, and the next thing Ashes saw the broomstick with the white T-shirt poke out from the window above the balcony of the House. It hung rather limply, like it didn't mean what it was trying to say; it was saying, 'Okay, nuh, give us a chance.' It looked like a rag, sorry for itself. Then Ashes realised that he *was* sorry for himself.

Hal came to stand next to him and said to him, 'You go with Breeze and take the Prime Minister away, go down with him together.'

Ashes felt like it was the first time in days that he had been asked something he was happy to do.

'He cannot stand by himself,' said Hal. 'You will need to support him down the steps.' Then his walkie-talkie crackled.

They both stared at it. 'Like it still have battery left,' Hal said.

It was the army; they'd seen the flag.

'Yeah,' said Hal. 'We sending the Prime Minister out. We go need a wheelchair. We sending him now.'

*

Ashes and Breeze each took one side of the PM, hooking his arms over their shoulders. Ashes had hold

215

of his briefcase too; it had been found amidst the rubble in the chamber. He was a big man and he was heavy and one of his legs was badly wounded. He shuffled and yet he was upright, still, in his manner and his posture. He had on a pair of dark black sunglasses to shield his bad eyes. An ambulance had already arrived in the street on the east side of the House of Power to take him away. Ashes and Breeze took care not to walk too fast or too slowly. Ashes felt out of himself, like he was watching this happening from the sky. He was setting the PM free and yet he had come to take him hostage. They had damaged the PM, maybe forever, and he'd turned out to be brave.

Breeze kept saying, 'Yes, Mr Prime Minister' to anything he said, keeping very penitent and formal. They had to walk down the mahogany steps, down into the cool terrazzo central court, and then they were at one of the side doors, a grille-type gate. The rain had stopped and in its place there was a razor-sharp glare. There was a wide sweep of gravel and a sculpted hedge and again Ashes had that feeling of normality and civil order being just inches away, on the outside. For days the House of Power had been a gaol and he now felt like how a newly released prisoner might feel. He blinked into the sun. The army paramedics had left a wheelchair out on the gravel for the PM. Ashes couldn't believe it. He didn't want to let go of the PM. *Take me with you*, is what he felt. *Don't leave us, don't leave us to this mess*, was what his insides were crying out. He glanced at Breeze; Breeze had a look of held-in regret. The young man seemed a lot harder than him. The young boy had toughened up early on. And now he'd shot someone inside. In some ways he was a much more experienced person than Ashes.

They managed to get the Prime Minister to his wheelchair and sit him down. Ashes carefully placed his briefcase on his knees. He wanted to say something but he could see that the PM didn't. There was nothing to be said. No words to exchange between a captor and his prime victim in the end. Breeze looked like he'd quite a lot of things to say, but he wasn't going to blurt anything out. Ashes wanted to say at the very least, 'Goodbye, Mr Prime Minister,' but it became apparent that their relationship was over. He would never see the PM again. They weren't friends. They had no links to each other. Ashes backed away. Breeze looked like he might faint. He stepped backwards too, then back again, so they were standing behind the grille of the House of Power, the gaol they had made for themselves. They watched the army paramedics move forward and fetch the PM, tending him, wheeling him around and back towards the ambulance. None of the three men so much as glanced backwards at Ashes and Breeze. Again, Ashes had that feeling of being utterly invisible. He was a man with no meaning and no importance in the world outside himself, the world of men and power. The PM was wheeled away, and soon he was out of sight. Ashes glanced at Breeze and he saw that Breeze needed to be alone.

He left Breeze to be quiet and then he headed for the only safe place in the House, the small library. He opened the wooden door and let himself in and then knelt on the floor and he looked up at Jesus on the cross gazing upwards at the sky. He bet Jesus knew a thing or two about sky. Silently, Ashes allowed himself to weep, for he'd completely lost track of why he was here.

'Who is this all for?' he said aloud. 'The Leader, the PM . . . whose power do I serve? Who?' He looked up towards the sky and felt desolate and unsure of everything in his life. He knew nothing. Everything was gone.

Then . . . an answer came. And it was beautiful and clear: *a man must serve his higher self.*

Ashes bowed his head. He gave thanks. He was grateful and he was miserable too; he knew the first part of his life was over. He had ruined it. Soon he would have to face a new life ... maybe even death. He wept for something about life or growth, something about himself he'd missed, and he said aloud, 'I surrender.'

IV. Fortress by the Sea

SUNDAY AFTERNOON,
THE HOUSE OF POWER,
THE CITY OF SILK

I comforted Mrs Gonzales in her loss. Even though it was what she'd wanted all along, even though she'd threatened suicide over his ill health, she now looked a little deflated that the PM was gone.

'A piece of me gone with him, praise the Lord,' she said. She looked tired and yet almost happy. Vindicated. 'I glad he safe. He not like these bandits. He a working man. He do things fair, by the book. He is a man of compassion. I does see how he care about people who work here with him, all the long hours he work.'

I nodded. I also knew the PM to be a hard-working man. The PM had good backup at home. He was old fashioned and maybe out of touch, or maybe he'd just been slow with things; maybe we could have been more transparent, yes. But all this mayhem? I looked at Mrs Gonzales sitting there in her wig, which was perfectly coiffed, stiff, from all the hairspray. The stiffness and precision and neatness of it reminded me of the PM. I could see why they understood each other. Things in Sans Amen had been run so formally once.

'I very happy I stayed to protect him,' she said, her mouth turned down in defiance. 'No regrets, man. I glad I stay here with allyuh. Is me who get the PM free. Me.'

I smiled at this. 'Sometimes,' I was thinking aloud, 'I can see the bigger picture of all of this . . . you know? It's all clear, what has happened here. All the connections and reasons for this kind of occurrence. And sometimes I feel like, no, Aspasia, you're dreaming all this up; you are imagining things. It's not really happening. And then, no, I'm back again: Sans Amen is such a small place. This *is* all connected. Something like this couldn't happen of it own accord.'

'Of course not.' Mrs Gonzales' face set in a smile of utter certainty. 'These badjohns know some of them politicians in here. How you think they come in so easily?'

'Everything is mixed up,' I said. 'That dead woman

back there. She is linked too, you know. You remember that young girl long time ago they call Bathsheba?'

Mrs Gonzales nodded. 'Yes. They shoot she when she was carrying a chile in she belly.'

'They shot her dead in the street for being a revolutionary – and yet not long later her sister went into politics.'

'Really? Oh, my.'

'Yes. She was a popular politician. She even became Sans Amen's ambassador to Cuba at one point. You see how things work here? One sister exterminated for her extreme leftist politics, the other sister celebrated. That is how things work here in Sans Amen. You go in one door, you leave by another. Everyone coming and going from this House of Power. They just using different doors.'

Mrs Gonzales clicked her throat and nodded. 'That is called corruption.'

I was grateful for her attention, an audience for my thoughts.

'You see that hard-looking man over there? The one swaggering and looking so tough?'

Mrs Gonzales nodded.

'He is Greg Mason. He is the last remaining member of the Brotherhood of Freedom Fighters. You remember them? After black power over, the marches crushed, they locked all of them up on that island off the coast? In its heyday there were three hundred members, twenty-four were active and about fourteen were shot dead.'

'You know all that?'

'Yes.'

'The government . . . shot them?'

'Well . . . you could say they were "eliminated", quietly, and not so quietly, one by one, here and there. By the police force, on the orders of the PM at the time. That man Mason standing there is the last link to the Brotherhood and to 1970. That was an actual revolution. Not like this mess.'

'*Serious*? He survive all that?'

'Yes.'

'No wonder he look so tough.'

'The Brotherhood began as a bunch of outlaws, really. Bandits, crooks. They robbed banks. They caused a nuisance. They had no ideology at first; it was only later they began to call themselves "guerilla fighters", and took to the hills to train. They had a middle-class leadership and some middle-class supporters. Doctors were sympathetic to them, lawyers used to provide free legal representation. You see the white minister over there?'

Mrs Gonzales nodded.

'It was said he even provided bail for members of the Brotherhood. The Brotherhood were popular with the intelligentsia. But then most guerilla fighters had this appeal.'

'Yeah, man,' said Mrs Gonzales. 'Fat Clay of Cuba – is his entire fault. He was too damn handsome.'

Aspasia laughed. 'You're right – he made it attractive to be a guerilla fighter. Fat Clay of Cuba was fat and yet handsome. Communism was sexy thanks to him. A man of the Caribbean.'

'You think Fat Clay was such a good man?'

'Who knows. He has become a saint, a man of virtue and an icon of revolution. But they say he was very violent too, that he shot many people, even some of his own comrades. He had wives and many lovers, official children and outside children.'

'A man of the Caribbean, yes.'

'He was a sexy communist.'

'You find communism sexy?'

'Not at all.'

'It take away my right to do as I please. Everybody different. In Cuba taxi driver or cleaner get the same wage as a politician. That is not fair, not to me, and I is a cleaner. And besides, they have no food to eat in Cuba.'

'Cuba is an extreme example.'

'Then what about Grenada? They try the same thing there too. Revolution. A revolutionary party, a time of change. Then the army shot their own revolutionary heroes. Crazy thing, man.'

I felt a surge of misery; it came up from my chest. Grenada, Cuba, Sans Amen – revolution in the Caribbean had mostly failed or backfired. I wanted to cry but there were no tears, nothing inside. Why were we killing all these people in the name of change?

'Is like we Caribbean people mess up real good every time we try this thing called revolution,' I said. 'Is like it too simple. Or like it too good to be true. Every time the liberators become oppressors.'

'True. Fat Clay and all them fellers needed to overthrow injustice back in the day. But now, they jus keeping people miserable, same, same. You ever been to Cuba?'

'Yes. It's a strange place. Havana feels like everything stopped working twenty-five years ago. The whole of the city feels like it's melting, like a big cake. Revolution happen and then everything got locked down. Embargoes, stalemate. Now the people suffer a different set of problems. Freedom to think, mostly. The state control everything. News, radio.'

'Things not like that here. Why these damn fellers come inside here and try to take control?'

'They figure they is liberators.'

'Well . . . something fishy about it all,' said Mrs Gonzales.

'In what way?'

Mrs Gonzales lowered her voice.

'Quite a few big-shot ministers are *absent*,' she whispered. 'Y'understand? Big names. You know. They *not here*.'

I nodded. I understood. I'd been thinking the same thing. I bet Mervyn had too. Neither of us had been able to bring it up; it meant the worst. Betrayal, treachery within our own ranks. Mervyn and I had left this subject alone.

'You don't think it is *obvious*?' said Mrs Gonzales. 'Why you think I stay? The PM get stitched up real good. He get his arse cut. He on his own with this.'

I'd been slowly, slowly threading together these same ideas. Something wasn't right at all, from within.

'Yes,' I said. 'I saw some of them here last Wednesday afternoon and is like they all *left*. The House was in the middle of an important debate about corruption in the last government. But is like some of the big names disappeared after the tea break.'

'The whole thing is *fishy*.'

I nodded. 'Fishy as *hell*,' I blurted, surprising myself. These had been my private, secret thoughts. But if

229

they'd been the same thoughts as the cleaner in the House, a woman who'd been around a long time, long enough to see who came and went, to overhear what others never could, maybe I wasn't so off in my thinking. The PM had been double crossed; some of his own ministers, even allies, may have had wind of this. And they hadn't intervened. They wanted to see him deposed. I dreaded to think of the who and what; it was a rat's nest inside the House.

'How could something like this happen in Sans Amen and not one person in the government know? Eh?' said Mrs Gonzales. She grimaced and nodded to herself and clicked her throat. 'You know what?' she said.

'What?'

'I here alone in this House all these nights. I sometimes come in on weekends too. I see many things and no one take any notice of me. Is like I is a ghost coming and going about here, minding my own damn business. No one notice me. Them big shots have more to think about than if this place is clean, but I hear many things said because no one care if I overhear. Except the PM; only he notices me. I hear one thing one time.'

'What?'

'I hear about the guns. I hear about them coming in.'

'You hear that *inside* this House?'

Mrs Gonzales nodded but her lips were sealed tight.

'Yeaaaah. Long time ago I hear about this. But it like I choose to forget it. I ent know what they talking about. Now it make sense.'

I looked around. A hotness spread in my chest and belly. *Who* inside here knew about the guns, or this plot? Which of the ministers had wanted this coup to succeed? I felt jolted, and I felt deceived. A sudden and new awareness sprang up inside me. Turtles. Protecting the environment. My job, everything about it, was meaningless. Politics was something else. I hadn't really seen or understood The Game of it till these last few days. I had been naïve only four days ago. Politics was about darkness, about reaction, about . . . yes, Mervyn was right . . . ego. It had something to do with a blindness rather than seeing.

Mrs Gonzales looked at me straight. 'You aks me? This one big dance. This is about men needing to claim status. This like animals squaring off, fighting for territory. The Leader, he feel he need a piece of the action; he make a claim for his share. But he come up against bigger men and bigger guns and a bigger will. He come up against true power and Godliness. The PM – he face him off. I hear he risk his life. It all done done after that. The greater man in all of this? He free all now. He in hospital.'

*

The Prime Minister had left a chasm behind him. His civilising presence and influence was missed and this also brought a new worry. Without him in the chamber, there was a vacuum; it felt as though anything could happen, even this late in proceedings. Apparently we were soon to be released, but I wouldn't be able to believe this until I was actually on the street, until I could see my children.

I wondered about what Mrs Gonzales had said. I knew the government had an 'intelligence unit', that we had stationed an army post right on top of the Leader's compound. The Leader was well marked out. He was being observed. But just how had they smuggled all these guns into the country, trained all these men, sent some to the deserts far away – I had heard them talking – and nobody high up knew? Secrets were impossible to keep in Sans Amen. Even Mrs Gonzales had overheard some of these so-called secrets.

I looked around and thought: *who? Who knew? Who isn't here?*

It was a fact. Everyone in Sans Amen, particularly in political life, was linked. They had met at school, or university, or were related by blood. Some of the ministers right there even knew Hal from school. If you were clever and male, you had come across one another. Many of the ministers in the House had been in various previous governments. The Leader? It was too simple to heap everything on him, isolate him and reduce him to a monster.

Sans Amen had made the Leader. And the Leader wasn't the only mad man involved in politics on the island, that was for sure. It was too easy to simply hang all the sins of the past thirty years on one man. The Leader hadn't worked entirely alone. The Leader had his part to play in the story of the making of a small nation. Many others had their fingerprints all over this half-realised failure of a plan. An official inquiry into these events would never be commissioned by anyone. An inquiry would implicate everyone.

*

Now we were facing our fifth, and hopefully final, night under the gun. No army convoy had arrived to take any of us away. The army now seemed to be stringing the gunmen along with negotiations as long as possible. No amnesty, just surrender. The piece of paper signed by the ministers had been photocopied by the gunmen on a machine in one of the offices; several had a copy of it in their back pocket – the army had the original. Hal also had a print in his back pocket. The signatures mattered to him; it had been signed by the PM after all. The army had kept up their demand all day through the megaphone. *Give yourselves up*, was their only demand. *Come out. Surrender.* I hoped it was now only a matter of time before this insurrection fell flat on its face. A few more hours of hell.

The July rain didn't make it cooler. The rain brought a sullen broodiness with it, a rancorous on-off drizzle which affected my joints. I hadn't eaten in days and the lack of nourishment had made me weak. We were allowed water and the women could use the wash-room, but nearly five days without food meant I could hardly walk straight. Any physical bravery was out of the question.

I watched the young boy Breeze as he painted words onto the wooden butt of his gun with white Liquid Paper. I strained to read the words and saw that he was slowly inscribing the words *God will prevail.*

Breeze had entered the House brainwashed and convinced of his plans. Now I watched him lose himself. Not just Breeze, many of the other men looked nettled and a little undone. Some of them had been killed or injured and it was interesting to see who still kept the bravado up. Most of them called each other 'brother'. Many still prayed and they did this together. I wondered if these men looked at us, the ministers, the elected politicians of the land, in the same way I had been studying them. Were we *all* now feeling uncomfortable; were we all dying to stop seeing so much of each other? Hal kept glancing at his watch and striding to the back room even though the phone line was now cut. Was he at all embarrassed?

Greg Mason still hadn't jettisoned his gun, his military combat garb or persona. He was still there to liberate the oppressed. In the same way all the politicians had met at school or at university, these men had met too, on the street, in gangs, in prison; there was an alternative criminal network which mirrored the network of so-called legitimate political life. Some men did things by the book; others did the opposite.

'Ay, you,' Greg Mason suddenly turned around. 'What you staring at, lady?'

'I beg your pardon?'

'Oh yeah? All you do is stare all the time.'

'I don't mean to. I am thinking . . . that's all.'

'Yeah, well stop with the staring.'

I was starving, fatigued, constantly on the verge of tears, but I had no intention of letting him see me as weak. If I moved my head too quickly the room span. Even so, I kept my cool around this dangerous man.

'Anyway, what you thinking?' said Mason. I studied him: hardman, liberator, badjohn, guerilla fighter, whatever he was, or thought he was. He was serious.

'We are at the end of the twentieth century . . . change is coming. A whole new century is round the corner. A New Society is arriving . . . why you so hasty to shoot up everything?'

Mason gave me a pitying look and steupsed. 'Lady, you not real sharp, eh? We does take cocaine off the streets. Eh? Flush it away. We does care for the young boys of the City, buy medicine for the sick who cannot afford it. We does organise ourselves and fight for the land we build on. You think anyone in this country really have power? You think the black man or the brown man have power in this country, or if *you* in here have power? Power belong outside politics. Power belong to the men we cannot see, big men. They running drugs up and down the islands from Colombia. Men in business in this country are part of it. Men with big money, their own army. We know who those men are – so do you. No one inside here have power. Money is power; corporations are the new colonisers. We taking power back. Change? You talking change coming? Bullshit.'

I felt cowed, and interested.

Mason glared. 'Allyuh politicians take a cut of the big men money and nothing ever go change. The Leader, he march in the streets, he march with the labour movement, plenty people think the same way as the Leader. The Leader represents the poor man, the humble man in the street. Allyuh politicians like to use him, associate with him. Allyuh like puppets,' and he made a puppeteer movement with his hands.

I actually nodded. He was right, there was big power outside politics. And this big power was all about drug money. Yes, those men Mason was talking about existed, and yes it was difficult to run a small country with them bribing everyone, including the politicians and the police.

The young boy Breeze came forward, anger in his face.

'Who is the Leader?' he asked Greg Mason. 'If he so friggin clever and important, why he not running the country?'

Everyone hushed and looked at Breeze. 'I tired of all of this. Big men, power. The PM, the Leader. Who run this damn friggin place?' Breeze steupsed and looked vexed.

Greg Mason was twitchy, like he'd been cooped up far too long. 'The Leader born poor like you,' he said. 'He work for the police force. He go away, get some teaching. He find the spiritual path he lose in slavery. He come back and he make space for himself in society in Sans Amen and for men like you and me. He doh really want to be the PM, or head of the country at all. He want a job, yes, maybe Minister of National Security. But the Leader, he come from another place. He come to start the purification process.'

Breeze stared.

I gaped.

Mervyn laughed out loud and shook his head. 'The Minister of National Security? That what he looking for?' he said, openly amused.

Then Greg looked a little ashamed, like he'd let a secret slip.

No one said anything.

Breeze said, 'Fock this shit.'

'Ay, watch yuhself,' said Greg.

'I leaving here,' said Breeze.

'Oh, yeah,' said Greg, 'and go where?'

Many of the younger men had come closer. They'd been listening in to the conversation. Now they gathered close. Some stood behind Breeze; many were as young as him or not much older.

'I going and walk outta here, plain so.'

'Oh yeah? Life done, boy. Where you think you going?'

Breeze looked blankly at Greg. His lower lip quivered and he squinted. 'Muddercunt,' he said. 'We should all shoot you and Hal. Is you they want. Not us.'

The words fell like bombs. The air around emptied, a space cleared. That feeling came back to me, which had evaporated for a while. Extreme danger.

'Young man, hush,' said Mervyn.

Greg Mason stared down Breeze. They were both holding their rifles.

Breeze glared at Greg Mason. He wasn't scared. He was angry and tense. He screwed up his face and sniffed up phlegm from his lungs and hawked it on the floor and then sneered. He gave Greg a hard, mean look from the streets. The Leader hadn't bred that out of him, hadn't even tried.

Greg threw down his gun and clenched his fists, beckoning Breeze. 'Come, nuh,' he said.

Breeze flung his gun down. He spat hard on the floor and cussed and lunged at Greg. In seconds they were brawling and kicking each other with karate kicks and round kicks and all kinds of action poses I assumed they'd learned from their training and from TV. And then Greg Mason had Breeze in a headlock and was jabbing hard punches into his ribs and Hal was shouting for order and the ministers all cowered and everyone in the chamber was frozen watching. No one wanted this. It was too late in the proceedings. Soon we were to be freed. *Ayyyy, fockin muddercunt*, Breeze struggled and swore, jabbing back, and then Greg had Breeze on the ground, punching him in the face, and the young man was still cursing and Greg was pasting him down with hard punches, shouting, rounding on the boy who was cussing and swearing he was going to kill Mason dead.

Shots rang out in the house.

Mason stopped mid-punch, heaving. They all looked across the chamber. Behind Mason and Breeze the gunman called Ashes was standing there with a rifle in his hands. He was staring at the men and clutching his gun, shaking his head. He'd fired two shots up into the ceiling.

Greg looked annoyed and steupsed. He was still heaving. 'Fockin put that thing down,' he gasped.

'Leave him alone,' Ashes said. He aimed his rifle at Mason. 'He a young boy, let him be.'

Mason shook his head with pity.

Ashes moved closer with his pointed gun. Greg Mason smirked. 'What, you going and shoot me with that?' he laughed. 'You ent even know how to use that thing. You coming like your brother or what?'

There was a silence.

The gunman called Ashes closed his eyes. It was as if he was praying or trying to steady himself. When he opened his eyes they were glistening. Then,

Bam.

'Jesus *Christ*!' screeched Mason, clutching his leg. Blood sprang. Mason looked incredulous, horrified. *'Jesus hell, you fockin prick,'* he cussed. Blood seeped instantly through his camouflage pants and he held his leg and writhed around on the floor.

'Get away from him,' Ashes said to Breeze. 'Go on, move away. If you want to leave, go. Get out of here.'

The young man called Breeze also looked surprised. He moved away from Mason and crawled across the carpet. Breeze was fine, roughed up, but okay.

Mason was still cussing.

Ashes pointed his gun at him again. 'I'll shoot you again, if you don't calm yourself down,' he said.

Mason was crying now, blood all over his leg. *'Shit,* man,' he cussed. 'Why you go do that?'

Hal looked wondrous, out of himself. 'Ay,' he said to Ashes.

Ashes wheeled around and pointed his long rifle at Hal's chest.

'Okay, okay . . . ayyyyyy,' Hal said quickly, backing away. Hal was unarmed. He put his hands in the air.

Everyone went deadly quiet.

'Ay, ay, look,' said Hal. 'Look, cool it, nuh. We all leaving this place soon. Okay? Anytime now. Cool it.'

The gunman called Ashes didn't lower his gun. It was as if he was listening to another voice inside him.

'Where we all going soon?' Ashes said to Hal.

Hal looked confused. He nodded. He still had his hands in the air. None of the other gunmen had come to his rescue. Every person in the room was at the end of their wits. No one came forward to help him. The group of gunmen stood huddled, not knowing their own strength. Breeze, the younger men, just stared. The older men didn't move. Hal's second in command was on the floor, shot in the thigh.

For the first time since the whole invasion began, I saw Hal was beaten. This Ashes wasn't a crazy hot-head like the man with the Santa hat. Tears dripped from his eyes.

'I lose mih life over this,' Ashes said. 'Lose mih home, mih family. Everything. Now you get us out of here alive. I want to live.'

SUNDAY EVENING,
THE HOUSE OF POWER,
THE CITY OF SILK

I felt queasy. Sick. I found it hard to breathe. Everything was too much by then. I'd been hallucinating,
having night sweats and day sweats too. My body was
five days without food and I could feel it straining,
shutting down. I was able to walk around but I had to
hold on to things to do so. In my hallucinations I saw
the wise, inquisitive head of a leatherback turtle sur-
facing from the sea, gazing towards the beaches of the
north coast of Sans Amen, ready to lay her eggs. I saw
many turtles, dozens, maybe even hundreds,
approaching to nest, huge, tentative and pregnant
with new life. I saw the Sans Amen of the twenty-first
century, the House of Power painted green. I saw a
female Prime Minister in the future, a woman perhaps

no different to the male leaders of the past. I had a gnawing desolate feeling in the pit of my stomach that it would be many decades before Sans Amen grew mature. This wisdom was coming, though, this change the gunmen so hastily grabbed for. It must come. Bathsheba, the freedom fighter, her baby shot dead in her stomach. A citizen murdered in the womb. Bathsheba had wanted this change too. *I will not run away from all of this,* I pledged to myself and to my own children, and the sons and daughters of the other mothers of the city. I was still alive. But everything was different now in Sans Amen.

I was hanging on, just. My ears rang with tinnitus, as though I could hear a distant screaming. A rage had struck up in me and it was as if my insides were shrieking. My outer ear could now hear this sound of inner distress. My body was damp with my own sweat and urine. The stench of this five-day chaos was omnipotent in the air. *Tomorrow, dear God. Tomorrow. Let it end soon.* The PM had been gone just a day and he'd kept things stable. The PM had kept us all alive. Now there was no battle, no tension between the gunmen and the army. The gunmen had been cut off from their Leader; there'd been a small mutiny. They had stacks of ammunition left, in boxes down the hall. They'd brought enough bullets and explosives to last another week at least; they could still blow up the whole place. But the army weren't negotiating and Hal, unable to speak to the Leader, didn't know what to do.

I could see Mervyn was now struggling with his legs and feet. For hours at a time he would unbuckle his braces and then he would crawl about on the carpet. He would rub and massage his shins. He never once complained or showed distress.

'Mervyn, are you okay?' I said. Mervyn didn't look at all okay.

'No.'

'I didn't think so.'

He laughed. 'I think we have survived the worst, hopefully we all going tomorrow,' he said. 'Five days. No food. Very little water. I figure every single person here now on the verge of collapse. It can't last longer. The gunmen are as dehydrated and exhausted as we are.'

I didn't want to bring up what Mrs Gonzales had said. It felt inappropriate right then. He was one of the few good guys in the cabinet, like the PM; it seemed the good guys had been hurt in all of this, on both sides. Five days ago he was a man I hardly knew. I wanted to hug him. Or maybe I wanted him to hug me.

'Let me give your feet a rub,' I said.

Mervyn shot me a look and he blushed.

I didn't give him a chance to say 'no' out of polite-ness. I pulled one of his feet towards me and rested it on my knee and I began to massage the ankle and arch with my fingers through his sock. I sensed he was embarrassed but I knew what I was doing, keeping my fingers moving slowly and in circular movements and this kept him quiet.

'I saw you tending to Mason,' I said.

'There really isn't much I can do. He's been badly shot. The bullet needs to be removed. They've lain him down in one of the back rooms. I applied a tourniquet. His leg will become infected if he's not seen to by tomorrow. He could lose it.'

'That bad?'

'Yeah. Boy, that quiet-looking feller with the glasses, I never figure he could shoot.'

'I could shoot a gun now, if I had to. This situation bring out a side in us we never use.'

'I bet you could shoot. I think I could too, by now.'

I kept massaging his ankle, the ball of his foot. He winced.

'The PM is on the outside, he will take charge. I guess they making decisions all now. But I still worry for these young boys. What will happen to them.'

'Aspasia, you *still* feeling sympathy for these crooks? Half of them would shoot you dead.'

'Not now.'

'Yes *now*. All of them is crooks. Including that boy Breeze you like so much and that spooky quiet one, Ashes. They are crazy fellers. Gunmen. Is like you can't see them.'

'I am a mother. Some of them same age as my own children. They should all be in school.'

'I suspect many of them *are* at school.'

'The Leader's school?'

'Life is school, Aspasia. Revolution is school. They getting educated right now.'

'I'm serious. What will happen to these young boys?'

'They will get justice.'

I kept massaging Mervyn's ankle; his foot was hard and stiff, like a piece of wood. Just walking, for him, was an act of defiance. I looked over to the other side of the chamber. Breeze sat by the window, rubbing the long neck of his rifle. He rubbed and rubbed, all the while staring out into the real world, where the army were encamped. He looked like he was trying to make his gun disappear. He looked skinnier, a scrap, a stick boy there with his stick gun. He had charged in, blazing, a crusader, a young knight storming and enveloping a castle. Now he looked emaciated. He kept pressing and patting his groin, as if it was tender there. He had hurt himself, maybe, or strained a muscle. He had been limping too. Only days ago he had been an innocent, a fool. Would he spend the rest of his life in fights, duels, trying to cool his wound?

*

Night was closing in and I felt the urge to get up and stretch my legs. I struggled shakily to my feet, and then I straightened my skirt. Mrs Gonzales got up too, her head naked, and the two of us supported each other towards the hall and down the corridor. Mrs Gonzales opened the washroom door and disappeared and I kept on down the corridor, one hand running along the wall for support, the other hand holding my scarf to my nose. I glanced into the room with the dead woman and grimaced; I walked past it and turned left into another room, equally ruined. I noticed a telephone on the floor, the receiver strewn next to it, and I stumbled past it, dragging a chair to the window. I wanted to sit and see if any of the lights would come on in the City of Silk. I managed to position the chair near to the window and yet at an angle to avoid the army snipers. I sat down on it and a cool breeze came in through the window onto my face. I breathed in and could smell a dim sea scent, the scent of mud flats, of the gulf beyond. Tears ran down my face in tiny

streams and the urge to retch came. My body hiccupped and spasmed but I brought up nothing. It was
the stench. And it was my body quaking in the early
stages of starvation. I sat on the chair and watched as
clusters of fireflies of lights began to appear, the lights
of our city, a metropolis by the sea in the middle of an
archipelago of islands.

I wondered about the other island nearby. They
must be aware of this chaos in the neighbourhood.
I thought of Cuba. Havana was nothing like the
City of Silk. It had an empty feeling. So much had
been cleansed, taken away from the common citizen; so much had been eradicated. Thousands of
poor people living in abandoned grandeur. Trees
sprouting from rooftops, a black market economy.
Salsa and sex were all that was left to the man in the
street, and yes, our old African religion, santeria.
Havana had been cleared of crime by revolution. I
had some notion that my own City, the City of Silk,
corrupt as it may be – dirty, drug-ridden, half-civi-
lised, Victorian in design, elderly, decaying, violent
– would never succumb easily.

Something moved. I broke from my thoughts and
turned my head towards the door. Hal was standing
there in his soiled camouflage fatigues. He looked
ravaged and tired, not the man who'd run in five days

ago, a tidy beret on his head, the man who'd kicked and shot the PM. He was staring down at the telephone.

I gazed at him and willed him to look at me and he glanced upwards. This man with so many big ideas had been to the same school my son was now at. I nodded at him and said, 'I look forward to tomorrow.'

Hal didn't reply. He was looking at me and past me, out the window.

'Lady, don't be so sure.'

'Why?'

'Because you don't know what we know.'

'And what is that?'

'You see this thing, what happen here?'

'Your revolution?'

'This nothing compare to what going to happen soon, this week, tomorrow, or the next day.'

'Oh yeah?'

'Yeah, something big going and happen soon, in the world. Big.'

'And this is part of it?'

Hal nodded. His eyelids were heavy and his eyes were hard. All he had now was a photocopied piece of paper with some ministers' names in his back pocket. And he had 'news' up his sleeve. Something big. I found that this didn't feel interesting at all. I was a politician, sure, but right then I was annoyed by the very thought of bigger news than this.

'We all have good intentions,' I said.

Hal was gazing down at the telephone again. I turned back to the view of the City, some of the lights now on, but there were holes here and there; the City now looked different. The police station across the road was wizened, its colonial arches tarred and ugly. I could see the army and their covered trucks everywhere, their nightlights, the cordon they had made around the House of Power. I was thankful for them, a force of loyal, well-trained men.

'I had good intentions,' I said to Hal and looked over to the door. But Hal had disappeared.

MONDAY MORNING,
THE HOUSE OF POWER,
THE CITY OF SILK

It happened very quietly. At dawn, on the sixth day,
the army convoy was standing there. Two white
buses. One for the hostages, one for the gunmen. The
hostages would be released and I was chosen to be
the first one to walk out. *Thank God.* I was ready. I
could have run down those steps, even in my weak
state. The final negotiations with the army had
happened overnight. Surrender. It was happening,
finally. Soon I would be outside, free. I would see my
children, my husband; it would be like a miracle. To
be out of that chamber, to be back in the world. The
last few days had taken me out of myself to another
realm. There had been numerous deadlines, several
moments when I thought I might be safe and clear,

only to be disappointed. I still had to be patient. I wouldn't feel free until I was away from the House, well away.

I found I wanted to say something to almost everyone in the chamber. Most of the ministers I wanted to thank, many I would. But it was the gunmen . . . it was the teenagers . . . I found them the hardest to leave behind. Their motives for being here were confused and complicated. The PM, he'd been on the outside for some time now; hopefully he was safe and alive. What had he decided? Everything would be done by the book; they would be dealt with honourably and well within the law.

I didn't want to look anyone in the eye. The ordeal had in some way been intimate . . . and humiliating. Hal wanted to send the two female MPs out first, me and then Lucretia Salvatore, and then Mrs Gonzales. They wanted to demonstrate they still had no war with women. They wanted this show of respect. The army buses were waiting, the press were too. Guns and cameras were trained on the House. The young boy Breeze was still sullen and skulking in the corner of the chamber, gazing out into the street full of army men with balaclavas on and press with long camera lenses. The man called Ashes had vanished.

Hal gave me a look which said, *Okay, it's time.* I

pressed Lucretia's arm, gave Mrs Gonzales a look which said, *We'll meet again.* I bent and kissed Mervyn's cheek and said, 'Thank you.' He had watery eyes and looked, finally, at the end of his good cheer. He smiled, thinly.

Hal led me out. 'There,' he said, pointing to the public gallery. 'You walk down those stairs and then the army will guide you at the bottom.'

I nodded. I wanted to say something to Hal. Something. What? I was sorry for him too. He had made the mistake of his life. He might be executed for all of this, hung like a rat. I didn't want this to happen. I couldn't hate him. I said nothing, there were no words fitting. Instead, I covered my nose with my scarf and began my descent, one step by one step down the staircase of the public gallery, out and down. My legs were shaking, but I had to get out. Visions of it all being a trick came to me, or some kind of trap. I'd become meeker, conditioned somehow to captivity. It was strange not quite knowing what to do.

Quickly I came upon the lifeless body of a man in uniform, his body black with congealed blood and buzzing with flies. The stench was overwhelming. I tried not to look but found myself staring and gagging; it was one of the security guards. He'd been shot several times in the chest, perhaps in the first minutes, when the men had stormed the building. There was a swipe of blood on the wall behind him from where he'd fallen, the blood now dried and caked. I crossed myself and said a prayer for him and his family.

I forced myself down another flight of steps, holding on to the railings. My eyes were blurred, sheets of tears fell down my face. I thought I might slip and tumble down the steps head first. I stank and was covered in blood, my own urine, a fine dust of plaster from the ceiling. I knew Hal's gun was at my back. He wouldn't shoot but he was watching me. I was soon free, and yet I might faint. My kids! My son and daughter, I was stepping towards them. My time on earth had been halted. It would start again. Only then, as I was escaping, the trauma began to emerge, in shakes, in overwhelming dizziness.

At the bottom of these steps was the ground. I walked slowly towards this idea of ground, holding my hand to my nose. I would be okay. *Keep walking*. Then the sun was pounding down on me. I was outside. And there – more horror. Strewn like toys, other bodies. Men and women lay dead on the ground. It looked like they had either jumped from the balcony of the chamber or from the windows, or had been shot while trying to do so. Three bodies, stiff and lifeless and swollen. New ideas gripped me. What had happened? How big was this?

A voice came at me through a megaphone, 'Mrs Garland, keep walking. Turn right.'

I was trembling. I did as I was told, turning right, and only then did I see the bus. My heart surged. Freedom! It would carry me away. My legs felt spongy, like I was walking on pillars of foam.

'Keep walking towards the bus,' said the voice. The bus was parked just beyond the perimeter of the grounds of the house. I saw the bright magenta walls, how dwarfed I was next to them, how astounding they were now. A wild colour, the colour of sex and carnival, it gave me a sudden surge of confidence. Slender green palms stood next to the House, their red berries showing under their skirts. I could have kissed the ground. Sans Amen was still standing.

The skies were the brilliant clear blue that screams down and says *good morning* much too loudly. Everything was too much. I feared I might topple over before I reached the bus. Men were everywhere, wielding rifles, in army combat uniform, their faces hidden by balaclavas.

'Keep walking,' I heard the voice, now at my back, through the megaphone. There were two men in army fatigues standing near the bus. One of them greeted me with a glass of water which I took and drank from immediately. These men with guns weren't my captors, they were my protectors; I smiled at them uncertainly. I still didn't know quite what to do. One of them saw I was disorientated and took my arm and helped me up into the vehicle. He escorted me to one of the rear seats. There were open windows but the heat was intense and dazzling. I felt amazed, blinded by the sun and by my freedom.

*

Parts of the City of Silk were still smouldering in the morning heat. Some of the looted buildings were clouded in a grey smoke and this made everything in the blackened and barren streets appear smudged. These buildings were in the act of being rubbed out. They'd been dismantled, raided, burnt down and now – six days later – what was left of them looked indistinct and blurred. The looters had invaded most of the lower end of town. Shops, offices, arcades, everything was now charred; broken glass was everywhere in the streets, the innards of these properties dragged out into the street: timber, sheets of metal, chunks of plaster, a power cable, like a giant skipping rope, hung limp across the road. Tears ran down my cheeks. No one spoke in the white hostage bus. The City of Silk had been burnt like razor grass. It had been seared off. Now it was a wasteland.

As the bus moved slowly down Veronica Street I felt like I was on a fairground ride; this was a Tour of the Macabre. Everyone on the bus could now see what had been happening in the City of Silk over the last six days. If the city could weep, it was weeping. It stood disrobed and humiliated and I felt its shame. I had been craving freedom, but now I witnessed another hell on the outside of the House. I found it hard to look at the damage; it was like looking too closely at a woman who'd only recently been raped. The City was standing in its own violation and it hung its head, raw and pitiful. *What had the people done to themselves?* What had the PM, myself, other ministers not seen? How could we have missed this? Here it was. Here was the people's anger and delinquency. An old anger. It was right here on the streets and now the streets were smouldering with contempt. The City of Riots. This city kept doing this to itself; its citizens had old wounds to discuss. *Stupid woman,* I castigated myself. Everyone in the bus was equally silent. The City of Silk was in mourning and, as we glided past, every single one of the ministers gazed out, unnerved, humbled.

'Jesus Christ.'

'Jesus, dear God.'

Low whistles.

Tears in my eyes. Shock in my nerves. Some of the ministers would survive; others would never come back. Mervyn could only click his throat and shake his head.

Where would Sans Amen begin again after this? There were helicopters in the sky, I could hear a not-so-distant *chop chop chop*. Like a big carrion bird hung overhead.

The bus stopped at the Square of Independence and I gasped. Soldiers everywhere now, more chaos. Only last week we were discussing plans to erect a statue here to a brave woman, a citizen who'd fought corruption in the past. Now the square was corrupted. The people of Sans Amen had beaten us to it; they'd made their own sculptures, from mangled metal and broken breeze blocks. Jab jabs had been here. They'd urinated, stolen, jeered and mashed up the place well and good. The bus turned the corner and sailed past an old woman standing in the street. She wore a simple housedress and held a human head in her hands. She proffered it up to us hostages in the bus as it passed. I gasped. The bus moved on and, moments later, when I looked back, I saw no woman. The streets were deserted.

I was beyond tired. I closed my eyes and pressed my fingers to my forehead and took several deep breaths and counted. The urge to retch came as it had so many times in the last few days. Nothing. There was nothing inside me.

The bus was now being trailed by two army jeeps, each with armed outriders. We were heading north, towards the savannah, away from the House, and yet everywhere there was this sense of dismay. No life on the streets; the City of Silk was being kept stable by the military. Something war-like had happened.

Then I saw the green rich field, the vast savannah playground gifted to the City by the white French Creole planters of another era. Nothing felt good or right or sane or safe or stable. Freedom tasted like ashes in my throat. The bus swept around the park and everything was grotesque and familiar; the Poui trees were laughing, the world was enjoying a sinister joke. I felt older and I felt ugly. I needed to urinate. I needed a hundred hours of solitude. I was in shock. And I needed a bath. I wanted to say something but my voice was lost. I craved my family. I was so grateful to be alive; I'd lived for them. But this was another landscape, another island now. The bus was heading out of town, away from the savannah, and then it swept up the hill towards the old upside down

MONIQUE ROFFEY

Hilton Hotel which clung to the hills above the City
of Silk.

*

In my hotel room I threw open the curtains and went
straight to the balcony and gazed out. From high up,
the view was different. I could see the deep glittering
purple sea; ships and tankers in the gulf. I could see a
horizon. The City of Silk was left and right of me, pan-
oramic, low and jumbled, old and young, and all of a
sudden there was perspective. This attempted revolution, this disaster, had happened in a squared-off mile
of town. I looked at my watch; it was just past noon. I
had been missing for six days. The sun was mired
behind thick clouds. The day was overcast and the colours of the city were hazy and muted. The rains were
coming again; they would wash the city, bath the tired
old city built on soil so loved by silk cotton trees. The
phone rang and I jumped. The gunfire had done that
to my nerves. Would I always jump like that? I found
the phone by the bed and picked it up.

'Hello?'

'Darling, it's me.'

Tears fell.

'Thank God.'

'Are you okay?'

I shook my head and choked. The sound of Marc's voice brought on thick emotions. I sat down.

'I'm not so great.'

'We're coming to see you as soon as we can.'

I nodded. Everything felt hot and light and fluid. Like I might dissolve. I might even expire, there, from relief.

'You're safe now.'

'Yes, I am.'

'I love you.'

'Good. I love you too.'

It felt like months since we'd seen each other. I felt like a teenager, my heart beating at his voice. Love struck. Needy. Dazzled. Weak. And safe. The army wanted to keep us at the Hilton for one night. We all needed to be debriefed, seen by doctors. I needed the privacy; I was grateful for this time before I met my family.

'Can I speak to the children?'

He handed the phone to my son, James.

'Mum?'

The flood came: the blessing of relief. 'Yes, it's me, my love. It's me.'

'We're coming to see you . . . tomorrow.'

'I *know*, I know,' and I rocked on the bed, holding his

voice in my hands, the voice of a son of the city, my son, *my boy*. The terror of the boys with guns engulfed me too; they were all related, these sons. Where were the mothers of those boys inside there? I was grief stricken and yet I was free.

'I'll be seeing you tomorrow,' was all I could manage. 'I love you.'

I put the phone down. My face was wet. I sat on the bed, not knowing what to do. I was still filthy and I stank. I'd been told food would soon be sent to my room.

I ran the taps in the sink in the bathroom and splashed cold water on my face. In the mirror I saw a version of myself, a person I recognised and used to know. The face in the mirror had a sullenness which reminded me of someone else . . . the young boy, Breeze. I looked like him now. Sullen and vexed. Six days, but the lines looked like they'd invaded for good; I was different. There was a storm in my face. I was angry. How long had I been angry? Before this had happened, or during the whole thing? My cheeks hung. My eyes were reddened where they were supposed to be white. I touched the skin on my forehead, just to make sure I could still feel. There I was again, Aspasia Garland, free, alive, back in the world. I could now do as I pleased, but I felt very ill at ease. As I stood looking into the mirror words came.

'I deserved this.'

The words fell out of my mouth onto the ground. 'I deserved this.'

That was the new sense, the mood of my new and future womanhood, a guilt and a responsibility associated with this anger on the streets and with that young boy, Breeze.

*

There was a knock at the door and when I opened it there was a uniformed member of the hotel staff standing there with a courteous smile and a tray at his shoulder. I thanked him and took the tray to the bed and uncovered the plates to find a mountain of hot stew chicken and rice and two different salads and bread rolls and fruit. My stomach rejected even the sight of the food. I sat down on the bed again and poured myself a glass of Coca-Cola from the bar and coughed on its fizzy sweetness. A large television sat on a table in the room and I switched it on and flicked to the local news and found nothing but a cartoon film about a little mermaid.

I flicked to other channels, quickly finding CNN, to see what looked like a line of armoured tanks in convoy rolling in the middle of a desert. Sand dust billowed from the tank treads. I could barely guess what I was looking at. Tanks? A desert, somewhere in the Middle East, far away? I found the control panel and turned up the volume.

A young, fresh-faced white male reporter in a flak jacket was saying something about an invasion. Tanks. Where was this? I picked up a bread roll from the tray and began to tug at it.

Apparently an invasion was taking place. The tanks were rolling in to a small fortress by the sea in the Arabian Gulf. The fortress was being bombed and the line of tanks were from a much bigger country nearby, a desert country ruled by a violent dictator. This much bigger country was invading its tiny neighbour, suddenly and without warning or provocation. One massive country was invading its neighbour by land and by air. Bombs were landing on a fortress by the sea . . . the young, fresh-faced reporter was saying that the fortress had been well defended once, from invasions by sea, but now the residents were helpless. People from another state were arriving to claim this smaller ancient fortress city for itself. An old dispute. There was news footage of lines of men praying in a masjid and a young boy saying something in Arabic, something about God. He was about the same age as Breeze. I stuffed some of the bread roll into my mouth and found myself chewing on cloth. What had Hal said to me? *Something big.*

I was stunned. Surely the two invasions weren't connected? They couldn't be. One was a bungled and spectacular failure on a tiny island in the Caribbean sea; and this . . . this was an altogether bigger bid for power. This involved the world: superpowers, jet fighters, NATO. I wondered about the news teams staying in Sans Amen; if they were already booking their tickets to fly out. Did any of these journalists notice a connection between the last six days and this bigger attempted coup d'état?

I coughed on the roll and swigged some Coke to get it down; I stared at the line of tanks and then I didn't want to see anymore. I turned the TV off. I lay back on the bed. I closed my eyes and it was only then I could hear it again, the noise in my ears, the sound of distant shrieking, the sound of an inner screaming.

V. The Hilltop

MONDAY AFTERNOON,
THE HOUSE OF POWER,
THE CITY OF SILK

Violence is man re-creating himself, said the psychiatrist Frantz Fanon. Ashes took this to mean that somehow violence could be a positive thing. But when he looked around at the empty and destroyed chamber of the House of Power, he felt despair. Their valuable hostages were now free, people had been killed. The place was shot up – and yet Fanon was suggesting this had some higher meaning, that there was a grander pattern, historic and purposeful, to this violence; it had been significant in the great scheme of things. It could lead to new creation. But Ashes didn't feel the least bit positive. He had lost track of his spiritual growth and his sense of selfhood had been crushed. He was going to be imprisoned or publicly executed over this. His children were now fatherless. No. He didn't feel any sense of purpose, any resonance with Fanon's words. He didn't want to die for others to grow. He was a stupid man. He had read too many books, too many words. He felt no pride and no vindication in what he'd been part of the last six days. And now there was no slipping away, no getting off lightly. No way out of the House but on the bus waiting for them outside.

It was their turn now to walk out. None of them could even talk to each other. Ashes knew he was no one special or important to his country. All those notions were ill-begotten fantasies of six days ago. He wanted none of this business with guns and bullets. He bet Frantz Fanon had never held a gun in his hands. He had said things that needed to be said. He was a black Caribbean man and he was only twenty-seven when he wrote it down: the white man does not see the black man. This was a revolutionary thing to say, then, in the 1950s. But Fanon had never held a gun. And now that Ashes had held a gun, fired it and shot someone, he felt it was irresponsible to write revolutionary literature and to stir people up.

When the PM was freed he'd felt abandoned. As the hostages disappeared he had felt relieved for them . . . and envious. Now it was his turn. He took his gun and didn't look around too much as he walked from the chamber. He didn't say anything to Hal or any of the other men. He took his turn in the line of those surrendering. Slowly he walked down the steps, and soon he came to the body of the security guard he'd seen Arnold shoot dead on the way in, years ago now. He nodded to the body in respect and for a split second he was caught in the blur of the chaos of those moments: Arnold screeching and shooting him dead, spraying the man with bullets. Now the man lay bloated and rotting and covered in caked blood. The stench made him gag.

He stumbled a little and then forced himself down towards the sun. At the bottom of the steps he was quickly surrounded by armed men.

'Put down your gun,' said a voice through a megaphone. Ashes did what he was told, placing the rifle a few feet in front of him. He took a large step backwards, to show obedience.

'Now put your hands in the air,' said the megaphoned voice. He did this too. Two army men wearing balaclavas came forward, gesticulating with their rifles for him to keep walking. He did so, the sun pounding on his back. Now he was captured, now he was helpless. His body was rigid and everything seemed to be happening a few feet away from him.

'Turn right,' they said, and he turned to see the bus,

aware that the snipers had their guns now inches from his head and back. One quick movement and they'd shoot him dead. The long white bus floated in the heat. His legs didn't seem to touch the pavement. He had his hands in the air, two guns at his back. He couldn't hear what the megaphone voice was saying; the men behind him were shouting orders for him to spread his arms and legs across the side of the bus. He did so, his body trembling. They patted him down and wrenched his head backwards. They were cool and mean and efficient in their manner. They found nothing on him and so he was marched to the front of the bus. *Keep your hands on your head*, one of the snipers barked. He kept his hands on his head as he mounted the stairs and walked to one of the seats at the back. He looked through the window to the left and he could see other men coming out now, also frogmarched by armed soldiers.

It all seemed to happen without sound. He lifted up his face towards the sky and then he closed his eyes and relaxed his chest. His heart slowed and then yes, a small feeling of peace came into him from outside and he breathed it in deeply. He fell quiet.

Then the other men were coming on to the bus, some still looking bad and serious, others with their faces closed and shut down. All of them stank and they were dirty and worn down from fatigue and hunger; they all sat with their hands on their heads and some of them stared straight ahead in a stupor and some watched what was happening with a curiosity as to their own fate. Ashes sat with his hands on his head and felt open in his chest and heart and he prayed for himself and for them. He thought of his wife Jade and his sons. His small lie, *I'll be back for dinner*. Regret wasn't quite the word for the way he felt. He'd read too much; he'd taken it all too seriously. None of these books came close to describing the way he felt now.

Every brother was searched, some against the flank of the bus, some spread-eagled on the ground. Ashes watched as the soldiers found and confiscated the photocopied pieces of paper some of them kept in their back pockets, the proof of a so-called amnesty; a piece of paper signed by members of the government under duress days ago. The world had moved on. There was a wall of press and photographers not far way and Ashes felt himself to be the object of much attention. It was humiliating; could Jade see him now, on TV?

Then almost all of them were on the bus. And then he saw Breeze come round the corner of the House, thin and wiry, and he had his hands in the air too and his face was full of contempt and there was a bound-up energy in his step. Breeze, the young boy, was angry to have been so caught out. Angry that he hadn't been told who the Prime Minister was. Breeze came out holding his mouth shut tight and Ashes could see he was full of a new fight. Breeze had snipers behind him, shouting orders. He was spread across the side of the bus, just under Ashes' window, and he could see the army men now patting him down and one of them brought a piece of white paper from the back pocket of his pants. They jeered and took it from him and said, *Yeah, nice try young man.*

Breeze looked upwards and when he saw that Ashes was looking down he couldn't meet him eye to eye. The young boy had far from surrendered. Ashes wondered if he was only just beginning to think for himself.

*

They were driven through the ruined streets. Everything had been destroyed by the people; town was chaos, the rubble so bad it was hard to recognise where he was. His mouth hung open with the sight of it all. *Books*: he'd read too many. Books didn't talk of this happening; looting wasn't discussed in Fat Clay's handbook of revolution. Or if it was, he'd missed it. Books didn't say enough about lying to wives about dinner, about satellite dishes being so easy to dismantle, about cleaning a human tongue off the carpet. About the sounds captors make, some as young as fourteen, tiny whispered whimpers, like cats crying ... and the sounds their hostages make too, some of them women, the soft moans they make at night as they call for their children. Books didn't talk of the smell of a ruined city. He could speak of that now and write it down if need be.

A ruined city smelled of ashes. And it looked cratered, like the moon. It had no sound. It was quiet, like guilt. And it tasted of bitterness and the shame of its own citizens, those who'd plundered the city while revolution happened only a few feet away. If he could reach out and touch it, a ruined city would feel rough and ramshackle, like broken bitumen, like burnt tyres; it would shred the hands that tried to explore and caress it. A ruined city was already a haunted city; Ashes could sense thousands of extinguished moments in this dead space. It was a city of leftover impressions. He could still feel the things that had disappeared: arguments, love affairs, street deals, games of cards, moments of revelation, bargains lost, friendships made, the pulse of everyday human endeavour and frustration somehow hung in the air.

His throat coiled into lumps and his eyes burned at the sight of the scarred streets. There was a supermarket which looked like a cave. There was a pile of rubble inside it and outside it too. He couldn't understand what had been done to it. Everything seemed to have been taken outside and then rubble seemed to have been brought inside; or had walls been knocked down by the looters? What had happened? One or two of the brothers let out a low whistle. There was an old gingerbread wooden shop on the corner of two main streets, a shop he knew well; it sold hardware. The windows had been pelted with bricks. They were all smashed and the shop looked like a face with many broken eyes and many broken teeth. Had the people in the street hated the shop so much they had abused it?

Trucks full of army soldiers were trailing them and the air was heavy and humid. Ashes felt hated. He felt stared at and guilty and hated. The bus was half full of brothers. Breeze had come towards the back to sit down. Sixty men sat with their hands on their heads. Sixty freedom fighters. Sixty mistaken men. There was no longer the stench of the House but there was now an overwhelming feeling of dread and an inevitable feeling of the power of the universe mounting its revenge. There would be severe recourse towards them and it was already happening. He had threatened life. They had abused and taken life itself. Death still followed the bus around on its tour of the City of Silk. There was sun and air and the feeling of being let out and yet also deprived of freedom, forever. He would actually never see the sun again. The army were everywhere on the streets watching the bus. Every man on the bus stared out into the City of Silk which they had personally destroyed. Ashes uttered his mantras to his God, begging for forgiveness, to be given another chance. He could start again, very humbly, again, again, dear God up there in the skies. He would start again on the ladder upwards.

*

They were being taken to the television station, Ashes guessed, to pick up the other brothers. They would be reunited with the Leader and the other men. They travelled some more and the hollow streets and their charred ugliness blurred and he remembered a time when he first came to the commune and met the Leader and felt he had met a teacher, a man who could add to and enhance the enquiry he was already making about his spiritual existence on earth. Maybe this was a man who could be of some special consequence on his path. He understood, immediately, the Leader would change his life. Very quickly he had been swept up. It felt like he had at last, on earth, found a band of like-minded souls, this was where he fit in. He had felt kinship, a sense of brotherhood, for the first time since his brother's death. He had felt a sense of belonging, at last. It had been a good time, early on, when he'd submitted to the Leader in the commune on the outskirts of town. His mother had named him Ashes and this, she said, was because she had a feeling about him, when he was first born, that he would live and die many times during this one life, and always survive from the ashes of himself.

*

Soon, the bus stopped again, in the street. The day was overcast and the grey-purple clouds in the sky squashed the heat down onto the tarmac. The steel-framed bus cooked them all slowly as they waited for the men in the television station to come out, again, one by one, laying down their weapons in the street. It was embarrassing. Everyone was watching, CNN, BBC, the local media, literally everyone in the world; journalists with cameras everywhere. This was their heroic failure, their shining mistake. This was their learning. How many of them would learn *anything*? How many of them would live, actually survive after this? How many of them had now felt the power of the gun and now had a taste for guns and for death? Ashes didn't like any of it at all. What would Jade make of this? She had married a man who had made this huge mistake. Could she ever love him now? He was out alive, and yet he had been part of this and it was shameful.

Each brother who filed out of the television station was searched; each one was marched at gunpoint to the bus with their hands on their heads. Ashes didn't even know who had gone to the television station with the Leader, and now faces of brothers he recognised came onto the bus ... some looked utterly lost and defeated, others appeared sullen and closed. All were tired, none looked too scared. Many looked as if they had been having similar thoughts to him.

Ashes waited for an hour, at least, in the hot bus. Eventually, all the brothers came out of the TV station. It was like watching a procession of concrete men, each brother looked grey and hard. He guessed that, as in the House of Power, a few brothers had been shot dead. He guessed that they had killed others too. Nothing was speakable. There were now almost the same amount of men on the bus as there had been last Wednesday afternoon during prayers at the compound. Hal was with them. Greg Mason was at the front near the driver, resting his leg which was turning purple in the heat. They were a band of brothers who had been rounded up after a war and there was no love in them at all. These men he had prayed with on a regular basis for years; they'd all attended the meetings at the compound, listened to what the Leader and his men had to say. There was much they had in common and had shared over time: the community school, the medical centre where he volunteered, the community shop. They had tried to self-organise. There was the dormitory for the young street boys like Breeze. He knew these men and some of their wives. They were family men; they were his brothers on earth.

It was all coming back to him, now they were together. Why they had done this thing called insurrection. It had been for a New Society, one like theirs.

*

The army weren't giving much away. There was a quiet, tense atmosphere to the way they were conducting their affairs and this felt frightening. What were their plans?

The Leader would be giving himself up last. And now it was his turn. Every brother in the bus watched the entrance of the television station for his well-known figure. Everyone wanted to see him again, if he was defeated or if, like them, he was having closed and quiet thoughts which involved regret. Cameramen and news teams were stationed all along the street. There were snipers on rooftops and Ashes wondered if they might shoot him.

Then he appeared, huge, dressed in robes of grey. Familiar. Family. 'Papa', some of the young boys called him. He was their Papa, their Leader and their spiritual guide. Ashes felt his heart lift from his chest. The Leader appeared like an angel, his clothes hardly creased, like he had been out for his daily stroll. Ashes saw his teacher come out into the sun, holding his gun tightly by his side, like a soldier. No army man came forward to frisk him or search him; it was as if even they were taking a good look, as though they were impressed at who he was and what they'd caught. The Leader walked like a general with his gun under his arm and his grey robes still immaculate through the centre of the hot street. He walked like a noble dignitary, a man who'd done justice to himself and his men, had even succeeded in his intent.

He stopped dead in the centre of the road and then he bowed, courteously, from the waist, to those watching him, the world's press, the national military.

'Put your gun down on the ground *now*.' There was a terse command from behind an army jeep.

With a casual flourish the Leader placed his rifle down in front of him in the road. He then stood and clicked his heels and smiled beatifically, handsomely, like he was still so sure of himself. Like Breeze, this was a man not surrendering. He had put down his gun *for now*. He was calm and he was graceful. The Leader was attractive, even glamorous – and only halfway through his life.

Ashes saw then that the Leader had lots more to do on the earth. He had more plans and his three wives and children to get back to, his foster sons, his work, the compound. He was still proud, unrepentant, and he was a thorn in the side of the government, any government to come in future years. How would they punish him? How could they punish them all? Ashes looked at Breeze and caught a troubled expression in his face; Breeze wasn't having the same thoughts at all. Breeze was gazing at the Leader with a look of considered dislike in his face. The young brother called Breeze, he could see, had come to hate his father.

*

They were driven from the television station back through the deserted city, to where the city met the sea, and then the bus veered right, along the highway on the foreshore, out towards the old American army base in the west. Ashes looked out of the window to see the world again, the city where he was born – yet it was nothing like it used to be. Everything looked familiar and yet also it felt like there was a great distance between his hometown and himself. Everything appeared smaller, the buildings and office blocks along the shoreline were all minute and far away. They had shrunk and condensed, or maybe they had walked away. He didn't like this feeling at all, this distance. It was already like a punishment, like it was all removed from him now.

It was mid-afternoon, around four, he guessed. The Leader was at the front of the bus, his hands on his head. Two armed soldiers were with them. They were being led and followed by several army vehicles. Again he had that feeling that they had made the country mute. They had silenced the place. His world had been made smaller and quieter. To the left there was the sea, flat and placid and pewter blue, and soon they came to the abandoned bauxite mine which always felt haunted to him, a giant gawky spider of fading steel, words barely visible painted on the side, another era. Then the road narrowed to one lane which snaked along the coast and they passed tiny rocky beaches. No one was out bathing in the shallow sea. He would come here sometimes, with his family; none of them knew how to swim well and so it was safe to come for a sea bath.

Ashes noticed every man on the bus was gazing out towards the sea. Sans Amen was an island, of course; they were looking out towards a sea which had held them captive since birth. None of the brothers had ever been sailors, he imagined. All of them were men from the city or from the hills. He had always felt respect for the ocean, but now he felt dull and shy seeing so much water. It felt hard to witness, or maybe the sea was bearing witness to them. He felt unable to look at anything. The bus began to slow and Ashes realised they'd arrived at the American army base which had been abandoned after the Second World War.

The bus turned a sharp right and this was unexpected. He'd imagined they were to be taken to the barracks or to the army base beyond. But no, the bus swerved right and then they were on a thin strip of broken up tarmac road. Then they were travelling in a silent green place, past gargantuan samaan trees with their beards dripping to the ground, past clumps of towering shafts of emerald bamboo and concrete benches where families or lovers might like to meet. They travelled along this road for quite some time; everything was very green and peaceful and he felt almost like he could relax; and then he felt a cold terror curdle in his gut. This wasn't right. This was the wrong way to go.

The army vehicle ahead of them stopped and turned abruptly. To the right there was a small side road leading into what looked like a tunnel of green bamboo. It was the road to the derelict tracking station up on the hill. There was an iron barrier gate across this road and more army vehicles stationed there, waiting for them. Their bus stood with the motor running as soldiers shouted orders to each other. One of the army men raised the barrier and then beckoned the driver of the bus. The covered vehicle that had been leading them moved off, and then they were following it again, this time down into a long green nest. The bamboo on each side of the road was so wild and dense and it had grown so high that the poles had bent over. On each side of the road the long shafts dipped and met in the middle. The green stems against the lemony light reminded Ashes of the stained-glass window of Jesus Christ nailed to the cross in the House of Power. It was pretty and the light moved and danced in between the shafts of bamboo. They could have been in a holy place. The bus moved slowly along the slim road and it was like they were being driven up through a gateway into another world of possibilities. His heart lifted a little and he said *Praise be to God*.

The road began to wind and climb upwards and then it stopped at the top of a hill. They had reached a perfectly flat plateau, as if the top of the hill had been sliced off, and Ashes guessed it had once been excavated to be so flat. To the right, on the edge of the flattened hilltop, stood an enormous rusted satellite dish. Once it had been white, now it was polka dotted with orange and saffron rust. It resembled a huge eye gawking awkwardly and blindly out to sea. It was an olden day thing and it was part of what the American army had left behind: spy equipment from before the war; he had heard the talk about NASA and how they and the FBI had come to these islands to plant their satellites. It was part of some kind of defence shield, defending the USA from communists. Ashes was aware that they'd arrived at a remote and deserted spot. They'd been followed by numerous army vehicles.

All of a sudden he didn't feel good at all. He felt bad. He felt badder, suddenly, than he'd felt during the last few days, then he had ever felt in his life. The driver of the bus turned the engine off. The army soldiers guarding them were wearing balaclavas. The afternoon sun had now disappeared and soon it would be dusk. Ashes felt sick. Why had they brought them up here? He looked at Breeze and saw that he was equally as anxious and puzzled. Every brother on the bus stared out the window at the satellite dish and at the perfectly flattened land. They were up on a hilltop, miles from anywhere. Everything was silent, muffled by bush. They were surrounded by jeeps and covered vehicles. Scores of armed soldiers were now filing out of the jeeps and trucks; every one of them was wearing a balaclava. They were not wearing green combat fatigues. They were wearing black.

Then the soldiers on the bus were barking at them.

'Now, *move!*' They were prodding and shouting at the Leader to get up off his *damn blasted arse and move*, and Ashes saw the Leader rise in his grey robes. He turned back to his brothers and his face was blank.

'Come on, move!' The soldiers began to shout and hustle them. Slowly, one by one, the brothers began to move from their seats. The soldiers outside were forcing them to walk towards where the hillside had been cut, where there seemed to be a natural wall. They still had their hands on their heads; the Leader was the first in the line of men now walking towards the green wall. When it was his turn, Ashes rose, with his hands on his head, and an image of a ladder came to him, as if he could climb up it and vanish through a trap door, up into the sky.

Breeze was ahead of him; Breeze who he had never

really known before. Breeze began to descend from the bus to the ground. They were the last two men on the bus. They had become friends in a way. Ashes followed him down. When he was on the ground he heard the sound of gunfire. It made him jump. His nerves were raw from the days in the House. Some of the brothers had begun to run away from the green wall and the army men in black were chasing them down, shouting, *Come back or we'll shoot.*

It was then that Ashes decided he needed to go home. He grabbed Breeze by the collar of his shirt and yanked hard. Breeze turned. Ashes put his finger to his lips and pointed towards the underbelly of the bus.

'There,' he whispered.

Breeze nodded.

The gunman minding them had turned his head away towards the commotion. There were brothers now running all over the place, trying to escape. One or two were shot and fell down. The Leader was shouting something, and then some of the soldiers in black pointed their rifles at the Leader and he went quiet again and held his hands up in the air. The soldier guarding them seemed to forget they existed completely; he had finished guarding the bus, he was hypnotised by what was happening. He walked away, towards the green wall and the armed soldiers in black.

Ashes and Breeze moved quickly. In seconds they were under the bus and Ashes' heart was beating fast and he was thinking okay, I will survive, just like my mother predicted, I'll live from the ashes of myself.

From under the bus they watched as more brothers trying to run away were chased down and rounded up. All of them were made to stand in a line against the wall of the hill. The light was fading now and everything was still. It was the time of day when the hills appeared gentle. Sans Amen is a city surrounded by green hills, amorous slopes that embrace the city during sleep. Ashes counted one hundred and twelve men, every one a brother; almost all these men he knew and could call their name if he had to. The soldiers wearing black and who wore balaclavas lined up opposite the brothers; some regular soldiers joined them too. There was a line of army men facing another line of brothers. It felt bad, all of this. Ashes knew it was wrong that he wasn't there with them. There seemed to be a commanding officer and he walked between the two lines of men. Some of the brothers were now praying, one or two had dropped to their knees. The Leader was standing there, his hands on his head, and Ashes had a sense he was praying too.

'Take aim,' shouted the commanding officer. Just like that. He put one hand up in the air. He had got himself well out of the way. The men in black aimed their rifles as one and when the commanding officer gave the second command of 'Fire', they all opened fire and their guns blazed.

Ashes could feel a collapsing inwards, a sense of the earth slipping from under his feet. The brothers all fell to the ground in a heap. They fell softly and the soldiers dressed in black and the army men advanced, firing again and again into the heap of brothers in case they might not be quite dead. Ashes could see Greg Mason in the heap. He saw the Leader in the heap too, blood on his grey robes; he'd been shot many times in the chest.

He turned to Breeze and said, 'We must go, now, before they come back and ketch us.'

Breeze nodded. The sun had fallen into the sea behind the hill. The huge dish blinked at them and said *Now go*. The new night air was thick with insects and the stink of gunfire and then Ashes found himself running away from the bus, slipping down the muddy hillside and Breeze was ahead of him. They fled downwards, coming down the hill through the bush, running and tripping and moving blindly, both of them dazed and weeping because of what they'd seen. They ran into the night for what felt like a long time. All the while, Ashes saw the line of men falling softly, quietly, to the ground. He saw their bodies collapse, almost like a line of women fainting. He should have been with them; he should not be running away in the opposite direction. He saw his friends riddled with bullets, like his brother River.

They came to the road and it was very dark by then; over an hour had passed. It was night. Ahead of them was the long, thin track which was overshadowed by bamboo. Then the two of them were running again, on the long, slim road, heading towards the entrance to the tunnel of green. Minutes passed. It felt like they'd done it; they had escaped. It was happening. They would live. Then they stopped for a few moments, getting their breath back. Ashes could feel his ribs quaking in a stitch. He'd never moved so fast, not in his adult life. Breeze was panting heavily, as he was. Breeze said, 'Where we going now?'

Ashes knew he was going home, back to his wife and sons. He was going to hide forever, or maybe even leave and go to Trinidad, listen to Lord Wellington in his tent. Or maybe he and his wife and sons would move to the countryside, live a quiet life. But he knew where he was going now, and as fast as possible, and he said to Breeze, 'I going home. Through there.' He pointed through the jungle of bamboo which was east, back towards the City of Silk. It would be an overnight trek, through the forest. He would stay close to the hills.

'Come with me, if you like.'

But Breeze said, 'Nah, man. Too slow, man. Too slow.' Breeze smiled at him, pensive, and sure of himself, a look which said I need my life and I need to go too, anywhere, and I'm going my own way. Then the young man tore off down the road into the cathedral of bamboo, running quick, quick, quick as the breeze.

VI. L'Anse Verte

23 YEARS LATER

11 APRIL, 2013

'Eh, eh, they find bones,' says his wife Pearl.

'Bones? What bones?'

'Amerindians. Last month. They dig them up.'

'Where?'

'Under the House of Power. Bones, nuh. Four humans, they say, and some animals, some pottery.'

Joseph looks at his wife sitting at the kitchen table, her face buried in *The Gazette*. Her ankles are neatly crossed; her elbows are on the table. She is wearing a housedress, slippers which are rubber flip flops worn thin under the balls of her feet. He can feel his heart beating a little faster in his chest as she mentions this news.

'They say they around seven hundred years old, maybe older. What a thing, eh?'

She doesn't take down the newspaper.

Joseph doesn't reply. He stopped looking at the papers some time ago. His wife loves them. Sometimes she reads snippets aloud to him and he tries to be responsive. Generally, he is evasive. Especially with anything connected to the House of Power. She knows about his past and yet she seems to enjoy reading out news about the place, as if she can't help herself. She is always trying roundabout ways, subtle, off-hand comments, these news reports. She's heard . . . most of the story, once, years ago, and that's all. He feels bad about being so unable to talk. But the truth is he can't; he isn't trying to be difficult. He's been over it once. And now he deals as best he can with her attempts to find out more.

'Bones,' she says, and he realises this is the first piece of news about the House he's ever heard which makes him feel interested.

There's a female Prime Minister now in charge of the country, but not like Aspasia Garland, not a real hand-on-heart type person. There's a woman in the House, but she can't stop the crooks. Same, same. Sans Amen has gone from bad to worse since all those years ago. The small island is now rich, the economy is booming, so much so that Sans Amen is no longer considered a developing nation. And yet corruption has increased; each government steals what it needs. One ex-PM was rumoured to be wiretapping the whole country. When he left, another senior minister was caught pocketing vast sums of money. The cost of living has soared while those in central and rural areas still scrape by. All the white people in Sans Amen do yoga while all the Indian people send their children abroad to study law and medicine. And the black man? He never again united or rose up and fought back or achieved any of those old heroics of ideology. Like anyone else, he wants to make a buck in this so-called rich island. The black man will make his money how he can. Resistance was tried, twice, and both times it failed – and so now it's as if his heart has been taken out of his chest and pounded flat and then re-inserted. That is how he feels about politics. Heartless.

But the *bones*? Four humans? He remembers the place felt haunted.

'Who find them?' he asks.

'They digging there. They renovating the House. Now they getting the bones examined in New York; they plan to bring a team down now, to dig up the place. Is possible there some kind of burial site under the House of Power, something so.'

'Oho,' he says, trying to show no real interest. And yet he's intrigued; he can't help himself. Bones? He remembers the ground floor of the House, the brother they called Ashes; he remembers the library, Jesus on the cross. *The first will be last and the last will be first,* Ashes had said. He said Jesus had been a revolutionary. Long, long time ago now.

*

At 8 p.m. Joseph starts his shift at the visitors' centre at the back of the hotel on the beach, behind the car park. His wife works at the desk selling permits; from March to August it's prohibited to walk the beach without a guide after 6 p.m. To start with, he goes out on to the sand alone to estimate how many creatures are already nesting. April, a full moon. Dozens will be on the beach and when he goes out to look, he's right. Sleek leathered black humps everywhere, like an invading fleet has landed from across the ocean, all of them pregnant females, their wombs swollen with eggs. All of them are bursting to bury their loot after their long migration from the cold waters. Every one of these creatures will be their own midwife. Each is a nursery craft. They have self-piloted all the way across the Atlantic to be here, right here on this tiny cove, L'Anse Verte.

His daughter Soleil and her friend Maria come with him tonight, two skinny girls, laughing and trying to be serious all at once. There are twelve visitors in his group tonight, all staying at the hotel.

He briefs them in the car park.

'Turtles are very startled by light, okay. So please, no flash photography. We cannot allow cameras on the beach. Or torches. You will need to stick close by me.'

The group nod as one. They are all carrying cameras. Most pack them away.

There are couples, a family with kids, an older man, the grandfather, two single women. It's midweek and usually the visitors midweek come from Sans Amen; the beach and the centre is famous now. People arrive from all over the world and from Sans Amen. That has been a great privilege of his job, showing his own people this sight of the turtles. As a child he didn't know much about them.

He leads them out down the lane to the beach which is damp from the river nearby. The small group follows him and his infrared light and quickly they find a huge turtle, maybe seven hundred pounds. She is digging her egg chamber and he settles the group around her to share the information he knows. He hasn't been much to school, let alone university, but he's studied these creatures for decades and he is as knowledgeable as the teams of American marine biologists who come here, and those from the BBC and *National Geographic*. He now calls himself a conservationist. It is like being a husband or a father to the earth.

This turtle has begun to lay, and so he holds her hind fins apart discreetly, like curtains, and shines his infrared torch into the chamber.

'The female turtles take around two hours to nest and lay. It's hard work, and so they cannot nest when it's day. It's too hot. Now she will drop around one to two hundred eggs. The chamber, as you can see, is about two feet deep. So the eggs are quite safe.'

The visitors peer into the chamber. Soleil and Maria crouch near the hole, watching. The white eggs look like hand-blown paper globes. They gently slide out of her cloaca into the chamber walls of sand. The young girls are quiet and reverent, like women scopsing jewels.

'The turtles will nest up to ten times in a season, maybe lay a thousand eggs and disappear. Reptiles aren't mothering creatures. Once they have dug and laid, they slip back off, into the sea. They don't see their young again. They need no contact with them.'

'Wow,' says one of the women in the group. 'They come all this way to lay, and that's it?'

'Yes.'

'The juvenile turtles will be born about eight weeks

later. They take five days to dig themselves out of their nest,' he explains. 'But once they are visible, if they hatch in the day, most will be eaten between the beach and the sea by corbeaux or frigates. One in a thousand live to adulthood.'

Joseph has spent a lot of his life hand-releasing hatchlings into the sea. When the hatchlings start to emerge, he's on the beach most of the day with his bucket, collecting the tiny black stars, but he cannot save them all. Many he finds dead, pecked to death.

'That's a minuscule number.'

'Yes. But the ones that do survive return to this beach twenty or thirty years later to give birth. Sometimes I think the reason why is because of the very miracle that they survived at all.'

Back in the car park, Joseph says goodbye to the visitors. Soleil and her friend Maria are tired and they are both so stick thin he could easily scoop them up in his arms together. He likes it when his daughter comes to help, that she is learning about these creatures too.

The older man in the group hangs about a little, as if he'd like to say something. He looks about sixty and he has a quiet pensive manner.

'Thank you,' he says shyly and yet with some considered intent. Joseph feels drawn to him; he has come to know he's often drawn to older men. He hovers, now holding the hands of two little girls who need to go to bed.

'Those turtles made me sad,' the old man says.

Joseph nods. He's seen people weep at the sight of them.

'I had no idea. No idea . . .' and then he says, almost with an absent mind, 'that so many come to Sans Amen.'

'Yes. That's because there's been a ban on hunting them. For fifteen years.'

'So now they come safely?'

'More or less.'

'One good thing happening here on this island, eh?'

Joseph smiles. 'It was the idea of Aspasia Garland, remember her? She was once the Minister for Environment.'

'Of course I remember her. She was one of the hostages. At the time of that attempted coup. She survived the ordeal, a great lady.'

Joseph goes silent. He wants to get away now, from this conversation. And yet he almost wants to boast too, *I knew her, I knew her, she gave me the idea to come here . . .*

The older man gives him a look which is deep and raw and also a little lost.

'I know something about that attempted coup,' he

says. 'My wife, she was caught up in it too. Unfortunately, she didn't survive like Mrs Garland. She was shot and killed . . . by those lousy murderers.'

Joseph freezes. He stares. How did this man come here? Why is this man standing in front of him?

'I'm sorry . . .' Joseph stammers.

He looks at Joseph, still full of anger and regret. 'Bloody ruthless bastards. I was left a single father of two children. It was a shock at the time. They were devastated and so was I. Hypocrites. I . . .' And then he pauses as if he's only just put his finger on what has come to him, with the turtles.

'She was pregnant when they shot her, you see. Three months pregnant. My wife. In the House of Power. You remember that terrible thing? Eh? The attempted coup d'état. She used to work there as a clerk and she was shot dead. She was pregnant. And . . . well . . . I've always been glad they executed all those bandits. They deserved what they got. But those sea creatures . . . made me sad. Sad for my wife and our unborn child. And also for . . . those men. I have never felt any compassion for those men before, ever. But some of them were boys. Those creatures . . . they gave me a surprise. Where do they come from . . . ? Is like they bring an old wisdom with them.'

Joseph nods, but he feels old suddenly, and hot in

his gut, a liquid feeling spills through him. The horror of it all never faded. The remorse has atrophied, and now it is melting into his blood.

'I'm sorry,' he whispers to the older man whose wife he shot.

*

Joseph finds his wife still busy at the centre, looking pretty, as usual, her thin locks tied back and hennaed red at the ends. She has amber eyes and a way of looking at him which can be soft and hard at the same time. Killer look in her eyes, which is why he married her.

'Please,' he says, 'take them,' meaning the children. 'Something's come up.' And she gives him that look and this time he gives her his look back and says, 'Not now. Ah goin,' and with that he's gone, out the door, and walking across the car park to his jeep.

His hands are shaking as he jabs the key in the ignition and switches on the headlights, shaking. Tears are falling too and he can barely see. He takes the jeep out on to the thin tarmac road and through the village where every single man who isn't on the beach guiding visitors to the turtles is drinking rum and standing outside the parlour; thank God the windows have an opaque strip which partially hides his face and he makes a gesture which vaguely says hello. All the men outside the parlour nod gently. He accelerates past them and keeps driving till he reaches the next cove and then he parks facing the oncoming surf. The beach here doesn't get so many turtles. The waves are rolling in, slick and black and silent. His face is wet with tears. The woman he shot dead was pregnant. The woman he shot dead as a teenager had a baby in her stomach. He wonders if he should just load his pockets up with stones, wade out into the surf. She will never go away, that woman. She has been with him all his life – it is as though he shot his mother dead. She was trying to escape out the window. There was a moment when she saw him and she begged. 'You are like my son,' she pleaded, and he shot her straight through the belly.

Joseph puts his forehead to the wheel of the jeep and feels his ribs shake, his stomach heave. She will not go away, that woman. And now . . . there were two of them. He's a double murderer. It happened so long ago that sometimes he almost can forget what happened. Sometimes, it's like he can pretend he is someone else.

All that was over eight thousand days ago. He has kept count in numerous ways: on walls, in sketchbooks, in his head. In footsteps. In breaths. In leatherback turtles. He has collected his days of so-called freedom in stones, in leaves on the trees. But she has never died on him, that woman from the House of Power. She has haunted him and he has often wondered if he should walk out into the sea to stop her infestation of his dreams. It would probably be wise to take his own life as a way of recompense. It would be a cancellation of a debt. He owed her his life. The others paid with theirs.

12 APRIL, 2013

He gets home very late and lies awake thinking it's time to go back. The House of Power. Amerindian bones. Jesus on the cross. He ran away and never returned and maybe it will be okay; maybe it will help. He has been so scared. He has been hiding. He saw what happened to the others. The commune was bulldozed and the brothers disbanded, joined other groups. The Leader's entire movement evaporated soon after the execution. Enough time has passed. Since then he hasn't prayed, he has led a secular existence.

He should go back.

At dawn Soleil comes into the bed and he makes space for her and he lies still while his wife and child are warm and fast asleep next to him. The light is creeping in behind the curtains. He dozes a little and as he dozes he dreams of running. In his dreams he is running through the City of Silk, down towards the sea. The pavement is hot and broken up and there are vagrants asleep on the ground and there is a mega-phoned voice shouting at him saying, *Give up, come back*. Then he sees a giant rusted satellite dish and men standing in a line, falling in a heap to the ground. When the men fall, his legs begin to give and then he finds he is running on his knees through the streets. He sees his mother, Mercy Green, with one eye. His mother says to him, *Give yourself up you wutless good-for-nothing boy*. His mother turns into the minister, Mrs Aspasia Garland, who is carrying a baby turtle in her hands. His mother says to Mrs Garland, 'He should give himself up, shouldn't he?' Mrs Garland is standing by an open window in the House of Power with the turtle and she smiles and says, 'I know where you went, I know where you disappeared in your adoles-cence.'

Joseph slips from the bed and he goes to the bath-room and splashes water onto his face. He brushes his teeth and stares hard at them. His teeth are perfect. His face has marks on it now, creases and small scars from accidents and acne in his later teens. He has the face of a man who people like. He learnt to smile more, trust people more, since he got married. He is aware that women find him attractive and that men are drawn to him too. He figures it is his teeth and his smile. His face breaks open when he smiles and he has learnt that this makes others feel good. It makes him feel good too, like he has a charm. He remembers the way Aspasia Garland spoke to him once, in the House, using her voice of authority, like she was an important person; it was a politician's voice, strong and clear. Over the years he has somehow copied this. Sometimes he speaks like she did: precisely, as if he has authority. It impressed him as a young boy. And now he uses the same technique and he impresses people too. Firm and yet polite; it gets people on his side.

He finds his jeans and a jersey and his baseball hat. He decides he will drive half of the way, then park in a private car park he knows and then he will catch two maxis the rest of the way, one across country, the second into town. He will be travelling south and then east, back to the City of Silk. It will take him hours, maybe half the day to get there. He will call his wife on the way, a small lie. 'Something came up last night . . . a family thing. Ah goin into town.' She will be very surprised. He's never been back to the City of Silk in all this time. He goes all shut down when she mentions taking a trip into town. She will be curious as hell. But he'll make an excuse; he will not say the truth, which is *I haven't told you everything. I shot a woman dead. I shot a pregnant woman dead. That is what I have been hiding from you for twenty-three years.*

*

The trip across the centre of the island is long and bumpy. Villages flash past. The road, in places, feels soft, as if the asphalt is warm from the core of the earth. There are jhandi flags outside colourful houses and there are old men sitting on chairs outside these houses and young pot hounds asleep on their sides. There is KFC and Subway almost everywhere and over-crowded Christian cemeteries, their tombs all lopsided from the earth which is slowly and mysteriously mobile. Sans Amen is not such a small island; it feels spacious and unknown. Fields appear, and hulking black water buffalo with cattle egrets standing on top of them like angels astride their chariots. And the spicey smell of *chadon beni* is everywhere, blessed thistle, a cilantro which grows like a weed. *Chadon beni* and the stink of car fumes as other maxi taxis weave in and out of the traffic, some letting out black puffs from the exhaust.

The countryside of Sans Amen is full of secrets – perhaps some just like his. How many others are hiding out here? How many failed, intimate, desperate stories are being hushed up and extinguished here? Just like his. Joseph remembers his city childhood, his mother, his first life, the life which ended in a bullet-hail. *Thank God* for all this countryside. It gave him cover. He thinks of the other escaped gunman, Ashes, and he wonders what happened to him. Is he still in the country, hiding? Did his wife forgive him? He watches, mesmerised, as the island flashes past: rastamen with towering wrapped dreads selling bags of pommeracs in the road, massive factories selling paint, sweet drinks, hardware. Villages where the maxi tracks into thin maze-like private roads, Julie mango trees standing laden and sturdy behind walls; he sees a young woman poking the branches with a long stick. And all along the way the mauve-green mountains hover in the background, like the curves of a colossal woman lying on her side, the slopes of a gen- erous lover. Joseph feels tense and screwed up and nervous the closer he gets to town. *It will be okay*, he whispers.

*

When they reach the City of Silk it is mid-afternoon. The savannah is parched to a crisp brown fuzz from all the hot weather and the Pouis are like delicate pink clouds erupting in slow motion from the tops of the trees. The ground beneath is all mottled pink and it looks like someone has dropped lots of tissues around them. The maxi flies much too fast down the middle lane and then it's round the corner and he sees the gargantuan silver domes which look like shells inside each other, or like a part of a space rocket has fallen off and plummeted to earth. Already he feels uncomfortable. The City of Silk used to feel village-like; he knew the place, he knew the streets, the people. It was for everyone. Now he wonders if it has changed too much, if it has become a City of the Rich. These silver domes look like they landed here from an alien universe. He thinks he has made a big mistake coming back. To do what? See what?

Joseph asks the driver to let him off close by, at the top of Francis Street, and it is then that he is glad of the baseball cap. His heart starts to beat much faster and he feels a tightness in his entire body as if it is trying to make itself smaller. The sky is high and open and blue and he walks down the pavement in the full glare of the sun, past many shops, most of which are opticians; it's like everybody has gone blind or short-sighted in the City of Silk. And then he passes some offices and government buildings like the Ministry of Finance and then, he forgot it was there, the big gaol, yes, squat and low and sweltering in the sun. In the middle of the city. The Leader saved him from a spell inside there, years ago now. It has a gatehouse and a low rusted galvanised roof and a tower and a spotlight and a small door in the big green metal door. A woman goes to the small door in the big door and rings the buzzer and waits. There is a man in uniform talking to another woman; a green army van is parked outside.

Joseph walks past the entrance to the gaol in the centre of town. Not one single person turns to look at him. Not the female soldier driving the van, not the armed guard in the tower, not the woman waiting for the small door to open. He strides past all this, floating inches from the hot pavement, past the water hydrant, past the big church on the right surrounded by fir trees and royal palms which resemble fancy umbrellas, past a set of balconies which he remembers well, the famous boys' school, a school he used to walk past all puffed up and furious when he was younger. This school only takes the very best scholars, men like Hal.

Joseph walks on, unseen. He is a visitor, or a tourist even, feeling uncertain, feeling like he has made a stupid decision to come all this way. He walks past more shops, the street getting busy with life, with people. He is deeper into town now, and the vibe he remembers begins to show itself. A man walks towards him who is bleary-eyed from drugs. There is a sleazy nightclub with laughing Buddhas out the front and a sign saying that patrons must dress *elegantly casual*.

The City of Silk is small, he realises, tight and packed and busy. But when he left *he* was small, a boy. Now he is grown it is as if he has put on the right pair of spectacles, or he has adjusted the lenses on his eyes to the right strength. The City of Silk is not so big at all. In his memory the streets were very long and wide, but this isn't true, they are narrow. A man with a straw hat on walks towards him and Joseph notices his short-sleeved shirt is empty on one side. Joseph dares to look into the man's face and the man looks back, a practised defiance in his eyes. The one-armed man is the only person to notice him at all, and that is because Joseph is staring at the space left by his arm.

Soon, he reaches City Hall and his innards freeze and there it is: the famous square, the main square in town, where old men go to socialise. It is surrounded by high wrought-iron railings. He can see old men still sitting there, playing chess, like they never left. The square has a bandstand and a fountain and it feels quiet and peaceful, like it is safe. And yet he feels bad, awkward and unsure of himself. He crosses the road and enters through the open gate and then he is walking calm so, through the square in front of the

House of Power which is still painted magenta after all these years. He forces his legs to carry him, to keep walking towards the end of the long narrow pathway. He feels sick and unsteady, like his nerves are all up by his head and his stomach is like soup. He remembers jumping out of the back of the truck marked W.A.T.E.R. with his new gun, running up the steps to the public balcony shouting, *God is our saviour*.

Joseph stops directly in front of the House. It is like standing in front of a monument to his childhood. He tries to remember who he was then. He has limped a little ever since those six days in the House, especially when it rains; he gets a stitch in his groin, a small stabbing feeling. Like he was stabbed then, not by Greg Mason, not by anyone. It's a phantom wound, he's been told: 'psychosomatic'. He has seen the doctor many times about it, and no one can find the reason for this pain. But sometimes he feels so bad and ill with it, this quiet hurt, that he has to lie down for days. *Bones*, he thinks. Four humans buried under the House, at least, from centuries back. An innocent woman, a clerk, shot dead, others gunned down too in the corridors. He remembers the bodies on the steps, rotting in the heat. Waving the white flag for peace. The House of Power is really some kind of ongoing and active grave. It is the House of Many

Dead. Archaeologists have found bones now. And, finally, it looks like they are repairing the panes of glass where bullets flew.

It's all he can do to stand still. The House of Power reminds him of a dignified old woman. Its outer walls are cracked and flaking and it looks like it hasn't cared for itself, like it hasn't washed its face for a dozen years at least. It is peeling. It is cordoned off by a high fence and clad with scaffolding. Ideas come to him: he could make a mad dash into the street, across the two lanes of traffic and announce himself, proclaim who he is and what he has done.

'Here I am! It is me, I am one of the gunmen. I'm one of those that was never punished. I survived. I'm here. I escaped.'

Or he could clamber over the corrugated wall and get himself arrested. Or he could wait till dark and sneak over the wall and explore the place, graffiti his cell number in the chamber. Or he could urinate against the cordon in an act of provocation. He feels sad and sick. The spaceship at the other end of town has no feeling to it and no presence, not like this. This building spreads itself out, it owns the City; it has a dome and a spike at the top. Then he notices that there is no dragon there on top. He stares hard. Instead, there's a bird. A dove. Made of bronze with an olive branch in its mouth. They must have swapped it for the dragon the man Ashes had told him about.

He remembers Aspasia Garland talking about saving leatherback turtles, about politics being about everything, about taking care of the earth, not just people. 'Breeze', that was his nickname. His big gun. He shot a lady dead inside that House; he was so excited and overwhelmed by all the action. He had wanted to kill her too, his mother, kill her dead for all the time she never gave him.

His groin begins to throb. He feels a jab in his side and also a dull ache in his heart which he will never erase and neither can Sans Amen. So, after all these years, they will 'reconstruct' the place, rebuild and renovate the House to its former so-called glory. They will reinstate its grandeur, its righteousness. This place of ruling in this City is built on the bones of others. Who were these others? Does anybody care? They will polish up the peace dove. He has a sense that this reconstruction is the opposite of progress; that the House of Power was not built for them; it was built for Victoria. Politicians inside the House are nothing like conservationists; they are not putting hatchlings back into the sea. They are not concerned with future generations.

Joseph walks towards what used to be the old fire

station. It is painted gentle pastel colours now. It was all crooked and dusty and abandoned the last time he saw it; now it looks like an attractive spot. Behind it is a dazzling building, an apparition of white, like a holy place. Tentatively, he draws closer and sees that in fact it is a library. It is the National Library of Sans Amen. It is magnificent, like a big white butterfly or a collection of sails. There is a small amphitheatre to one side which makes it look as though it could be in Rome. It is a place for books, for studying. When he was fourteen he couldn't read properly.

In the time of the attempted coup there was no library here; it was an old building on the other side of the square. He remembers Ashes telling him that books liberated people, the common citizen, from poverty of spirit. A man who read books was a man who was freer than most.

Joseph walks left, behind the library, towards the sea. He should never have hidden at all, not for all these years. Hiding is cowardice. Hiding is not going to help him or the country heal. And yet he saw little alternative than to keep his head down. Has his real father been hiding too, from him, from all his other sons and daughters? Who is he the son of? His mother told him so little. His father was one of ten men who never stayed long. Maybe he could start to ask around; there must be public records, a register of some sort. Who, who, was his father? There must be relatives or half-siblings around he could track down and ask. What does his father look like, fat or thin, short or tall? Does he have good teeth?

It is then that he sees the new promenade, a long stretch of sculpted public space – trees and a walkway – and he realises that now he's in another place, a city he doesn't recognise. This part of town was rough. Now it looks like a vibrant bustling square. It has been recreated, renewed. It used to be full of vagrants and beggars and men drinking rum in parlours. It was a violent place, edgy and unsafe. It was where the men used to send him to drop money and drugs. He came here for the men in the pizzeria on the east side of town. He came to do their deals before he got bailed from prison by the Leader. This is where he got caught, picked up by police and locked up. On a night run. Right here, where there are now trees and umbrellas and a wide open feel. He was entrapped here – and now it feels spacious. The sea is still there, though. It is like gun grey satin on the other side of the square. The small white lighthouse on the foreshore stands like a man he once knew. He is still standing there, alone, and he says now, 'So there you are again. What took you so long? Hello, Breeze.'

Joseph puts his hands over his ears. He walks through this busy square he doesn't know anymore and he starts to walk faster. It is now coming to him, who he was. Breeze. He was worthless once, lost, abandoned, hard, a criminal, a fighter, rude and sour and difficult and proud and ugly and bad – and he starts to run, run up Chanders Street, run and run, fast fast fast.

'Breeze,' he hears the name everywhere now, everyone noticing him as he runs.

'Breeze!' shouts a voice through a megaphone outside a shop called Rattans, 'Breeze come up and check us out, everything must go today.'

'Breeze!' as he runs past the Golden Windows plaza, past a woman on the street with two buckets of pickled green mango.

'Breeze!' as he runs past KFC, past the car park, the fruit vendors, the man selling handcrafted leather shoes. And then he cannot see, he is running too fast, up and up, past the spaceship and its silver domes and then across three lanes of traffic. He runs and stops cars and then he is in the middle of the brown savannah, the trees everywhere, like strawberry ice creams, erupting and clapping as he passes, petals like wedding confetti, like he is running through a party. Then he is running fast as he can across the savannah. There are children with brightly coloured kites and he keeps running across towards the centre. There are hills all around, gentle slopes, and he remembers now, running through the tunnel of bamboo, yes, he ran away, fast fast, like an athlete sprinter. He ran for days, ran for nights, ran to the centre of Sans Amen, away from his old self.

LATER THAT AFTERNOON

No one knows what happens to leatherback turtles between the day they hatch and the day they return to the beach where they were born to give birth. It's a mystery only known to God. No one knows where they go for twenty years, where and how they live and how they survive. They simply disappear into the great oceans of the planet. Humankind hasn't been able to find them in their adolescence or early adulthood. They survive, somehow, and have done for millennia. They outdive killer whales who hunt their prey in packs for days, and great white sharks who can snap them in half. Over time, they can grow enormous.

Like the turtles, no one knows what happened to him either. Those first fifteen years of his life – what were the facts of his existence as a son of the City of Silk? The young boys who were gunned down, who cared? Now Joseph wants to remember. What happened to him? He wants to retrieve his life, all of it, before and after what happened in the House. He must find the only other man who escaped the execution, the strange quiet one with the spectacles, Ashes. The one who took him to pray and who said that intelligence lived in the heart.

For a while he's had some inkling of where this man Ashes lives. He's heard some talk, over the years. On the way back home from town towards L'Anse Verte he will again cross central Sans Amen, pass through towns and villages. He can get dropped off, ask around. He heard something once, from those who left the compound, those who were never involved. After the Leader was shot, his followers quickly left the compound and separated. News drifted his way that the army quickly realised two gunmen had escaped; they searched for them that night and for weeks afterwards. Years later, a rumour had come to him, via some of his ex-brothers, that one of the escaped gunmen, the older one, had become a librarian in a small village . . . a village called Liberty.

5 P.M., THE LIBRARY,
LIBERTY VILLAGE,
CENTRAL SANS AMEN

It would be easy to sneak in, just take a look. Then sneak out. The library is a modest affair, just three large rooms, a reception desk and some filing cabinets; there is an area with some desks and a corridor with some doors, one marked AV, one marked washroom. It is late afternoon and it is empty, near closing time.

He is a lot thinner now, and his hair is grey and his beard is long and frizzy, and he is wearing exactly the same round spectacles, has the same slow way of moving around. It occurs to Joseph that this man Ashes won't recognise him. Joseph pretends to browse the shelves, taking books out, using the slots left as a spy hole from which to watch. The man Ashes is moving along with his trolley, absorbed in re-shelving books.

Joseph can feel his breathing slow in his lungs; the old librarian floats past like a ghost. The man is putting books back on to shelves, taking pleasure in doing so, reading the spine of each. Joseph feels himself go in to some kind of trance. The air seems gluey. His tongue is thick in his mouth. His kidneys are suddenly active, he is itching to piss. He fights the urge. Again, his heart, it begins to race and then slow. All of him feels weak and faint and he realises he needs to sit down.

He gets to a chair by the wall and sits. He feels like an old man too, like his heart is slowly quaking and rolling around. He remembers the line of men falling, the sound of machine gun fire, the way some were already on their knees. Running blindly along the road, through the bamboo.

'Hello.'

He hears a voice. He looks up to see the man Ashes standing there with his trolley.

'Sir, are you okay?'

Joseph presses his hand to his groin and blurts, 'It's me, remember me? In the House . . . it's me.'

The man bends closer to hear him.

'It's me. Breeze.'

A small seizure of shock spreads in his face, 'Oh!' And then . . . a furtive glance backwards.

'Wait,' he says and hurries to the door. He turns the

open sign to closed and locks the door with a key. He pulls down the blind.

The man comes forward towards him, his arms outstretched, tears flowing and Joseph stands. Then he is in a crush of arms and beard.

'Thank the Lord, give thanks, give thanks,' the man Ashes repeats again and again into his ear, like he is whispering these words to a long-lost child or relative. 'I'm so glad to see you, thank you, thank you for coming. I have been hoping. Hoping and waiting and praying for you, my friend. Oh, my friend, my young friend, *oh, oh,*' and Joseph is overcome with relief. Feelings slide through him of wonderment and pent-up longing; tears flow and the two men stand and hug each other for several long minutes.

Then Ashes takes him by the shoulders and holds him at arm's length and examines him, as if concerned for his health, as if checking his teeth. Behind his spectacles his eyes are alert and piercing, like they've been taken out of his head and polished. It is then, gazing back at him, that Joseph can see something has changed with this man called Ashes. Now he has a different face, alive and animated.

'Is *you*,' Ashes says. 'I can see you become a man. Oh, look at you! You got so *big*. Eh, eh, gorsh, nuh, very tall and big. Are you married? What happened to you, eh, come, come and sit down with me, here in the back. Come.' He keeps glancing backwards and pressing his hands to his lips and smiling at him and saying, 'Oh, thank the Lord. He lived. He lived.'

Over cups of sweet mint tea they sit and talk freely, both of them needing to, both full, everything and anything falling out. It is a joy for Joseph to see this man; he is so different now. Energetic and somehow younger, not older. Their conversation is in fits and spurts and long monologues and each listens to the other with intense curiosity.

'I have felt alone all these years,' says Joseph, 'all this time. I have a good wife, a daughter, but . . . there is a part of me that is on fire, that is restless since those six days in the House. I care for turtles now. I found my way to a small village on the north coast. I ran that way, getting there three years later. One of the female ministers gave me the idea and so I went to look for where leatherback turtles go to nest. I was lucky, I got work picking cocoa at first. The men of the village didn't run me out. I was still young, about seventeen by then. I found the men on the beach guarding the turtles, and so I joined them.

'But . . . is like the House, what happened there, killed part of me. I find it hard . . . to sleep. My side aches. I have a wound no one says exists. I fill my life and I enjoy my work. I have love in my life. And also is like I suffer an absence. I am a loner, still.' Joseph looks away. He thinks of Mercy Green, his mother, who died alone, eventually. She possessed this kind of singularity too, despite all her children; like she was always distracted or somewhere else. His mother's bones were laid to rest in the large cemetery on the outskirts of the City of Silk.

'I went back to the House, today – first time ever – just to look – to see if it could give me back . . . you know . . . I figure I lost myself in there.'

Ashes sips his tea and nods and says, 'When my brother River died, I felt the same way for many years, most of my adult life. Like something get lost. Is why I get mixed up in that mess. To prove something or get part of myself back. I get devastated when I was a boy, something left me then. The House? For me, something else happened.'

'What?'

'I get *saved* there, I find my way out. Back to home, to roots. To self and service. I ask the right question then.'

'Oh yeah? What is the right question?'

The man called Ashes looks into a middle spot between them.

'I cannot give you that answer, my friend, every

man need to come up with the right question when he gets to a certain age.' And then Ashes goes quiet. 'Go an see the King,' he says.

'King? What King?'

'The King of the castle.'

'Who you mean?'

'The Prime Minister.'

'Eh? You crazy?'

'I serious.'

'Which Prime Minister, that woman in charge now?'

'No.'

'Then, who?'

'The man we meet all those years ago. The PM, the man Hal shot in the legs.'

'Him? You mad or what?'

'No.'

'How?'

'Never mind that. Go see him and ask him the question you must ask.'

'I have no idea where his house is, where is it?'

'Go left,' says Ashes.

'Left?'

Ashes smiles. 'That's all I can say for now. Left and over the bridge. Keep walking. Then ask.'

'You speaking some kind of code?'

'I speaking simple. Go left and cross the bridge and

you will find the PM. He an ol man now, a recluse. He no longer go out in public affairs. He get his confidence shaken. But he is the founding King of a big court now, court of human rights and international justice. He an ol King. Wounded. Go and see him. He walks with a limp. Go – and then ask the right question.'

'Shit, man.'

Ashes laughs. 'He's not difficult to find, my friend. His address is in the phone book. He lives in a quiet suburb of the City of Silk.'

Ashes is so different somehow. Peaceful and manlike. His advice sounds crazy, though. It is most unexpected advice for his loneliness, and it is extraordinary to see this man again, strange at how he is transformed. He was a man depleted of power, who had a famous brother, that was the talk. Now he seems strong.

'You been reading in the papers about those bones?' Joseph says.

'What bones?'

'Amerindians. Under the House.'

'Oh. Yes.'

'That place haunted, no arse.'

'Yes. I had a dream when I was there. About bones.'

'Well, seems like they going and dig up a whole other parliament under that House.'

'What . . . the elders of the past?'

'Or maybe just regular people. That place haunted. Like I is haunted.'

'Yes. I can see that.'

'I murder two people. I am a double murderer.'

'Go to see the King,' says Ashes.

'Yeah, an ask him the right question, right?'

Ashes nods and his eyes are inquisitive and alight.

*

When Joseph gets home Pearl gives him the silent treatment. His disappearance was too secretive, too puzzling, and she is repaying him with silence and he doesn't blame her for this. She will refuse to be generous with him, in bed, in conversation. She will be cool, cool, and he knows she will stay so for a while even though she has never won any of these stand-offs; she has never been so silent with him that he has spilled the beans. Part of him clamps shut – and when she goes silent in response he clamps up even more. He goes insomniac too. The rocks in their marriage are all about this: his past. He is evasive; she demands more – and he cannot give her more. It is a stale old rigmarole. They are both tired of it.

Soleil is in bed, fast asleep. His wife, he knows, is

faking sleep. It is 1 a.m. and he decides to go out on to
the beach. Sometimes he talks to the turtles, they remind
him of Aspasia Garland. Her ban on hunting and eating
them has been effective. The beach has become a safe
haven, as have others on the coast. In the moonlight he
can see the beach is now empty of other humans. All the
guides have gone home. It is just him on a beach which
is long and narrow, a river at each end. The waves are
choppy and roll in from the Atlantic. And there are hundreds of turtles on the beach, massive, like trucks, like
armoured tanks, coming up on to the sand, like they are
bringing parts of another continent with them on their
backs.

He stoops by one and shines his infrared light on to
her face. It's all spotted and mottled pink and she looks
all greasy-eyed and tearful and he thinks of the dove
on the House of Power. He remembers how confused
he was to find out who the Prime Minister was, the
elected head of state. He felt elated with his gun, the
chaos and the shooting; and then it was a shock to find
out that the Leader wasn't so important. It was the PM
the army came to save. It was the PM who ordered all
the men to be shot, including the Leader. He remembers coming down out of the House, his hands in the
air, the feeling of contempt for his father-Leader. He'd
been used. When he ran out the tunnel of the green

bamboo he ran and ran, into the future and the hell of knowing he'd been so let down – again. The Leader was a madman and the PM had had them shot. His own father he never knew; he'd abandoned him before he was even born.

'Go left,' said the man called Ashes; what de ass did he mean by that? 'Go over the bridge. Go and see the King.' How does he go and see such a man, a man who made the order to have him shot?

2 MAY, 2013

He wrote a letter in the end. Short, mentioning the Monroe Doctrine and his nickname Breeze, saying he was one of the two that escaped the execution. Saying he shot the woman and would like to turn himself in. He was part of a treasonous and vile act that hurt others and the country. He is a murderer and cannot live. He asked to be granted a meeting. He expected nothing would come of it; he found the old PM's name and address in the phone book, plain so.

Weeks later, an envelope arrives. Formal looking, a square card of some sort in a satiny envelope. He snatches it from the postman on his way out of the house and smells it, pressing the satiny sheen to his lips. He opens it in his Jeep. It is an invitation, the writing is raised up in gold letters: *His Excellency requests . . .* a small coat of arms at the top with three

Spanish galleons and two hummingbirds; so . . . he still retains a title. *He limps,* said Ashes. He is given a date and a time to arrive. Nothing personal. It hasn't even been signed by him. Just a date and a time to be there, an RSVP contact for his secretary, an address. His heart is beating faster as he stares at the square card; it is like the possibility of a love affair. He puts the jeep into drive and leaves for a meeting with his colleagues about a new scheme for schoolchildren nearby. This time he will tell Pearl where he is going and why; and he will promise to tell her everything once he returns. Everything.

*

Joseph is nervous by the time he arrives. He is even half an hour early. It is 11 a.m. and they are to meet at 11.30 a.m. He is wearing his only suit and tie. In some ways he considers it his lucky suit and tie because he only wears it for weddings and special occasions, and so every time before this he has worn it, he's had a memorable time. Pearl even offered to take it to the dry cleaners. Since he told her where he is going she has sunk into a space he doesn't recognise. Like she's gone off into new territory, no longer doing what she generally does: sulk, get vexed, refuse sex. None of these things. She has gone different. Silent – and yet soft. Like she is really waiting this time.

Eventually he presses the buzzer to the tall wrought-iron gates. The jeep is parked further up, half on the grass kerb. He speaks his name *Joseph Green* into the intercom and soon after the gates begin to slide back in a rickety kind of way and he notices a guardhouse to the left, two Dobermans chained up, gazing at him with their ears pricked. As he steps over into the electronic high-gated world of the old PM, he thinks just what does he want from this? The old PM didn't come calling; *he* has sought out the old man. The old man has said, *Yes, come.* And now he, 'Breeze', Joseph Green, a killer, a double murderer, a father and a married man, a conservationist and once a radical extremist, a thief, a badjohn from the streets of the City of Silk, a common crook, they should have thrown his ass in jail and done, is now walking up the driveway to see a very important man. Just what the ass is it, after all these years, he has to say? He feels shame and he also feels okay; there is some kind of offness here, an offness of centre which makes him trust himself, that this will go well.

He is greeted at the door by a young man, about eighteen, who speaks quietly and says hello and explains that he's a grandson. The grandson is

339

wearing formal-looking black pants and a pale shirt buttoned to the neck. The grandson leads him into a hallway. A woman appears, dressed in pink, wearing coffee-coloured stockings and big square spectacles and she also speaks in lowered tones, and all of a sudden Joseph feels awkward, but it's too late to check his appearance, too late to turn back. 'Thank you for your punctuality,' she says, shaking his hand. 'I'm Clarissa, his secretary. He is expecting you. You have exactly one hour. He only sees one person a day, if that. He is very keen to meet with you. So many people have asked, over the years, to speak to him, interview him about . . . that time. He always refuses.' And she looks him up and down, 'You must be very important, then.' She doesn't quite say *Who are you*, but that's in her eyes. 'You will address him as Your Excellency.'

Clarissa takes him to a large sitting room with heavy green silk curtains which run from ceiling to floor and lots of polished wooden furniture and a crystal vase of anthurium lilies on a small table. There is a gold-framed mirror on the wall and some silver candlesticks on a ledge, some silver boxes on a coffee table. He sees himself in the mirror, looking scared and handsome. The place smells of wax polish and of mothballs and he realises he is in some kind of formal reception room, a part of the house for visitors, not for family. Joseph has his back to the door when the King enters. He hears a muffled whispering and turns round.

The grandson is holding on to one arm. In his other hand he clutches a walking stick. His hair is white and he is bent over but he isn't limping. He shuffles with a slow but dignified step and it all comes back to him, who this man is. The old King is slow and cautious as he makes his way over to where there are two armchairs set out for a conversation. Joseph can feel a tremor spread through his entire body, a feeling of sympathy floods his veins. Like he might cry or indeed hug this man, crush him to his chest. The old man hasn't seen him yet; his eyes are fixed to the ground. He is making his way over in his own time. Joseph stands there waiting to be seen. It's only after a few moments of watching him that he notices there is something wrong. Not only is he shuffling, precisely, even proudly, with intent, but he appears unsighted.

The grandson sits him down. He says, 'Can I get you anything, Grandpa?' The old PM shakes his head. 'No. I'm fine. Is he here?'

'Yes, he is standing next to you.'

'Oh,' and he turns his head to face Joseph and he peers hard and he says, 'Oh, there you are.'

Joseph stares. The young man leaves the room.

'Please sit down. My sight isn't very good. My hearing is worse. Speak clearly.'

Joseph sits in the armchair next to him. Their knees are inches apart and he guesses the chairs are arranged this close due to the old PM's deafness. He has composed himself and is looking downwards into his lap, as if his eyes are useless and he now only uses his ears for sight and sound. That, or the old PM refuses to look his way. Joseph realises he is expected to start the conversation and that this isn't an unreasonable expectation. Except that he is awestruck, as awestruck by the old man now as he was when he was fourteen. He can feel there are tears in his eyes and he is glad the old man cannot see them. There is too much to say; where does he begin? He feels the need to tell the whole sorry story of his life and realises the PM will not and cannot listen to it. He remembers taking the PM down the stairs to his wheelchair out onto the gravel, how he wanted to say something then, *Save us, don't leave us here*. How bad he has felt ever since those days. How bad. And he can see the old PM isn't well either; maybe he can start there, about this pain, in the groin.

'Well, come on then. Don't just sit there,' the old PM says gruffly. 'You are that little boy Breeze, aren't you?'

'Yes.'

'That little badjohn. You say you shot the woman who died in the House.'

'Yes.'

'You should be ashamed of yourself. She left behind a husband who went to pieces after she died and two small children, both motherless. I understand both have had tough lives. Many people were left without loved ones after what you did. You want to turn yourself in, is that right? You've had enough of hiding?'

This isn't how Joseph had hoped things would go. 'I . . . met her husband recently . . . by chance. Yes.'

'Good. So you should. I can give you the name and address of the right person in the police force to do so.'

Joseph wants to say, *Wait! This isn't right . . . or fair. I'm not a badjohn. Or . . . I'm not one now.*

The old man has his head bent as if expecting a reply. Joseph wants the old man to *care* about him, he realises. But he doesn't. He doesn't. That is clear. Maybe this is what he needed to check on. If the old PM just didn't care, had them shot – just like that. He didn't care about Joseph at all; no one ever has: no man, no father, no Leader.

'Your Excellency,' he begins, and clears his throat.

The old man cocks his head.

343

'I have to ask you about what happened. About the execution. Did you give the order? Was it you?'

He doesn't reply immediately. He has heard the question; he is thinking.

'No,' he says firmly. 'It wasn't me who gave that order. I was in hospital. It was taken by others, the army and the proxy government on the outside.'

Joseph is relieved. Somehow he knew it hadn't been him. That was what he needed to know most.

'But if I had been more . . . *compos mentis* at the time, who knows. Maybe I would have said yes too. I cannot say. I was very ill.'

'But it wasn't your decision?'

'No. But, young man, make no mistake. I would have signed papers to hang those at the top, at the very least. Others would have received the strongest sentences. Locked up for life. Throw away the key. Make no mistake, it was a gross act of villainous treason. A violation against the state and the humanity of our nation. But I was in no fit state to make decisions after I left the House. Yes, I recall you helped me out, down the stairs. Of course I remember you. The Monroe Doctrine. You were one of the most trigger-happy of all those young boys. A real bad mouth. A little bad man. I hope you didn't come here expecting sympathy. All of you, in some way, had a hand to play in it. No I

didn't make that order . . . I left the country soon afterwards . . . to . . . recuperate.'

'Oh.'

'We lost the next election, thanks to what happened.
Game over. The City of Silk was ruined and laid waste.
It has never fully regained its confidence. You men
wounded the *country*. Deeply. Has it ever healed? Eh?
Little gunman, all grown up?'

Joseph is feeling numb. A massive guilt has welled
up and assaulted him. He has been so naïve. Politics,
the Big Game; it's not really about people, the common
man like him. It is over there, in the distance. Power.
He was confused then and he still is. Something terrible happened. Years ago. And yet he has always felt
innocent somehow. He realises he doesn't have that
much time and that the old PM is now looking impatient. This is no happy meeting, no reunion. So much
for his lucky suit and tie. What was he thinking? *Ask
the right question*. Okay, then.

'Power . . .' he begins.

'Yesssss?'

'I was very confused about it at the time. I didn't
know who you were, for instance; I didn't know a man
needed to be elected by the people to serve. I was a
boy. I knew nothing. It was a great shock to see I was
. . . wrong.'

'You had been brainwashed and exploited.'

From nowhere he feels defensive of what the Leader gave him.

'The Leader taught me to read and write. That is something.'

'What are you trying to say?'

'Power. You, the Leader, is like I was serving the wrong man. I was foolish then.'

'Yes. You were a young fool. And it looks like you still are . . . if I may speak bluntly.'

'*Who* then?' Joseph feels himself go dumb, urgent. 'Who should I serve? Who – or what? Who has real power? Who do *you* serve, Your Excellency?'

The old PM actually smiles at this. Broadly, and with great peace in his face. For the first time his gaze rises upwards and he looks at him squarely.

'You and your kind,' he says. 'Spiritual knights. Warriors, men who feel to change things up so quickly, using violence. You, yes *you*, were part of things. Big things. A chain of events stretching back now over twenty years or more. 1990. Not so long ago. Then 9/11. Now it is 2013.'

Joseph can feel his ears go hot. It is hard to bear the fury in the eyes of the old man.

'The *world* lost its confidence after 9/11. Of course we know now, what happened here was connected.

Big thing man. *You*. Young man, you are part of it all. You and your so-called "brothers". This thing that happened here in our small island was just the first event; we can look back and join the dots. *You*. You are directly part of it all and now you come back here to ask me who to serve? Eh? Little badjohn from the slums, shooting the place up?'

Joseph is shaking. 'Yes,' he mutters. He is lost now, out of his depth. What was he thinking?

'Here,' says the old King, and he taps his chest. '*Here* is who to serve. And what to serve. The best part of self. The spirit. The Light. It has many names. It is the universal force, a truth which lives in every one of us. We must serve that.'

Joseph stares, knowing this and yet still trying to understand. He puts his hands to his chest as if this might help him breathe. The old man's blind eyes are ablaze.

'True power lies away from man's grasping and greedy ego and towards a higher self. Only God has power, my friend. Our life's mission? Eh? To turn away from what we want. To relax this pursuit of need. Power already lies within every man.'

Joseph nods, as if he was on the tip of this very understanding. The old PM is revealing something he already carried inside him, an ancient wisdom.

'It lives in the heart, my friend.'

The old man stops speaking, abruptly. Joseph remembers his bravery; he'd been willing to sacrifice his life for his country. He had understood power, then. Power is love. Joseph feels this love sweep through him, a great release. The devastation of the woman on the ground, under the table, who bled to death, the child in her stomach. The others that were shot. The heavy, indescribable feeling which he's carried since then. The stabbing pain in his groin, near his testicles. As though the part of him destined to create new life has been eternally tortured. He's lived a life of enduring self-hatred. His feelings of self are shrouded in the violence of those six days. The City of Silk looks different now, resurrected. Restored. A promenade and a fancy library which looks like a big white butterfly. But violence hasn't caused any core change. The old King is right; he, Joseph Green, 'Breeze', the little bad mouth, the boy soldier, the man, conservationist, the person who puts hatchlings back into the sea, is a link in a chain which stretches across the world. A chain of violence.

The ex-PM flattens down his shirt in a manner which says he is done now. He glances at his watch. As if on cue, his grandson appears from the door and says, 'Thank you for your visit. My grandfather must now go and rest.'

Joseph rises. He wants to say something, maybe even shake the old PM's hand, but he is struggling to get up. They are not friends; they are not colleagues or brothers.

'Your Excellency,' he says, surprising himself. 'Why did you . . . want to see me? Allow me here? There must be a reason. You didn't have to let me in.'

The old man is now on his feet.

'Reason? Yes. Of course there was. I am dying. I have numerous ailments. My dreams are still rich, though, and yet I know the end is soon. I had a feeling you would come. I can die now, you see. I can go to the grave quietly, having met you again. I will die soon and the City of Silk will flourish after my death. I needed to see you too, you see. Just like you needed to see me. I must go. Goodbye now.'

Clarissa has also appeared and Joseph waits until the old man has left the room and then he allows her to usher him out into the hall. At the door she pauses and puts her hand on his arm and says, 'His Excellency wants you to have this.'

He looks down. On a small white card is the name of a well-known police superintendant and two numbers, a cell and a landline.

'He said it is what you came for. He wrote this before you came. I'm assuming it's still what you need.' She

349

looks at him studiously, as if she's just worked out who he is, and then she closes the door quickly on him, a short sharp push out into the world. He steps on to the driveway; the two Dobermans are still chained up. Joseph takes the card and slips it into the pocket of his lucky suit. He walks towards the high gates. They begin to slide back in a rickety kind of way and he remembers his promise to his wife, to talk to her, tell her everything. He thinks of the leatherback turtles, how the great oceans of the planet provide them with cover to grow to mature. Okay then, I will confess my sins to the mother of my child. I will start at the beginning and take my time in telling her my story, all of it.

ACKNOWLEDGEMENTS

In January 2011, a lengthy Commission of Enquiry into the events of 1990 began in Trinidad. The many witness testimonies were crucial to the writing of this book. I would also like to thank those who I was able to talk to personally: Raoul Pantin, Jones P. Madeira, Raffique Shah, Ralph Brown, David Millet (in particular his essay on NUFF); also Satya Crystal and Kim Johnson for enlightening conversations early on. Also many thanks to Jerleanne John at Udecott for letting me into the Red House in Trinidad in April 2012, even though it was under reconstruction, and to Sharon Miller for the photographs which helped. Thanks to Judy Raymond for use of *The Trinidad Guardian* archives and being so helpful with contacts. Also a great thanks to Bunty and Rory O' Connor for their companionship during my stays at their cottage in

Chicklands, Carapichaima, in early 2013. Much writing was done there, as well as at Man O' War Cottages in Charlotteville, Tobago. In Grand Riviere, thanks to Len Peters for his knowledge of the history of the conservation of the leatherback turtles in northern Trinidad. Also a big thank you to Lou, David and fellow commune-ista Piero Guerrini, owner of Mount Plaisir Hotel for space to write, edit, draft and think. For reading drafts and pages thanks to: Joanna Pocock, Sean Thomas, Lisa Allen Agostini, Ira Mathur and Angelo Bissessarsingh. Thanks to my agent Isobel Dixon and my editor Clare Hey at Simon & Schuster UK for making this a better book. Thank you also to my brother, Nigel Roffey, for much support and insight into this story, and to my mother, Yvette Roffey, once again, third time round, for giving me a place to write.